Praise for the works of K

T0273542

The Lucky O

This is a story about love, and not just romantic love. It is about the love of family, friends, and yes, even a love of a community. This is also a tale of hope. For me, this is a feel good story, one that made me feel happy at the end. It is well-written, with a vibrant setting, well-developed characters, both main and secondary, and a story that left me with that feeling of hope.

-B. Harmon, *NetGalley*

A Proper Cuppa Tea

A Proper Cuppa Tea is a smart and sexy romance featuring two professional women. While their relationship first stutters from the distractions of their lives, when they decide to pursue it, the romance develops in a realistic, charming, erotic, and organic manner. These characters are well rounded and fully depicted. They have careers and responsibilities as well as relationships with other people. The blended plotlines and complications are integral to the potential for Lark and Channing's future together. MacGregor's newest romance is a marvelous, entertaining, captivating book as complex and full-bodied as that perfect cup of tea. Put the kettle on to boil, find a cozy chair, and settle in to enjoy *A Proper Cuppa Tea*.

-*Lambda Literary Review*

The author did a remarkable job of bringing all of the characters to life for me. I was able to form a vivid image of each delightful character in my mind and I felt as though I could hear the witty banter between Channing and Lark. There wasn't a lag in the storyline or any unnecessary drama and I am very pleased to admit that the author made me fall in love with the charming English landscape. This story entertained me from the first word and I can't tell you how many times I had to suppress my laughter while I kept sneaking a read when I was at work. I adore British humor and I tend to fall in love (quite deeply, I must say) with quirky and sarcastic British characters who have a wicked sense of humor. If you love books with picturesque landscapes, feisty women, meddling and well-meaning friends coupled with countless cups of delicious tea, then this story is definitely for you!

Moment of Weakness

Moment of Weakness… is a romance that doesn't follow the usual track of a les-fic romance. The author's use of time in this story keeps the pages turning as the reader learns bit by bit how Zann and Marleigh met, what happened to Zann in Afghanistan, and who they are. I loved the story and the way I learned about Zann and Marleigh's relationship–not in a straight timeline, but moving backward and forward in time. KG MacGregor's characters are well developed and have flaws. I love that. I loved the romance. I highly recommend this book to KG MacGregor fans.

MacGregor has written a story that lulls the reader into thinking it will continue along a certain trajectory, then—wham!—we're thrust in another direction with a startling revelation we never saw coming. Every scene skillfully moves this tale along, adding to the tension. From desperation to longing, anger to disappointment, unconditional love to fear, all those moods and emotions and more are well portrayed. The superb writing, characters, and well-timed plot twists are skillfully done to make for an entertaining and revelatory story. *Moment of Weakness* explores the often unexamined tragic aspects of war, the power of true love, and gives the reader a thrill ride that lingers long after the last page has been turned.

-*Lambda Literary Review*

The Touch of a Woman

What makes this an interesting read beyond the standard plotline are unusual back-histories. The characters are well drawn, complex women, who will resonate with many. And their tender attraction is a reminder that real life isn't always about the grand passion, but a gentle falling.

-*Lesbian Reading Room*

Anyone But You

More than a sizzling romance, a well researched and well written eco-thriller... I loved the way the story was written: fast-paced, with great punch lines, a tidy, well thought-out and thought-provoking plot, at times witty, at times dramatic. Dating the archenemy added zest to the romance and both heroines were very believable and easy to like.

-*Curve Magazine*

Etched in Shadows

Well written, well edited, thoroughly enjoyable read... The loss of memory and feelings she once had gives Ms. MacGregor the opportunity to show a woman before and after a life changing event, and to explore how starting from scratch as an adult might allow us to make different choices... Johnelle and Alice are strong characters, well drawn and developed.

-*The Lesbian Reading Room*

Words Unsaid

Other Bella Books by KG MacGregor

Anyone But You
Etched in Shadows
The House on Sandstone
Just This Once
Life After Love
Malicious Pursuit
Moment of Weakness
Mulligan
Out of Love
Photographs of Claudia
Playing with Fuego
A Proper Cuppa Tea
Rhapsody
Sea Legs
Secrets So Deep
Sumter Point
T-Minus Two
The Lucky Ones
The Touch of a Woman
Trial by Fury
Undercover Tales
West of Nowhere
Worth Every Step

Shaken Series
Without Warning
Aftershock
Small Packages
Mother Load

Words Unsaid

KG MacGregor

Lambda Literary Award-Winning Author

BELLA
B O O K S
2021

Bella Books, Inc.
P.O. Box 10543
Tallahassee, FL 32302

First Bella Books Edition 2021

Editor: Katherine V. Forrest
Cover Designer: Kayla Mancuso

ISBN: 978-1-64247-281-3

Dedication

For Jenny

PROLOGUE

A grimy light fixture cast a dim glow over the steep wooden stairs to the basement. Why did it always have to be a dark basement? This one smelled of rot. Mold, sewage, dead rodents.

Without a rail to grip, Anna slid her hand along the wall, amassing cobwebs as she picked her way down and through a curtain of darkness. The only light ahead came from a far corner, where the voices of two men and a woman were muzzled by a rap tune.

All ice no thaw Ima drop ur call
Don't gimme no cheata cause I can do betta

As Anna drew closer, she realized the woman was Tawna Cooper, the police detective they'd sent to negotiate for Andy's safe return. "You have to talk to Hal. He's the finance guy, Anna's brother-in-law. If you want money from Anna, you have to go through him."

"I want at least a million dollars. She owes me that."

Anna recognized the voice of Mickey Cheung, the general manager of the BMW dealership in Redondo Beach. Like the others, he blamed her for losing his job.

"We worked our tails off to make her rich and she left us high and dry."

Try to climb my wall Ima watch you fall
Ringside satisfied its Isaacs law applied

Anna inched closer to the group to see Andy sitting cross-legged on the floor beside a pizza box and an empty soda bottle. He wore a greasy jumpsuit over his school uniform, and his hands were bound in front with duct tape.

"Mom only cares about herself," he said flatly. He didn't seem at all concerned about his predicament. "Tell her you're sorry. She makes you say sorry even if it's not your fault. She might give you the money then."

Why would Andy be helping his kidnappers? Anna knew she was missing something… unless this was a dream. She double-checked her surroundings. The concrete floor, a stack of tires that smelled of fresh rubber. It had to be real—those were the same tires Andy had knocked over. Surely she wouldn't dream she was dreaming.

"What should we do with him?" the other man asked.

Anna couldn't see his face from behind, only his beefy arms covered with brightly colored tattoos. This had to be the gang member Tawna had arrested. Why wasn't he in jail?

"If he testifies we'll go to prison."

The detective moved between Andy and his captors as if to protect him. "You have to let him go. Anna won't pay you a ransom but if you let him go she might give you a reward."

"He's a witness," the gangbanger growled. "We're not supposed to leave any witnesses."

As they discussed coaxing Andy to change his story, Anna watched to see if he'd stand up to them and refuse. His lying made her furious. Maybe this was why he did it so often, because other people pressured him to do it.

He told them, "You should ask my other ma for the money. She's the only one my mom ever listens to." He looked at the detective. "Tell them—she's nicer. Ma can make her give them the money. She's always sticking up for me."

That much was true, Anna had to admit. It drove her crazy when Lily sided with Andy, always making her the bad guy. All she wanted was for their son to live up to his potential.

Andy was right though. Lily would fix it. She always fixed it. That was the only way to end this.

With a sigh of relief, she stepped out of the shadows and offered her phone. "I have Lily's number if you want to give her a call."

Mickey shook his head. "It's too late. You already missed the deadline." He turned to the tattooed man and said, "You told her what would happen. She never listens to anyone else. Go ahead, do it."

The gangbanger raised his weapon, a hook-shaped dagger.

Anna shouted, "Andy, I love you!"

He looked back with narrowed eyes, his lips pressed tightly together—refusing to answer.

"I love you, pal. I love you."

"*Anna!*"

She went limp as Tawna grabbed her by the shoulders and shook her hard.

"*Anna!* Anna…wake up, sweetheart. It's just a dream."

Breathless and shaking, she opened her eyes to find Lily looming over her in their bed. "A dream…"

Was she awake for real now? She sat up and looked around the room. The bed, the alcove, the clock.

"Honey, are you okay?"

"How am I supposed to be okay when we don't know where our son is?"

CHAPTER ONE

February 2019

The brain trust of Premier Motors sat huddled in the back of a stretch limo, a sliding window sealing their conversation from the chauffeur. This secretive group consisted of owner and CEO Anna Kaklis, chief financial officer Hal Philips, vice president for human resources Vivian Zhao, and general counsel Lupe Segura. They'd spent the past week holed up with other executives in a conference room at the posh Beverly Hills Hotel where they'd drawn up the basic framework for a deal that would spell the end of the Kaklis family's auto empire. Their presumptive buyer was Pinnacle Auto Corporation, a publicly traded management group that owned hundreds of car dealerships up and down the West Coast. For now, complete secrecy was required to guard against the potential for insider trading, the kind that had led domestic maven Martha Stewart to prison for perjury.

"It's hard to wrap my head around the idea of that much money," Anna said.

"For a minute there I thought you were going to faint," Hal said with a laugh. Since he was her brother-in-law, he could get away with teasing the boss.

She felt alternately thrilled and sick to her stomach. After taking the helm from her father fifteen years ago, she'd grown Premier Motors from a single dealership in Beverly Hills to twenty-two throughout Southern California, all selling German cars: BMW, Volkswagen or Audi. Following industry-wide consolidation, Premier was still a small but valuable player in the Southern California market—streamlined, efficient and reliably profitable. Though Anna had taken on considerable debt at purchase, each acquisition had been carefully vetted to boost revenue and increase the company's value. This was her chance to extract that value and reward herself and her team for a job well done. Given the volatility of current trade partners and tariff wars, now might be just the right time to get out of the sales business and turn her attention to new opportunities.

The challenge was divorcing her emotions from the deal. Premier Motors had been started by her maternal grandfather in 1956, the first year BMWs were sold in the United States. After her mother's death when Anna was only ten, it was held in trust until she inherited it outright at age eighteen, though her father had run the company with her blessing until he retired fifteen years ago. She'd practically grown up at the dealership, walking the few blocks from school every afternoon to watch the service and sales teams at work, proud to see her dad make deals on just a simple handshake. If anything was holding her back from the sale, it was nostalgia.

"Just so you all know, I might still change my mind about this. If it keeps me awake after my head hits the pillow, I won't be able to go through with it."

"Pinnacle delivers virtually everything you wanted," Vivian said, checking the other faces for confirmation. A labor attorney by profession, she had joined Premier Motors eight years ago, the only corporate holdover from Anna's acquisition of the four Audi dealerships. "A seamless transfer of pension and benefits, and guaranteed severance for anyone downsized in the first eighteen months. I don't have to tell you, Anna—that's a fantastic deal for everyone."

Taking care of her employees was paramount to Anna's decision, but so was the fact that she stood to pocket well over a hundred million dollars. It was mind-blowing. At forty-eight, she was in her prime, with plenty of years left to make her mark in a second career. She already had an intriguing prospect.

It was dark and drizzling by the time they pulled onto the lot of the BMW dealership where they'd left their cars. Though most of the lights were off, Anna spotted Andy in the dimly lit showroom wiping down the flashy i8, BMW's plug-in hybrid roadster that retailed for $180 thousand. He came to the dealership almost every day after school, shadowing her sales team much the way she'd shadowed her father. Losing Premier Motors would be hard for him at first, she figured, until she showed him the doors the sale could now open.

Before stepping out into the steady rain, she said, "Good work, all of you. Remember, we need to keep this under wraps until the offer's signed by both sides. There's still a lot of work to do in the weeds." Addressing Hal and Lupe, she said, "Get your teams together and go through the fine print. Offsite, so people don't ask questions. But keep Vivian and me in the loop."

As they headed for their cars, she tugged Hal's sleeve and asked him to come upstairs for a private word.

Andy met them at the employee entrance in the back. His growth spurt had slowed at five-four, same height as his other mother Lily, who also happened to be his biological aunt. "Hey, Mom. You ready to go?"

"In a minute. Tell Holly she can go home," she said, a reference to the dealership's general manager, and one of Anna's best friends. "We'll set the alarm when we're done and go out the back. First I need a quick chat with your Uncle Hal."

Hal tousled Andy's curly brown hair as he walked by. "Somebody needs a haircut."

"So I can look dorky like you and Jonah?" he replied cheekily.

"Hey, what's that?" Hal asked as he caught Andy's hand and admired his commemorative gold ring for the Class of 2020. "That's your senior ring—a whole year early. What if you don't graduate? They'll make you give it back."

"Is that what happened to yours?"

Anna laughed. "He's got you there, Hal."

"Can I drive home, Mom?"

"In the rain after dark?"

"Come on, please. I need at least eight more hours at night. I've gotta learn sometime."

He'd gotten his learner's permit last summer but was well short of the fifty hours he needed to qualify for his license. Though he was already sixteen, Anna continued to hold him back, concerned about his maturity level after a disappointing report card and a fight at school. As he brought home better grades on exams and papers, she was gradually allowing him more time behind the wheel.

"I'll think about it, pal. You got your homework?"

"Who can think about homework? I'm starving to death." He raised a hand to his forehead and added, "I feel like I'm going to faint."

"Probably best not to let you drive then. You might pass out and run us off the road." She mocked his dramatic gesture with one of her own—the world's tiniest violin—before passing him a couple of bucks for the vending machine.

With Hal on her heels, she trudged upstairs to her office and closed the door. "So what do you think? Is this Pinnacle deal going to happen?"

He helped himself to a bottle of water from the small fridge beneath her bookcase. Nearing his fiftieth birthday, he'd lost the hair on his crown, but he still was a handsome man. "It's obvious they really want it. The real question is, do you?"

That, in a nutshell, was why the lurking headache behind her left eye had been threatening for a week to become a full-blown migraine. "It almost feels like an omen, getting this offer out of the blue. I keep thinking about our worst-case scenario. The industry's stable right now, but we can't count on US trade policy to remain that way. If Merkel says something that bruises you-know-who's ego, the whole German sector could get torpedoed overnight."

"Maybe that's your answer. You'll look like a genius for getting out when you did. What does Lily have to say?"

"Mmm, just that she trusts me to make the right decision. We try not to talk about this at home. I can't deal with it all day and all night too. Besides, I'm not ready for the big family discussion yet. Someone isn't going to take this well," she said, gesturing with her thumb toward the door.

Hal snorted. "Not just Andy. George won't take it lying down either. I know he technically has no say over this deal, but he could sure make our lives miserable."

Her father probably would make some noise at first but he'd see the wisdom in it eventually. It was Andy she worried about most. Since the day he came to live with them twelve years ago, Anna had encouraged his dream of taking over Premier Motors someday. This move might very well leave him feeling betrayed, but what choice did she have? A sale would spare him from the truth—that she had serious doubts he could ever run as complex and demanding a business as this.

Careful to keep his voice low in case Andy had followed them upstairs, Hal asked, "Any more word from Helios?" referring to the German automotive startup on the cusp of bringing solar-powered vehicles to market in Europe. They'd approached Anna two months ago about heading up their California initiative—exactly the sort of challenge she had in mind for life after Premier Motors.

"We spoke last week but I put them off so I could deal with the sale. But I'm seriously thinking about it."

"Helios could be fun for a motor nerd like you," Hal said.

"Not until I know exactly what they have in mind. I'd drop everything to be part of something revolutionary, but not if all they really want is a pretty face to charm investors."

"Nobody who knows you would hire you as a pre—" He cocked his head and wrinkled his brow. "Wow, I can't believe I almost said that."

"No kidding. Be glad you weren't talking to your wife."

"Oh God, don't even joke about that."

Anna's stepsister Kim, normally a good-natured wisecracker herself, was in the throes of menopause. A remark like that would have landed Hal in the pool.

She snorted and said, "See you tomorrow."

* * *

Five-year-old Dreama Doe had been a ward of the state since being found two years ago, dirty and hungry, abandoned in a downtown park. Today she was getting a new start in the home of Prince and Tamara Peavine, her foster parents for the last eighteen months. One day she would look back and call this the luckiest day of her life.

If there was one person in the courtroom who understood what an auspicious day this was, it was Superior Court Judge Lilian Kaklis. Like Dreama, she'd been neglected and abused as a toddler, and shuffled off to a series of foster homes. On her luckiest day, she walked out of the courtroom holding hands with her new mom, Eleanor Stewart, who'd helped her become the woman she was today.

Child services supervisor Sandy Henke, Lily's longtime friend, rose to represent the State in today's proceedings. In their respective lines of work, there was no greater success story than the adoption of a child like Dreama into a loving family. "Your Honor, the State of California is satisfied these petitioners meet all necessary criteria to complete this adoption."

"And is the State also confident this permanent placement is in the best interest of this child?"

"Oh, we're ex*treme*ly confident, Your Honor."

"All right then, it looks like we have some celebrating to do." Smiling broadly herself, Lily peered down from the bench at the excited child. "Dreama, would you like to come up here and help me make this official? Who's taking pictures?"

"I am." A gray-haired Black gentleman—Dreama's new grandfather, Lily guessed—rose from the gallery flaunting an expensive-looking camera. Quite a few members of the Peavine extended family had turned out for the happy occasion.

Wearing a lavender crinoline dress with patent leather shoes, the girl skipped up the steps to the bench, where Lily pushed back her chair to make room in her lap. With Dreama settled on her knee, she picked up her pen. "Do you know what happens when I write my name on this piece of paper?"

Dreama's brown eyes danced with excitement. "It makes me a family," she said, causing a chuckle around the courtroom.

"It makes you a family! That's right. Should we ask your mom and dad to come up here and help us?"

Without waiting for an answer, the couple hurried up to join them. Once they were in place, Lily signed the order to a chorus of cheers. Dozens of celebratory photos later, she adjourned the court for lunch.

Sandy squeezed through the side door before it closed. Now in her mid-fifties, she'd finally surrendered to the extra thirty pounds that clung to her under her well-tailored suit despite years of dieting. Lily couldn't help but note how much more relaxed she seemed. Holding up an insulated bag, Sandy said, "I hope we're still on for lunch, Your Honor. Suzanne made us chicken sandwiches on fresh sourdough."

"Bless Suzanne!" Lily looped their arms and led her down the narrow hallway to the labyrinth of judges' chambers. Best friends for twenty years, they always relished the occasions when their work brought them together. "You don't have to call me Your Honor back here, you know. High Priestess of Familial Justice will do when it's just us."

"High Priestess it is, then. It still blows my mind every time you walk in wearing that robe. Don't get me wrong, it suits you. But it seems like just yesterday you and I were juggling impossible caseloads, going to battle every day against the system."

"We're still juggling impossible caseloads, but now we *are* the system," Lily said, "and all these young, idealistic lawyers and caseworkers probably feel like they're out there doing battle with us."

Lily's surprising appointment to the Los Angeles County Superior Court bench had come just five months ago following the retirement of persnickety family court judge Rusty Evans, who'd championed her to his colleagues as his replacement. Though Judge Evans had been notoriously tough on attorneys, she'd always held him in grudging esteem for his consistent focus on what was best for the children who came to his court. Lily was determined to follow in his footsteps.

At forty-five, she was among the youngest of the hundred-plus judges in the Stanley Mosk building, the downtown courthouse where for years she had argued family law and criminal cases in her work at Braxton Street Legal Aid Clinic. As a relative newcomer to the bench, she had a windowless office that could barely hold three guests without one getting into another's personal space. Still, this was her "chambers," and she'd decorated it with her diploma from UCLA and framed photos of her family, including her favorite candids of sixteen-year-old Andy and twins Georgie and Eleanor, who'd recently celebrated their tenth birthday.

"I like your hair, by the way," Sandy said. "Funny, it looks even blonder now that you aren't coloring it anymore."

Lily ran a hand through her fresh cut. Anna liked it short, said it made her green eyes look bigger and brighter. "It looks blonder because it's starting to come in gray. At least it saves me a couple of hundred bucks a month. And a lot of time."

Sandy cleared a space on the desk and unpacked the lunch bag. "I passed Claré Zepeda and her entourage in the hall earlier. She did *not* look happy."

"Oh, she wasn't." Zepeda—or simply Claré, as she preferred—was the hottest thing going in Latina hip hop, and Lily had caught her divorce case. "I strongly urged her to go to mediation and try to reach a settlement. Someone's blowing smoke up her ass if she thinks she's going to leave her husband high and dry. Her attorney should be disbarred for malpractice. It's bad enough he let her marry her pool boy without a prenup. Now he's got her convinced she can buck California's community property laws. She'd do well to give her ex the pool and the house around it. Walk away from her mistake and be done with it."

"I bet you never thought you'd find yourself in the middle of that media circus. Can't you just see Rusty Evans catching a hip hop case? 'What's all this got to do with rabbits?'"

Lily laughed as she hung her robe on the back of her office door. "I always thought that was just his schtick. Ol' Rusty knew a lot more than he let on."

"Absolutely. I swear he played that naive card just to make us look like idiots. Like that time he kept interrupting me when I was trying to place a six-year-old named Compton with an uncle named Compton who lived—guess where."

"Compton," they said together, dissolving into laughter.

Wiping her tears, Lily said, "I bet we could tell Rusty stories all day."

"He was one of a kind. You making any new friends here?"

"I already knew a lot of these folks. I've been darkening their courtrooms for ages. To be honest, no one has time to socialize. There's so much minutiae to handle with filings and transcripts. And the dockets have to run like clockwork or it all breaks down."

"Sounds a lot like being a caseworker…or a legal aid attorney. But you still like it, right?"

"No," Lily paused thoughtfully before her smile leaked out. "I *love* it. This is my dream job, Sandy. The absolute top of the pyramid…though I wouldn't mind having one of those big offices across the hall someday."

They both knew that would be a while. Superior Court judges were appointed by the governor and served six-year terms before coming up for reelection. In the absence of a shocking scandal or controversy, voters almost always retained incumbents, so an appointment to the bench was all but guaranteed for life.

Lily peeled back the bread on her sandwich to find sliced apples and soft white cheese atop thin slices of roasted chicken breast. "Suzanne makes the best sandwiches. My mouth is watering already."

"Speaking of significant others, how's yours? We haven't seen Anna since the week before Christmas."

"I've hardly seen her myself, but that's February for you. She goes straight from year-end sales to tax season."

"Why don't you guys come over next weekend? Suzanne has the whole weekend off. She'll fire up the grill."

Lily checked her phone's calendar and saw a yellow bar, the marker for a family event. "Sorry, next weekend's no good. Georgie has a tennis tournament in Newport Beach on Saturday, then Sunday's a big birthday bash for Hal. He's turning fifty and their daughter Alice turns thirteen the day after. You guys are more than welcome to join us for that. We'd love to have you."

"I'll check with Suzanne, but she's turned into such a homebody these days. I doubt I can get her to leave the house. I still want to get together though, the four of us. At least have Anna look at her schedule and let's try to make a date."

"Will do." Lily silently congratulated herself for successfully dodging more questions about her wife. She was on pins and needles about letting something slip about Pinnacle that could land them all in prison.

* * *

Lily relaxed on the couch, where she called out seventh-grade spelling words to fifth-graders Georgie and Eleanor. She loved these moments after dinner when they all hung out together in the family room, though Anna was working late tonight so she and Andy had missed dinner. It was understandable since a lot was at stake. She'd be so glad when this grueling process was finished, no matter what Anna decided.

"Your turn, Georgie. The word is laboratory. Eleanor conducts experiments in her laboratory."

"L-A-B-O-R-A-T-O-R-Y."

"Correct. Ellie, your word is tournament. Georgie has a tennis tournament this weekend at Newport Beach."

"It's a match, not a tournament," Georgie complained. "I should have gotten that word."

As Eleanor spelled, Serafina Casillas entered from the kitchen, drying her hands on a tea towel. She was petite like Lily, with dark hair and wide brown eyes that lit up whenever the children were near. "Everything's clean and put away. And I put two plates in the oven for the stragglers."

"Thanks, Serafina. They don't deserve you." Lily nudged Georgie with her foot. "You guys go say goodnight to Serafina."

Eleanor rose first and ran to give their housekeeper a hug.

Lily couldn't imagine their household without Serafina. Her husband Enzo, who'd worked in the service department of the BMW dealership for over fifteen years, died unexpectedly from insulin shock while visiting her parents in Mexico. As a natural born US citizen, he'd sponsored Serafina for a green card soon after they married, but her march toward citizenship had been derailed by his death and now was bogged down in a system deliberately slowed by politics.

Feeling a duty to Enzo, Anna had offered Serafina the job of managing their household, since the twins were starting kindergarten and Lily was itching to go back to work full-time. In a matter of weeks, they built her a private apartment above the garage and gave her a car to ferry the kids to their activities. Now after five years, Serafina was family.

"Whose turn is it?" Georgie asked when Serafina had gone.

"Yours," Lily said, noticing a flash of headlights in the driveway. "The word is negotiable. Your bath and bedtime is right now and it's not negotiable."

Both children groaned but lumbered to their feet and collected the papers they'd scattered.

"I'm going out to meet Mom with the umbrella. You guys run on upstairs and we'll be there in a few."

Georgie asked, "What about Andy? I can get another umbrella and go meet him."

"Andy can get wet. It's your bath time. Up you go."

Andy burst through the door and raced past her on his way to the kitchen.

"Hi, Ma. How was your day?" Lily yelled sarcastically. "Serafina left two dinners in the oven. Don't you dare eat both of them."

Carrying a wide golf umbrella, she dodged puddles in the driveway to reach the garage, where Anna was folding her silk jacket inside out so it wouldn't get spots from the rain. Behind her was a 230i, BMW's entry level coupe. Anna usually borrowed this demo for Andy's practice driving, but she'd taken him out a few times in her M4 so he could learn to drive a manual transmission.

Though Anna was soon to be fifty years old, she still made Lily's heart race. She especially loved when Anna swept her long dark hair into a loose bun at her neck. Her business look, she called it, but Lily found it chic and sexy. Even standing in the rain. Her face was gently lined with laughter, showing off her high cheekbones and sterling blue eyes.

"You let Andy drive home in the rain? That's brave."

"He has to learn sometime, or so he says," she said, bending down for a kiss. "Sorry I'm late. It's been quite a day."

"Good or bad?"

"Possibly excellent. I'll give you the details when we get upstairs. But first, I'm starving."

"Too bad. Serafina saved you some but Andy went straight to the kitchen. He's probably eaten it all by now."

"Are you saying I might have to cook something for myself?"

Hooking their elbows, Lily conjured the string of kitchen disasters Anna had wrought over the years. "I'd never let you do that, sweetheart."

* * *

Next to the family hour after dinner, late evening was Anna's favorite time of day. The house was quiet, homework was finished, the kids were in bed. These were her precious moments alone with Lily. Once their bedroom door clicked shut, they connected as best friends, as partners, as lovers.

They'd renovated the master suite a few years ago, giving up space in their bedroom for a larger bath and two walk-in closets. The window alcove, which years ago had held the twins' cribs, was now a cozy TV nook with a small L-shaped sofa and ottoman, and colorful throw pillows. The rest of the bedroom held only a platform bed and a pair of nightstands.

Lily emerged from the bathroom, adorable as ever in her usual sleeping attire, flannel boxers and a worn tank top. "Sounds to me like you've made up your mind already."

Anna had laid out the substance of their meeting with Pinnacle along with the pros and cons of accepting their offer. The more details she shared, the more convinced she was of its merits. "The whole reason I bought all these dealerships was to grow the company and increase its value. I've done that. But it's only worth something if I'm willing to sell it."

"It's so wild to hear you talking like this," Lily said as she drew back the comforter on their king-sized bed. "I can't imagine Anna Kaklis *not* in the BMW business. You're like a kid at Christmas every time a new model hits the market. What would you do with all that pent-up energy?"

Excited by her growing resolve, Anna wrapped her arms around Lily and they crashed together onto the bed. "How about I lavish it on you instead?"

They laughed as they wrestled, each trying to pin the other on her back. When Lily finally surrendered, Anna noticed raised eyebrows that flirted and dared. After fifteen years of lovemaking, she knew that look—Lily was up for it tonight.

"Where should I start?" Anna teased as she playfully began to walk her fingers across Lily's collarbone, knowing how much the anticipation of being tickled somewhere would wind her up. Suddenly she buried her face into Lily's neck and pretended to devour it. "Chomp, chomp, chomp."

Lily squealed and wriggled, trying to protect her neck. "Not there, not there. Please, not there." She gasped for breath and braced for the next assault.

"If not there, then…" Anna lifted the threadbare tank top and drew a spiral on her breast, each ring bringing her closer to the stiffening nipple. "I think I'll start riiiight…"

"Good God, just bite it already!" Lily tugged Anna's head down until her lips finally met the nipple. "I want teeth!"

Anna obliged, nipping and tugging as Lily squirmed with delight. It thrilled her to hear Lily plaintively voicing her desires, unabashed about her wants. As Anna's excitement surged, she gave up their playful game and covered Lily's mouth with a hungry kiss. Their bodies followed, with legs tangled and writhing.

"Tell me what you want," Anna murmured. "Anything."

Lily was swarming every part of Anna's body her hands could reach. "Stay here with me. I want to look at you."

As Anna kissed her again, her hand slid inside the waistband of Lily's shorts and cupped her sex. She knew exactly what Lily liked when they lay face-to-face like this. Two fingers gently tracing… teasing… opening. Every stroke growing wetter. In and out, up and around. Lily's hips rolling like waves in the ocean. Then the tremors started and her nails dug into Anna's skin.

"That's my girl," she said, their eyes connecting as Lily climaxed. After barely a moment, Anna tested her readiness for another.

"I'm good, babe," Lily panted, covering Anna's hand to hold it still. "Just give me another couple of minutes to enjoy this."

This too was a part of their familiar coded dance. If Anna wanted to be touched, she could signal that with a simple word or gesture. She had something different in mind for tonight. "It's fine. You can lie there and relax. I feel like touching myself."

"Oooh." Lily shuddered so hard it shook the bed. "Keep talking like that and you'll make me come again."

CHAPTER TWO

Andy, still in his school uniform but with his tie in his pocket and his jacket who-knows-where, entered Anna's office bouncing a tennis ball that happened to slip from his hand and knock over a framed photo on her bookshelf. "Oops. You wanted to see me, Mom?"

"Please shut the door and take a seat," she said sternly, nodding toward the chair in front of her desk.

"Sounds like I'm in trouble. What'd I do now?"

"I should hope you already know what this is about, Andy. Jason Frick is furious, and he has every right to be." She'd practiced this in her washroom so she could get it out without losing her temper. "In the first place, *you* don't get to jump the line in the service department. We work by appointment so our customers can plan their day and we can schedule staff accordingly."

"I've seen you do it for your friends, like that Clemmons guy."

"Craig Clemmons buys two new BMWs every year for him and his wife. If anyone deserves quick service, it's Craig. Do you not see the difference?"

"I guess," he said sheepishly as he twirled a pen on her desk. "I was just trying to make Jason feel special."

"And I'm sure he did…until Dean came out and told him his front axle was bent and a new one would cost him two thousand dollars. He said you told him it was the driveshaft and not to worry because it was under warranty."

"Wasn't there a recall?"

"The recall was only for the X models, and besides, a bent axle is body damage. He probably hit a pothole or drove up over a curb. Those things aren't covered under warranty, but thanks to you Jason is convinced the damage was caused by a faulty driveshaft, and he expects us to eat it." As her temper started to get the better of her, she snatched the pen he was twirling and slammed it on her desk. "And since when do you speak for the service department? You haven't spent five hours in there in your whole life. You can't possibly learn how to diagnose problems without working alongside a mechanic."

"It's boring," he whined, and in a mocking voice added, "'Hand me that wrench, Andy.' A moron could do that."

"A moron." Anna was dangerously close to telling him only a moron would make an uninformed guess about a car repair. "You're saying one of our mechanics took the time to show you which tools they used—and gave you the opportunity to watch so you'd learn something essential to our core business—and you couldn't be bothered because you were bored."

"I don't like that kind of stuff, okay?" He began to pace in front of her desk, once again bouncing the tennis ball.

"Please put that ball away before you break something. This isn't a playground." This conversation was long overdue, but also moot if she followed through with the sale to Pinnacle. On the other hand, if she could get Andy to admit that he wasn't interested in pursuing the skills he'd need to run the business, it might soften the blow when she broke the news. "To be honest, pal, I'm trying to figure out what it is you actually *do* like. I've tried to get you to spend time with Holly so you can learn what it takes to run a dealership, but she says you glaze over every time you go into her office. Holly's a top-notch general manager, the best we have. Do you realize how lucky you are to have someone like that willing to teach you what she knows?"

"But I don't have to know that stuff as long as I can hire someone who does. That's what you said about Uncle Hal, that you didn't have to think about finances anymore because he does all that."

"*Waaait* a minute," Anna said, rolling her eyes dramatically. "How will you know who's good at their job if you don't understand what it is they're supposed to be doing? Just think about that for a second. What if your foot traffic dried up because your GM implemented a lousy ad campaign? If you don't know what kind of ads work for what, how are you going to fix that?"

"Simple. You fire that GM and hire a new one."

"But how can you be sure the next one knows their stuff if you don't know it either? And what if the finance manager you hire is skimming your profits? You could be cleaned out before you knew what hit you."

He almost bounced the ball again but wisely pocketed it instead. "I feel like I should focus on what I want to be good at—selling BMWs. I want to be the best there is. I figure the more I know about which cars have what options and packages, the better I'll be able to help a customer buy the car that's right for them. That's what it's all about really. Right?"

Anna's anger dissipated as she grasped where he was coming from. Her son—with the world practically laid at his feet—aspired to be a car salesman. The *best* car salesman, to be fair. But there was nothing in his words to suggest that he even wanted to run the company. Which was all the more reason to sell it.

"From now on, Andy," she said, "I want you to stay away from the service department."

* * *

LA winters weren't terribly cold but they sure were dark. Lily couldn't wait for next month's return to Daylight Savings Time. She'd gladly give up an hour of sleep to get home before dark.

Seeing the back gate ajar, she veered toward the French doors of the patio. Anna was in the kitchen stacking plates and setting out glassware. To the casual observer she might have been cooking but Lily knew better. Wednesdays were family night, a tradition they'd started a couple of years ago when Serafina started taking night classes for her nursing degree. Anna knocked off work early and picked up Chinese takeout from Chin Chin. They ate together in the family room and took turns choosing a movie.

Anna paused to deliver a hello kiss. "Were you sneaking up on me?"

Lily opened a carton and snitched a crunchy snow pea. "Just making sure you weren't sprinkling roofies on my dinner so you could take advantage of me later."

"Ha! I'm not stupid, Lily. I'd roofie the kids, not you."

"How'd it go with Andy?" she asked, her voice low so it wouldn't carry. Anna had called earlier to fill her in on Andy's fiasco with the service department. "You sounded like you were ready to go ballistic. Not that I'd blame you."

"I managed not to throw anything but he didn't make it easy." Anna shared the gist of their conversation with a surprising conclusion. "What's interesting is that I've worried all this time about Andy getting upset over the sale. Now I realize it doesn't matter. He has no real interest in running the company anyway. All he cares about is selling cars, and he can do that anywhere."

Lily didn't doubt Andy would make a terrific car salesman, but she believed he had far more potential than that. Furthermore, she expected Anna to be on the same page when it came to their children's futures.

"Let's not give up on him just yet, Anna. He needs to go to college first and get exposed to the arts and anthropology and political science and"—she ticked them off on her fingers—"you get what I'm saying. If he does all that and still wants to sell cars, fine. But I'd like to see him challenge himself, not just take a job he could practically walk into today."

"Hey, Ma."

Startled by Andy's voice behind her, she was relieved when Anna shook her head to indicate he hadn't heard their conversation. She turned and greeted him with a hug. "Hi, sweetheart. How was school?"

"Fine. Can we eat now? I'm starving." He swiped a chunk of beef in brown sauce with his fingers, avoiding a scolding from Lily since she'd done that herself.

"I need to go up and change clothes. What about Georgie and Ellie?"

"Not my job to watch 'em."

Anna sucked in a breath as he returned to the family room. "This is how he responds to being called out over something. And to top it off, not one word of apology for all the trouble he caused with the service department. And he wonders why we won't let him get his driver's license."

"Teenagers. Can't live with them, can't smother them."

"To answer your question, Eleanor's in the living room with a book and Georgie's doing his homework in his room. Everything's ready for dinner. I'll go help him finish up."

In her closet upstairs, Lily checked the coffee stain on her favorite houndstooth blazer and tossed it in the hamper for dry cleaning. She donned her softest sweatpants and a red flannel shirt that had belonged to her mom, and was rinsing off her makeup when Anna joined her.

"Georgie's done with his science questions so we're ready when you are. I didn't even ask how your day was."

"If it's true what they say about everyone having fifteen minutes of fame, mine's probably coming tomorrow in the supermarket tabloids. You know Claré Zepeda, right?"

Anna did a shuffle and rapped the hit tune, "*All ice no thaw, Ima drop your call*."

"Yeah, that one. She released it a month before she filed for divorce, so her ex is owed half the royalties—forever. We're talking millions. I tried to get her to work it out with him but she wouldn't listen. She thinks she'll get a jury to side with her, but the law's the law."

"Wowza. Her fans are going to hunt you down."

"Apparently it's already started. Perfect strangers on Twitter hope I choke on pool boy's penis. It's ridiculous. My poor secretary has more important things to do than screen obscene emails and flag the ones that look like a genuine threat." She instantly regretted saying that since Anna would worry about the threats. "Speaking of messages, did I tell you Eleanor's been texting me pictures of kittens up for adoption? Three this week."

"I guess being subtle hasn't gotten her anywhere, and those big brown eyes of hers are getting harder to ignore. Maybe we should think about it. Alice is getting one for her birthday this weekend. Besides, it's been three years."

"I don't know, Anna. Last time was just so hard on all of us."

Last time meant Chester, the basset hound that had belonged to Lily's mom. He'd lived to an extraordinary age of fourteen, with Anna and Andy carrying him up and down the stairs in his final years. While Andy had taken it quite hard, Georgie had been especially traumatized by his introduction to death.

"The kids are older now," Anna said. It was obvious she was trying to sound objective, but Lily could tell she was starting to cave. "They'll be adults before they have to go through it again."

"The problem as I see it is if Eleanor gets a kitten, Andy will want another dog. And then Georgie will want something he isn't allergic to, like—God help us—a pig." She pretended not to hear Anna snort. "Next thing you know they're off to college and we're living in a…"

"Ee i ee i oh."

"Exactly. So you need to think long and hard before you go collecting stray animals."

Eleanor's commanding voice sounded through the door. "Mom, Georgie's eating all the shrimp right out of the carton. Come on, we're starving to death."

Lily sighed. "Our poor neglected children. It's a wonder child services hasn't taken them away."

CHAPTER THREE

The gaudy pink tour bus had slowed to a crawl down what many considered the prettiest of all the palm-lined streets in Beverly Hills. This one came like clockwork three times a day along with half a dozen others.

Creeping behind the bus in her car with Anna, Lily drummed her fingers on the steering wheel waiting for her chance to pull through the gate of the Big House, their name for the stately mansion where Anna grew up. "Have you ever thought about taking one of those tours? For all we know, they could be telling people this is Taylor Swift's house."

Anna replied, "When we were kids, Dad would play along with it. Every time he'd see it coming, he'd go out there in his Ray-Bans and pose like he was some big Hollywood star."

"It takes so little to entertain your father." Finally Lily was able to pull around the brick circle and wedge her X3 into the row of BMWs belonging to Anna's father George, her sister Kim, and Hal.

Sadly, their weekend birthday celebration had been interrupted by a funeral.

Lily killed the engine and waited quietly for Anna's cue to exit. It was rare to see her looking so vulnerable. The birthday party would be a comforting counterweight to their solemn morning, a service in Pasadena for Anna's ex-husband, Scott Rutherford. They'd only heard of his death the day before through a mutual friend.

Sensing Anna's heartbreak, Lily grasped her hand. "Is there anything I can do, sweetheart? Anything I can say?"

Anna inhaled sharply and blinked several times to disperse a new wave of tears. "I'll be okay. I keep getting these waves of disbelief…and regret. He was such a nice guy. We traded notes on Facebook, but apparently he didn't feel close enough to tell me he had cancer. Why didn't I just ask how he was doing? It would have been so simple. Instead I don't show up until it's time to grieve. His family must have wondered what the hell I was doing there."

"No one thought that, Anna. You were friends and you had every right to be there. Scott wasn't just some guy you knew. He was an important chapter in your life."

"A good chapter, I think. I learned a lot about myself."

"And in the end you both went on to better lives and you were happy for each other."

To their credit, they'd ended their marriage on friendly terms and stayed in touch for years through social media. Scott left behind a wife and four children, the youngest only eight.

"Sara really appreciated you being there. She said so. I think their oldest son did too."

"Matt…Scott was so proud of him. I wonder if he's done the math by now and figured out he was born while his dad was married to me…so he'd know why we got divorced." Her voice creaked with emotion and she choked back a sob. "If he did, I hope he forgave him. I did."

Lily hated to see Anna hurting but she wasn't the only one whose emotions were in turmoil today. Funerals were hard on her too. Since losing her mom, she could hardly bear to see the suffering of loved ones left behind. To make matters worse, today's funeral mass had stirred up spurious fears about Anna's mortality. It horrified her to imagine sitting there like Sara with their children. Cancer could happen to anyone. So could a host of other diseases or accidents. A long life wasn't guaranteed.

The raindrops tapping the windshield grew suddenly into loud pelts. Anna said, "There goes our chance to make it inside without getting wet. Sorry."

"It's all right. We can sit out here as long as you like, or I can run inside and give you some time alone. Just tell me what you want."

Anna stretched over the console and kissed her softly on the lips. "I'm sure I'll feel better once we get in the house. There's not much five rowdy kids can't cure."

"Six, if you count your father."

* * *

The Big House bore little resemblance to the elegant, finely appointed home Anna had known all her life. These days it was a hub of barely contained chaos, home not only to her father and stepmother Martine, but also to Kim's family of four. They'd lost everything three years ago when a wildfire swept through Benedict Canyon. What started as a temporary shelter became permanent as Alzheimer's ravaged Martine's mind and body. Now in the end stages of the disease, she struggled most days even to recognize her loved ones.

"I'm off to find Kim," Anna said to Lily as she prepared to exit her father's study, having changed into jeans and a long-sleeved knit top that hung off one shoulder.

"I'll be along in a sec." Lily zipped her jeans and squatted all the way to the floor to stretch them out. "Tight jeans aren't as desirable as they used to be."

Anna eyed her up and down and winked. "They are to me."

Eleanor met them at the door. Tall for a ten-year-old and gangly, she bore a striking resemblance to Anna but for the brown eyes of her Hispanic father, the anonymous sperm donor she shared with her brother Georgie. Grasping Anna's hand, she exclaimed, "Come see what Alice got for her birthday!"

"Anna?" Lily tugged her back and whispered, "Ee i ee i oh."

Alice proudly presented her prize, a tiny longhaired calico kitten with a white chest and feet. A patch of black covered one eye on what was otherwise a darling golden face.

"She's adorable," Anna said, unable to resist cupping it in her hands and nuzzling its fur. "Does she have a name yet?"

"Gracie."

Eleanor added, "See how her face looks like a pirate? We looked up pirate names and there was this woman pirate named Grace O'Malley."

"She looks like a Gracie, don't you think?" Alice said, her natural voice low and husky.

"Gracie O'Malley. That sounds *purrr*-fect," Anna replied with a laugh.

She and Lily loved that Eleanor looked up to her cousin Alice, who was outgoing and mature for her thirteen years. Good grades, fun personality, and she got on well with adults and kids alike, though she had zero interest in boys. Lily cautioned against drawing conclusions, but pointed out that Alice's main pastimes—basketball and girl bands—were common among girls who later came out. Kim saw it too but Hal was clueless as usual.

"Where's your mom, Alice?"

"I think she's in the blue room with grandma."

A cozy parlor off the seldom-used formal living room, Kim liked the blue room for its two chaise lounges, perfect for reading while Martine watched travel and cooking shows on TV. That was exactly how Anna found them, with a small space heater that kept the room at what felt like eighty-five degrees for Martine, who still shivered beneath a couch throw.

Kim lit up when Anna appeared. "Look who it is, Mom. Say hi to Anna." She was usually careful to fill in blanks right away rather than quiz their mother about names and faces, which caused unnecessary anxiety and embarrassment.

"Hi, Mom. You look beautiful today. Did Kim fix your hair?"

Her hair was freshly cut and colored the same honey auburn as Kim's.

Martine's eyes darted between them with confusion until Kim signaled with a nod. "Yes."

"It's very pretty." Anna took a seat at the foot of her mother's chaise and stroked her leg. "Yours too," she said to Kim.

"Thanks, I've discovered it's just as easy to do two heads as one. We never know when some handsome fellow is going to ask us out on a date." She clutched Martine's hand and smiled.

Though Kim was the same age as Anna, she didn't look a day over thirty-nine thanks to her delicate features. Years of yoga and a healthy diet had kept her trim and fit, and her sense of style was impeccable. Anna and Lily both sought her fashion advice.

"I was really sorry to hear about Scott," Kim said. "How was the funeral?"

"About what you'd expect. Three or four hundred people, a lot of them from the business school at Southern Cal. Plenty of tears…especially for the kids."

"Nobody's ever ready, are they?" Kim said, her own tears welling as she gazed solemnly at their mother.

"No, they aren't." Anna took a deep breath to shake off the sadness of the moment. "So…I just met Alice's birthday present. Thanks for that. Ellie's going to want one now."

"Lucky for you, I happen to know where you can get six more just like it."

"I'll give you a thousand dollars if you'll keep that information to yourself."

"Come on, don't be heartless. I know you guys miss Chester. I still miss Peanut, if you can believe it." Anna laughed softly at this reference to the rambunctious puppy they gave equally rambunctious Jonah for Christmas when he was four. He grew into a hefty border collie/pit bull mix who adored everyone and broke all their hearts when he died young from bone cancer. "As soon as Jonah heard we were getting Alice a kitten he asked for another dog, but no way we're going down that road. Three years from now, he'll either be off to college or in jail."

Anna suppressed a laugh. Kim fiercely loved her children, but she wasn't blind to her son's behavior problems. Mostly it was simple mischief, like trying to sell his biology teacher's car on Craigslist. Jonah's saving graces were his charm and his talent for shooting a basketball, which kept him from being expelled.

"By the way, did Hal tell you Jonah got his driver's permit on Friday? We're entering a new phase of hell."

"Ugh. Get ready to age twenty years in six months."

"It can't be worse than Alice getting her period at eleven years old. Wait till it hits you that your daughter's old enough to bear children." Kim crossed her eyes and rolled her head. "What's wrong with Andy's driving? Lily says he's pretty good."

Anna shook off traumatic thoughts of Eleanor reaching puberty. "Sure, but then he stopped being good at anything else. His grades went straight into the toilet. I let him practice driving whenever he brings home an A, but at this rate it's going to take him another six months to get the hours in."

"Come on, Anna. Give the poor kid a break. He's like you. Cars are his life."

The last thing Anna wanted was a parenting debate with her sister, who was far more permissive with Jonah than they were with Andy. And in her opinion, it showed.

She stood, wafting her shirt to cool off. "I don't know how you can stand this heat."

Kim raised a spray bottle and misted herself. "You should try it with hot flashes."

"No thanks. I'm off to the family room. Apparently it's the world championship of ping-pong doubles. By the way, did you book your flights to Los Cabos yet? We're going down Friday night to check in since the villa's in my name. I figure we'll put the girls in one bedroom, the boys in another, and Dad and Georgie together."

"Poor Georgie. Let's hope he has earplugs. Oh, and speaking of Dad…did you get my note?"

Anna shuddered and shook her head. "I don't have the capacity to deal with that right now. I'm choosing to ignore it in hopes it's just a phase."

* * *

After kicking off her shoes, Lily sat on the end of the bed and massaged her ankle, the one she'd broken two years ago when she slid off the bottom step in her sock feet. She'd felt a twinge that afternoon while running from the car to the house in the rain.

Despite the birthday celebration, it had been a trying day. First the funeral, then an ugly fight on the way home between the boys over Andy's insistence that Uncle Hal and Georgie had cheated at ping-pong. Georgie used to idolize his older brother and agree with everything he said, but lately the two of them had been pushing one another's buttons. The result was lots of yelling and insults that upset Eleanor and made everyone miserable.

Anna appeared in the doorway to their master bedroom and called out over her shoulder, "Goodnight, urchins. Love you bunches."

"Did you get everyone settled?"

"Hard to say. We have a truce if it holds." She closed the door and retrieved her satin pajamas from the bureau.

"I have a feeling you won't be needing those right away, lady."

"Is that so?" Anna struck a coy pose for about a second, but then disappeared into her walk-in closet. "I need them in case someone breaks the ceasefire."

"Still that tenuous, huh?" Lily followed her into the bathroom and kicked off her slippers to enjoy the heated porcelain floor tiles. "What's up with Andy? I saw you guys talking out by the pool. He's been on such a short fuse lately. Are you sure he hasn't got wind of you selling the business?"

"I don't see how. I think what pissed him off today was Jonah talking about getting his learner's permit last week, and Hal's already let him drive three times. Now Andy's freaking out over the possibility of Jonah getting his license first. I told him he needed to start taking more personal responsibility for his own life and quit worrying about everyone else. Naturally, he took exception to that. He says we baby Georgie and Eleanor, but I pointed out that we babied him at that age too."

"Growing pains…I remember those. You want to be treated like an adult, but without having to take on the responsibilities that come with it. And deep down you're scared you won't be able to cut it." Lily considered her words and added cheekily, "I bet you never experienced that. George says you were thirty years old when you were born."

"That would make me, what? Seventy-eight? Some mornings it feels that way."

As Anna tossed her clothes in the hamper, Lily seized the moment and wrapped her naked body in an embrace. "Don't go talking about my wife like that. She gets more beautiful every day."

"Says the woman who admitted she needed new glasses just last week."

"The better to see you with." Lily snaked her fingers through Anna's hair and guided her head down until their lips met. Intimate kisses such as these—slow and intense—were their usual prelude to lovemaking. She was heating up when Anna broke off their kiss and pecked her forehead before turning away to dress.

* * *

Anna blinked at the darkness and weighed her options. She could remain still and hope Lily would finally fall asleep, or she could speak up and try to help settle whatever was keeping her awake. Lily made the decision for her when she rolled over yet again, this time nearly knocking foreheads.

"Honey, what's wrong?" Getting no immediate reply, she snuggled closer and ran her fingertips along Lily's collarbone. It worried her that she might have hurt Lily's feelings when she brushed off her romantic overtures as they were getting ready for bed. With Scott still on her mind, she hadn't been in the mood. "Can I help?"

Lily sighed deeply and turned to face her. "Sorry, I just…I was almost asleep and it hit me that we're in for such a hard time with Martine. It's going to be tough on the kids to lose their Gran. You and Kim too…all of us, really."

To Anna's thinking, the kids had already lost her. She hadn't been Gran for several years. "I'm worried about how Georgie will handle it. He's so sensitive. But we've always gotten through hard times by leaning on each other. Like when your mom died, and the Benedict Canyon fire. We're teaching our kids they can always count on family, yeah?"

"But can they?" Lily snatched a tissue from the bedside table. "Scott's kids were counting on him and now they can't. What if…"

"No, *do not* torture yourself with that." Anna's own thoughts had gone there during the funeral but she'd shaken them off. Sitting up in bed, she drew Lily into a firm embrace. "None of us knows what life's going to throw at us, but here's what I do know: The biggest challenge I've ever faced was getting out from under that mall after the earthquake. I thought it was over. Then you showed up and made me fight through it. It's why I married you, because you were the strongest person I'd ever known. I knew I could count on you."

"Oh, Anna…I love you."

They held each other and rocked gently before settling back beneath the covers. Anna delivered a long kiss to Lily's temple and added solemnly, "Honey, if anything should ever happen to me, I know you'll get our family through it. And you can trust me to do the same."

CHAPTER FOUR

Lily blinked several times before squinting at the bedside clock: *5:28AM*. Untangling her limbs from Anna's, she stretched to turn off the alarm before it pierced the quiet, and eased herself out of bed.

"Please don't tell me it's morning already," Anna mumbled, half her face still buried in the pillow.

"Okay, I won't tell you. Go back to sleep. You're not the one who has to be at work by seven." LA traffic was both horrendous and unavoidable, which was why Lily tried to stagger her work hours when she could. Early in, early out.

Anna threw back the covers and sat up. "Nope. That's not the deal, Your Honor. My days start and end with you." Though she usually didn't go to her office until nine, Anna always said she liked keeping the same sleep schedule as Lily.

Lily relished their morning routine, the forty-five minutes they had to themselves before she had to leave. While she showered, Anna fetched coffee and a protein bar from the kitchen, allowing Lily to eat as she dressed for the day.

With a towel cinched around her torso, she applied face cream and a touch of makeup, especially mindful of how she looked on days she appeared in court. "Sweetheart, thanks for talking me down last night. You always know exactly what to say."

"I had all the same thoughts during the funeral, so it was good for me to work through it too. I finally got to sleep by thinking about Los Cabos. Nineteen days and counting."

Their spring break family retreat was a highlight of the year. They'd long ago given up ski trips to Tahoe since the cold weather sometimes triggered asthma attacks for Lily and Andy. Besides, it seemed a bigger treat to hit the sunny beaches after what had been an unusually chilly and wet winter in LA.

"Like you need another excuse to think about Los Cabos. You're even more excited than the kids."

"Guilty as charged," Anna replied. Wrapped in a terry robe, she sat on the marble deck of the spa tub sipping her coffee. "Kim's a little anxious about leaving Mom this year but I doubt she'll even miss us."

"I think Kim's more worried that being gone a week might break that tiny thread that still holds them together."

"It could happen. She didn't have a clue who I was yesterday. Or Dad either. Kim said she calls him Claude sometimes."

"That'll bruise the old ego," Lily said, remembering Claude as Martine's first husband, Kim's father. He'd been dead almost forty years. "Is George coming with us to Los Cabos?"

"He hasn't said for sure. We need to have lunch or something this week, assuming he can make room for me on his busy schedule. It's time to talk about the Pinnacle deal…and the other elephant in the room."

George was harboring a secret that wasn't as secret as he thought.

"Sure you're ready for that conversation?"

"I guess," Anna said drearily. "Though I'm thinking about wearing earplugs so I don't have to actually hear it."

* * *

Teen heartthrob Sawyer Clarke and his entourage cheered as the showroom doors opened so Jeremy could drive the i8 roadster out to the delivery circle. Outside, paparazzi were on hand to capture the pop singer and his supermodel girlfriend driving off the lot. Money couldn't buy advertising like that.

Anna, taking it all in from the second-floor landing, thought it a shame such a powerful, precision machine was rolling out beneath a nineteen-year-old kid who'd only started driving a couple of years ago. He would certainly enjoy the i8, but he'd never appreciate it the way an experienced driver would.

Andy looked positively despondent as the sports car rolled out. Cutting edge vehicles like those were hard to find, but as a high-volume dealer in Southern California, Premier Motors always managed to secure a few. In fact there were two on a container ship set to dock in Long Beach tomorrow, but they would take a week or more to clear customs.

"Anna, your cell phone's ringing," Hal called from the hallway behind her. "Want me to bring it to you?"

"Thanks, I'll get it." She wasn't quick enough to catch it, but seeing it was Lily, she called back. "Hey, babe. You on your way home?"

"Not quite. That's why I'm calling. Can you leave work a little early and pick up Georgie from the tennis center?"

Anna checked her inbox and the clock. There was nothing that couldn't wait till tomorrow. "Don't see why not. Andy's here already so we can leave whenever."

"Thanks. I, uh…I haven't been to a meeting lately. Thought I should check in so people can see that I haven't fallen off the wagon and rolled down the hill."

With nearly fourteen years of sobriety under her belt, Lily seemed confident in her recovery. The only time she attended AA meetings was when something got under her skin and stirred her anxieties. Clearly Scott's funeral had done that.

"No problem, love. We'll leave here in a few minutes. See you at home."

Outside her office, rapid footsteps on the tile floor drew closer until Jeremy appeared in her doorway, wringing his hands and looking distressed. "Anna…"

"Let me guess. Sawyer Clarke wrecked his car driving it off the lot."

"Not Sawyer." He winced. "Andy."

She bolted down the stairs and out the side door where a small crowd of salespeople had gathered. A brand new Z4 convertible, San Francisco Red Metallic, sported a cracked windshield and a pronounced dent on the hood. Andy stood off to one side looking sheepish, his head down and his hands in his pockets. To Anna's relief, Sawyer Clarke's i8 was nowhere to be seen.

"What happened here?"

Jeremy answered, "He bumped into a stack of tires outside the service entrance and they fell over. Looks like a couple of them landed on the hood."

"It was my fault," Holly said quickly. "I was talking with Andy about what we ought to put in the showroom and we agreed on the Z. I asked him to go get the key. He must have thought I said go get the Z."

Anna didn't believe Holly would be so careless. Even if she were, Andy knew better than to get behind the wheel of one of their vehicles without her express permission.

"Andy, get your things and meet me at the car."

Sulking, he trudged into the media room for his backpack and jacket.

Holly continued, "I'll price the repairs and put in a claim."

"Never mind the insurance. They won't cover an unlicensed driver. This is coming out of Andy's pocket."

Guarding her temper in front of her staff, she turned on her heel and started back upstairs to collect her belongings from her office. Already dreading the ride home, she turned out the lights and took a moment to calm herself.

"Anna?" It was Holly again, her face grim with what Anna guessed was even more bad news. "Can we talk a minute before you go?"

* * *

Thirty days was forever to a mother separated from her kids. Lily knew that from the time the twins had spent in the neonatal unit after a car accident had caused them to be born two months premature. It was five weeks before Eleanor came home, and another two for Georgie. She remembered that feeling every time she ruled from the bench to separate a child from its mother.

Crawling in the traffic along Wilshire Boulevard, she was haunted by the sobs of Selena Cortes, a mother of two who'd lost custody of her two daughters sixty days ago after child services responded to a complaint and found drugs in the home. Police later determined the drugs belonged to the woman's brother, who was living there at the time. Lily was set to return the girls today, but the caseworker reported that Ms. Cortes had allowed her brother to stay at her home for two nights, violating the terms Lily had set down for getting her children back. Child services had asked for sixty more days. Lily gave them thirty but left the door open for thirty more.

Skirting the campus of UCLA, she turned into the parking lot at St. Agnes Lutheran Church to find a cluster of cars near a door leading to the community room in the basement. This Monday night meeting of Alcoholics Anonymous was the Over 40s, a group that usually included university faculty and staff, and other professionals like herself.

She was mildly surprised to recognize a couple of faces, given that she'd been to only one meeting since picking up her thirteen-year chip last spring. Dan was still the group's leader. He'd set a dozen chairs in a circle, an arrangement that usually encouraged participation.

Lily typically kept to herself and listened to others tell their stories of how they'd fallen out of control before they finally hit bottom and admitted their lives had become unmanageable. She honestly believed alcohol was no longer a problem for her—she hardly thought about it—but the specter of how it once had gripped her was always there. Indeed, it had nearly cost her everything she held dear. These days, however, the temptation to drink was merely philosophical, a pondering of what catastrophic events could possibly lure her back to the bottle. Yesterday's reflections over losing loved ones—of losing Anna—had scared her enough to come to the meeting and share her feelings.

"Lily, would you like to say something to the group?"

"Actually, I would," she said, staring into her lap as she twirled a paperclip she'd found in the pocket of her suit jacket. "I've been doing well. Most days I feel determined to stay the course. I don't get anxious about going to social events or feeling alone. Heck, I've got three kids. I've forgotten what being alone is like."

That drew a chuckle from Diana, an African-American woman Lily vaguely recognized as a social worker she'd encountered in court during her days with the legal aid clinic. Social workers knew very well what a hectic family life was like.

"Right, so I don't worry about it much. But every now and then it hits me that I could be just one disappointment away, one disaster, one loss…and those old habits could come roaring back and make me lose control again. It actually kind of helps to know how vulnerable I am. Like the saying goes, just one drink away from being a drunk. That never changes."

"Amen, sister."

Lily finally looked up from her lap and smiled at the faces around her. "I know I don't come very often, but I'm really glad you're here for when I get bogged down worrying about stuff. This program feels like my suit of armor."

She left the meeting newly fortified, as though she'd plugged the hole where her willpower might trickle out unnoticed. Everyone faced hardship at one time or another, but she felt certain she could face hers without that old crutch.

* * *

Four hours had helped to calm Anna's anger about the accident, but her frustration over Andy's lack of candor was another matter. After a quick chat with Lily in their bedroom, they'd agreed on a plan to turn this into a tough lesson about taking responsibility for one's actions.

"It was like Holly said. She asked me to bring the key, but I thought she said bring the Z," Andy explained earnestly. "I figured it was cool as long as I had her permission."

The twins were upstairs in bed already, leaving Anna, Lily and Andy to hash out the day's events around the kitchen table. Lily looked tired from what she'd described as an emotionally trying day.

Anna wasn't having her son's casual nonchalance. "You're sticking with that story?"

"It's not just my story. It's Holly's too."

"See, here's the problem. Holly came up to my office before we left and admitted that she only told that story to help you save face in front of the others. But she wanted me to know the truth."

"It *is* the truth!"

"Excuse me, are you now calling Holly a liar? Because she told me she asked *Jeremy* to bring the Z into the showroom when he finished the paperwork on Sawyer Clarke. And that you were standing right there beside him, and she very clearly asked you to get the keys *for him*. How could you have misunderstood words as plain as that?"

His face was turning redder by the second. "I must've heard her wrong."

"Just stop it. You need to own this, Andy—right now." She punctuated her words by jabbing the table. "Because lying about what happened only makes it worse."

Lily jumped in, her voice calm, her tone reasonable. "Andy, even if it happened the way you said—"

"Which it didn't," Anna snapped.

After a sideward glance, Lily continued, "I think you know there was a better way to handle that situation. What you should have done was remind Holly that you didn't have your license, and that your mom never allows you to drive cars on the lot. Am I right?" Getting no answer, she continued, "I happen to agree with her on this. It's very disappointing that you're refusing to come clean about it."

"Let's not lose sight of this, pal—you caused a couple thousand dollars damage to a brand new car. So the best thing you can do for yourself now is accept responsibility for this mess so we can move on."

"Move on to what?"

She exchanged nods with Lily, who answered, "This is serious, so you deserve to face some consequences."

"Great, so I'm grounded till I'm like, thirty. Whatever."

Anna slapped the table sharply. "You need to start taking this seriously, young man. What you did showed very poor judgment. Clearly you aren't ready for the responsibility that comes with a driver's license. So we're going to put your driving on hold till summer, and only if you can prove to us by then that you're capable of making better decisions."

"Wha—" he sputtered, looking ready to explode. "You treat me like a little kid. All the guys at school got their license as soon as they turned sixteen. I'm almost sixteen and a half and you keep making excuses for me not to get mine."

Lily reached for his hand but he jerked it away. "Andy, this is a *reason*, not an excuse. Just like your report card was a reason."

"I don't care what you call it...you always come up with something." He was fighting back angry tears. "I'll pay for the damage myself. Just take it out of my trust."

Lily shook her head. "A trust doesn't work that way. You can't touch it till you turn eighteen." The trust was worth two hundred thousand dollars, a settlement from the city of San Francisco as compensation for the police shooting that had accidentally killed his biological mother, the half-sister Lily hadn't known she had. "Besides, this isn't about the money. It's about you learning to be more responsible."

"No, it's about punishing me. That's all you really care about. You both sit around thinking up ways you can punish me so it hurts. I can go a thousand days without messing up, but you jump on me the one day when I do, and that's what you judge me on. I can't be perfect every day." He crossed his arms defiantly and slumped back from the table, clearly fuming.

"Pout all you want, Andy," Anna said, her patience dried up. "The more you pretend this is our fault, the further you are from getting behind the wheel. You're already at June. Want to try for August?"

He growled under his breath and stormed out of the kitchen and up the stairs. Moments later his bedroom door slammed.

"That went well," Anna deadpanned.

Lily flashed a look of annoyance before shoving her chair back and following him upstairs without a word.

* * *

Lily slammed drawers and stalked around their bedroom, angrier at Anna than at Andy. Parenting was hard enough without one of them undermining the other. What was the point of talking things over in private if not to present a united front?

Anna entered the room and closed the door. "I made sure Georgie and Eleanor were tucked in. And I said goodnight to Andy through his door but he didn't answer."

"I'm not surprised. I doubt he'll speak to either of us in the near future."

"That's up to him."

"And us too. I couldn't believe you going off script like that. We agreed on a month. Now you're telling him he can't drive till June...or even August. That's forever for a kid his age."

"Yeah, well...a month would have been plenty if he hadn't sat there and lied to our faces. And not one word of apology either. In my book, that's a nonstarter."

Lily followed her into the bathroom and pointedly said, "*Your* book. That's the problem right there, Anna. It's supposed to be *our* book. If you changed your mind, you should have waited and talked it over with me in private, and we'd have come up with another plan together. Instead, you just issued your draconian edict from on high and that was that."

"My edict from on high...that's nice. Tell me how you *really* feel."

"How I feel is disrespected. It so happens I had a different opinion, which I would have shared if you'd bothered to ask."

"And now you're being a drama queen," Anna said flippantly as she shrugged out of her clothes and tossed them in the hamper. "We agreed on a month because we expected him to own up to it and show a little remorse. The fact that he didn't do either *obviously* means he deserved more."

"Do you not hear how arrogant that sounds? As long as it's obvious to you, who cares what other people think?" She shuffled between Anna and the doorway to command her attention. "Did it occur to you that I literally make decisions like this for a living? I have the power to be a hard-ass bitch, slapping fines on people and sending them to jail for looking at me sideways. But that's not me. Instead I try to find the path that gets people where they need to be. We could have done that with Andy if you hadn't dropped the hammer on him."

"Great, so I'm a shitty mother too. Anything else on your checklist?"

Lily was surprised by the intensity of their bickering, but now she blamed herself for the sarcastic tone. Her edict on high remark had been over the top. Anna had no way of knowing that her guilt over keeping Selena Cortes from her daughters was behind her heightened sensitivity to questions about fairness.

Even so… it didn't change the fact that Anna had come down too hard on Andy. Still fuming, she climbed into bed and rolled over to face the wall.

Clearly Anna was angry too. Upon coming to bed, she turned out the light without even a goodnight.

Lily rolled onto her back and tried to calm her emotions. This wasn't the way they treated one another, this tension crackling as they lay side by side. Not speaking, not touching. Somehow, they always found their way to a peaceful stasis before sleep, whether by resolution or truce.

One of them would have to breach the divide. An apology, a concession. She was choosing her conciliatory words when Anna's cool finger brushed hers beneath the blanket. A pinkie, deliberately teasing hers until they hooked. Lily answered with an open, upturned palm before rolling into Anna's arms.

"I'm sorry, babe," Anna said softly. "I should have talked to you first."

"I'm sorry I was being so self-righteous. Turns out being a judge gives you a god complex."

Anna kissed her forehead and climbed out of bed.

"Where are you going?"

"To tell Andy that we'll talk it over again tomorrow when we've all calmed down."

CHAPTER FIVE

Lily watched the action on the court from a folding lawn chair, huddled in a wool sweater with her back to the morning sun. She and Anna alternated weekends at the Pacific Palisades tennis complex, which was set aside each Saturday for youth match play. Georgie, who preferred George when his peers were present, had reached the top level for the US Tennis Association's 10 and Under Group (10U) and was focused now on making the jump to Junior Team Tennis when he turned eleven.

Up two games to one in a four-game short set, he tossed the ball high above his head, arched his back, and whacked a slicing serve that spun out of his opponent's reach. An ace, his third of the match.

"Thirty-love," the chair umpire announced.

Lily clapped enthusiastically. "Nice one, George."

"Looked wide to me," a man in front snarled over his shoulder. The infamous Kurt Lockhart, easily the most obnoxious parent on the 10U circuit.

Spread along the sidelines were a dozen others, families of players awaiting their turn to take the court. Some days Lily sat with them and chatted about their kids, but Georgie had asked her to watch today's match closely in case of a flare-up. All the parents were wary of Kurt, who had a reputation for arguing line calls and harassing his son Brandon's opponents. Most of his ire today had been directed at Brandon. A shame, because the kid was pretty good for a ten-year-old.

Unfortunately for Brandon, Georgie was really on his game today. It was amazing to remember this was the same child who'd spent his first seven weeks fighting for life in the neonatal unit. Now he was the picture of grace on the court, a trait he might have inherited from his father, the anonymous sperm donor. They'd chosen a Latino donor for the twins based on the social worker's report that Andy's late father had been from El Salvador. The twins had brown eyes but their similarities ended there. Georgie had Lily's blond hair and athletic physique, while Eleanor was tall and slim with Anna's fair complexion. Only Andy, with the bronze skin of his father's ancestors, was distinctively Latino.

On the court, Brandon chased down a lob and went for the overhead smash, only to hit it into the net. Another unforced error.

"Forty-love."

"You gotta be kidding! He served it up on a silver platter, Brandon. Pull your head out of your rear end." Kurt shook his head and muttered, "All that money wasted on private lessons…I might as well have flushed it down the crapper."

Lily wanted badly to call this man on his bullshit, but the way he treated his son gave her pause. She knew too well the potential danger for kids whose fathers came home in a rage. Her two cents wasn't worth the risk of making it worse for Brandon at home. That wouldn't stop her from putting a bug in Sandy Henke's ear to look into reports from his teachers. It wouldn't surprise her at all if others had raised concerns about Kurt's obvious mean streak.

The next point was a decent rally that ended with Brandon scooping a half-volley cross-court that caught Georgie on the wrong foot. All the parents, including Lily, clapped loudly and cheered, "Great point!" Probably the only positive feedback Brandon would get all day.

Georgie finished off the game with another spinning serve that Brandon returned into the net.

Kurt jumped to his feet. "That was a mile wide!" he yelled, his wrath now aimed at the chair umpire. "Are you blind or just ready to go home?"

Lily again bit her tongue, but one of the fathers behind her had reached his limit. "Come on, Kurt. It's not Wimbledon. Let the kids play."

As Kurt left his chair to confront the other man, the boys passed beneath the umpire's chair for the changeover. Georgie waggled his empty sports drink bottle and Lily met him at the fence with her cooler bag.

"You got any extra, Mom? Brandon doesn't have any."

"Here you go." She squeezed two bottles through the fence. "You're playing great, honey. And tell Brandon he's made some killer shots too. All the parents think so."

"Not all," he said, rolling his eyes as he walked away.

Back at her chair, Lily placed a call to Anna, who was picking up Eleanor at her Saturday STEM class. Science, technology, engineering and math. Eleanor was following in her mother's footsteps. Her *other* mother.

"Hey, what's up?"

"Nothing. I just wanted to tell you how proud I am of our son. We've raised a really nice kid."

"By my count, we've raised three of them. What's Georgie done?"

Lily described the scene at the tennis club, from Kurt's crass behavior to Georgie's kind gesture. "And by the way, today's the best I've ever seen him play. He's in a real groove."

"Good for him. We went over the rankings last night. If he wins today, he should crack the top twenty."

Georgie continued his dominance on the court, breaking serve to win the first set.

"Only three games to go if we survive it. Are you going home?"

"I thought we'd stop by the Big House so I can talk with Kim. We need to figure out how we're going to handle this stuff with Dad and his so-called secret."

Lily laughed. "Good luck with that. Just so you know, I think I'm with your father on this one. Sorry."

"Probably doesn't matter anyway. He's done exactly what he wanted all his life. He's not going to stop now."

* * *

Anna warmed herself in the sun outside Boelter Hall, the hub of UCLA's science and engineering programs. Most parents picked up their kids on Westwood Plaza but she liked the atmosphere of the quad, where she could study the faces of future Grace Hoppers and Sally Rides. Eleanor had that look too, a mix of curiosity and determination.

The weekend workshops were designed to build a STEM community among girls ages ten to seventeen so they could encourage one another in their endeavors. Eleanor had been accepted into the program after excelling in the university's summer STEM camp. She especially enjoyed computer science, which tapped both her logical and creative sides.

Eleanor exited the library alone, her backpack slung over a shoulder and a sweatshirt tied around her waist. Her face lit up when she spotted Anna.

"Hey, how was it?" Anna called.

"Awesome. You know that blogger I like, Kylie Redeker? She was our guest instructor. It was livestream, but still. She showed us how to build a data set using apps."

Anna often glimpsed pieces of herself in her daughter. At Eleanor's age, she could have catalogued all the parts of the E21s, BMW's first generation 3 Series. It fascinated her to discover Eleanor's similar interest in technical specs at such a granular level. "What kind of data set?"

"We used one of those step counters that keeps track of how many steps you need to take to be healthy. Kylie showed us how to write a program that saves the data from your steps every day between noon and one o'clock and puts them in a chart."

"What's so special about noon to one?" She smiled to herself as Eleanor groaned, obviously because her idiot mother couldn't grasp something so simple.

"*Nuhh*-thing. It was just the example she used. Like if that was my phys ed class or Georgie's tennis practice."

"Or like now, when we have to climb the stairs to the top floor of the parking garage because the elevator's out of order." As they reached the roof, she wheezed, "Got any plans for this newfound knowledge?"

"We're supposed to try to make one at home, a data set from one of our apps. Maybe Ma will have a good idea for what to do."

"Oh, right." Anna pushed out her lower lip to feign hurt feelings. "Because *this* mom never has good ideas."

"It's just for practice, Mom. Your ideas are always too complicated."

Anna stopped abruptly and put her hands on her hips. She'd noticed they usually went to Lily for help choosing topics for essays and research papers. "So that's what it is. I've been wondering why you guys never ask me those kinds of questions. I make you work too hard."

"It's not that." Eleanor bit her lower lip. "Well, maybe it is a little. But I always ask you when I have a math problem. Mom's pretty useless with those."

"I'm telling her you said that."

"She already knows."

They climbed into her car, a Mineral Grey M4 convertible, one of the few remaining BMW models that still offered a manual transmission. "I need to go by the Big House and talk about something with Aunt Kim. You want to come with me or should I drop you off at home with Andy?"

"I'll come. Can we let the top down? My brain needs to cool off."

Anna laughed. "I'm totally stealing that."

It was a short ride from the campus to the Big House. Eleanor skipped up the stairs to find Alice and her kitten while Anna scanned for Kim.

The weekend nurse Gloria, wearing pale lavender scrubs, emerged from the laundry room with a basket. "If you're looking for your sister, they're sitting out by the pool. Would you let Kim know I'll come get Martine as soon as I get her bed turned down? Two minutes."

"Sure thing, Glo. How's Mom doing today?"

"Not one of her better days, I'm afraid."

Better days used to be when she recognized and interacted with her family, even if she showed confusion. Now they were days without fear or hostility.

Despite the sun, the air was crisp. Anna found them sitting side by side in lounge chairs with Martine wrapped in a tartan wool blanket.

Kim looked up from her magazine. "Look, Mom. Here comes our waitress. We'd like two vodka tonics, please. You can hold the tonic in mine but I'd appreciate an olive."

Though dressed in leggings and a baggy sweater that belonged to her husband, Kim still managed to look chic, especially in the bright sun. Large sunglasses covered half her face.

Anna bent to tuck the blanket around her mother's neck. "Is this lady bothering you, Mom? I can have her thrown out of the bar if you like." Martine's reaction was hidden behind dark sunglasses, but Anna knew the playful banter was lost on her. "Look, Glo's coming to take you back inside where it's nice and warm."

"That's good. Have a nice nap, Mom. I love you." Kim watched wistfully as the nurse escorted her inside. "I miss her so much."

"I know you do." The two of them had always been close. "Somewhere in there she still loves you."

"I just hope she knows I love her too. I tell her all the time, but...I hope I said it the last time she could understand, you know?"

"I'm sure you did." Anna squeezed her shoulder before falling into the vacant chair. "I thought we could have a chat about Dad. You up for that?"

"What I'm up for is that drink you didn't bring me. Except make it a double and drink it yourself. I get the feeling you're going to need it."

"I hate it when you have to warn me before you tell me something. What is it this time?"

"Dad mentioned over coffee this morning that he was on the fence about Los Cabos. Any guesses as to why?"

Anna blew out a ragged sigh as she slumped into Martine's chaise. "Christ, that means this is an actual *thing*."

"Of course it's a thing. You're the only one who can't seem to see that."

"That's because I refuse to look."

"You may have to. Here's what I know. Her name is Lois Townes and she works at the Getty. Dad saw her eating lunch alone in the cafe and the rest, as they say, is history."

Anna couldn't fathom how her sister could approach this so breezily. "Does this Lois Townes not realize Dad already has a wife?"

"I have no idea what she realizes, but to be honest—now don't kill me—I'm starting to see this from Dad's perspective. He's been trapped in this nightmare with Mom for six years, and Dr. Adams says her body could keep going for who knows how long. Meanwhile Dad's healthy, he's vibrant. And he's seventy-four years old. Who knows how many more years he has? It's not really fair to expect him to put his life on hold for the sake of appearances, especially since Mom doesn't even know who he is anymore."

It would be just like the old Kim to deliver that heart wrenching soliloquy, only to finish with "Just kidding!" Since losing everything in the fire, she'd grown circumspect, showing more of her serious side. Though if Anna dared to point that out, Kim would probably blame it on menopause.

"He still loves Mom, you know," she went on. "He comes down to her room every morning and helps her with breakfast. Butters her toast, blows on her coffee. You should hear how he talks to her. It's so sweet it'd make you cry."

Anna was close to tears just hearing about it. "That's what makes all this so uncomfortable. He's almost acting like she's already gone."

"It's not that, Anna. I think he just needs someone to appreciate him, who lets him be happy for a little while without feeling guilty about it. Lois gives him that. They meet for lunch, go for walks. She even rode along in his golf cart the other day."

"Dad actually told you that?"

"Of course not. He talks to Hal, but he has to know Hal tells me everything. I figure he's not saying anything to us because he's afraid we'll judge him."

"He's right. I can't help it." Anna rubbed her face briskly with both hands, trying to clear her competing emotions. "What are we teaching our kids if we just pretend this is normal?"

"Compassion?"

* * *

A pair of flameless candles flickered in the TV nook, the only light in the master suite. Lily cradled Anna in her lap, smoothing her hair and dropping the occasional kiss on the top of her head. It was tough to see her struggle with her emotions, but the only cure was to let her make peace with herself.

"I get how Dad feels, honest I do. He deserves companionship. I just wish he'd kept it secret so the rest of us wouldn't have to deal with it."

Lily smiled to herself, thinking of all the parents who wished their gay kids had stayed in the closet—including Anna's father. Anna had been a nervous wreck back then while Lily wanted to shout from the rooftops that they were in love. "It's hard to keep a secret like that. When you find someone who makes you happy, you want to share it. Especially with your loved ones. You remember how that was."

Anna groaned. "Fine, so call me a hypocrite. But *all* of us are going through this business with Mom, not just him. Lois might be making him happy, but she's giving the rest of us a lot more to process on top of our grief."

"Are you going to talk to him?"

"Not unless he brings it up. We've set our lunch date for Thursday. Hal's coming too. It's time to tell Dad about Pinnacle."

"Don't forget—"

"I know, we're meeting Andy's counselor at two. I'll be there. Would you believe Dad had the nerve to suggest we meet at the Getty? Probably so we'd conveniently bump into Lois and he could introduce us." She sat up and scooted close enough to rest her arm around Lily's shoulder. "I put the kibosh on that. Told him this was a business lunch, to meet us at the Four Seasons."

Lily recognized the shift in Anna's body language. It wasn't like her to want comforting and she could only stand so much. Her nature was to be the comforter, the one ready to take charge and fix whatever was awry.

"Does this mean you've decided to go through with the sale?" Lily asked as she nestled into Anna's strong shoulder.

"Ninety-nine-point-nine percent. Hal and Lupe had the accounting team drill down to make sure we're at the right price. If that pans out, I'm thinking we'll probably sign the papers this week, after which we'll go public about the negotiations and open our books to their accountants. The whole process could take several months, but once it goes through I'll be walking away with quite a nest egg." She tentatively shared Hal's after-tax estimate and watched for Lily's reaction.

"Holy shit, Anna!"

"What, you thought I was kidding? I told you it was a crazy offer."

Crazy didn't even begin to describe it. When they'd moved into this house together fourteen years ago, they'd had a frank discussion about money, prompted by their enormous income disparity. A year later, before they married, the Kaklis family attorney had pushed for a prenuptial agreement, which Anna resisted until Lily persuaded her it was a sound idea for both of them. At the time, Premier Motors had consisted of four dealerships and a ton of debt.

"Lily?"

She realized her mouth was still agape. "Whatever happened to our prenup?"

Anna threw her head back and laughed. "Don't you remember? I voided it the day we adopted Andy."

"Whew!"

"Why, are you already spending your half?"

"You betcha." Lily grabbed the finger that was playfully poking her in the ribs.

Their lifestyle was admittedly expensive—three kids in private school and Serafina—but hardly on par with the A-listers in and around LA. Their Brentwood house was a home, not a monument to opulence like the Big House. Importantly, she and Anna had agreed that spoiling their kids meant helping them reach their full potential. Georgie's tennis lessons, Eleanor's STEM classes, Andy's obsession with cars. Theirs was a comfortable yet unpretentious life.

"If I can be serious for a minute," Lily said, breaking a long silence, "you know I've never been in this for your money. I have everything I could ever want under this roof. And the sex...mighty fine."

CHAPTER SIX

The waiter brought Hal's vodka gimlet, which he clinked to Anna's glass of sparkling water. "This already feels like a celebration, Anna."

"Go for it. I'm driving." Anna had decided this morning to proceed with the sale, signing a letter of intent that barred her from entertaining other offers while the deal was being finalized. Since Pinnacle was publicly traded, a purchase of this magnitude required approval from the Securities and Exchange Commission, which could take several weeks. In the meantime Anna would work to elicit buy-in from her dealership managers to effect a seamless transfer.

"I have to say, Anna...I'm having a hard time wrapping my head around the idea of you not being in the car business anymore. I've never known you when you weren't laser-focused on selling somebody their dream car. I know you're thinking about the solar thing with Helios but that's different, you know?"

"Yes, but my end of the business changed a long time ago. I can't remember the last time I actually sold a car. What I do is run a company while other people are having all the fun." Her conversation with Andy had reminded her of the things she loved about Premier Motors, especially selling BMWs. "I feel like I proved myself as an executive with all the acquisitions, but I need to find some joy again. Maybe that's Helios…maybe not."

"Are you still planning a trip to Germany?"

"I suppose I'll have to go eventually. I don't want to complicate Helios with the sale, or vice versa. I figure one life-changing decision at a time is plenty."

"Kim said she can't picture you in a job where someone else is calling the shots. Maybe Lily will let you be in charge at home sometimes."

"I doubt that." She sipped her water and scanned the restaurant for her father's face. "What about you? Have you given any thought to what you want to do next?"

"I'd love to take a few months off to sail around Baja and up the Gulf with Jonah. Kim's been wanting to do Victoria and the Puget Sound, but going off the grid right now isn't really an option, not with Martine the way she is. So what I'll actually do is anyone's guess."

"You've done an amazing job for us, Hal." She grasped his wrist as he looked away sheepishly. "I'm serious. Bringing you aboard was the smartest move I ever made. Any company would be lucky to have you, including Pinnacle. I could try to make that happen if you want."

"Yeah, I thought about it." He slowly twirled his drink before tossing it back. "The problem is what I've always liked most about my job—in fact, the reason I took it in the first place—is working with you. It wouldn't be the same without you across the hall, or Andy running up and down the stairs. Premier's always been a family thing to me."

Anna's heart broke a little to think of starting a new endeavor without Hal's steadying hand and unwavering support. She couldn't love him more if they'd been blood. "Believe me, I get it. All my memories there are tied in with my grandfather and then Dad. And now Andy and you." She looked up. "Speaking of Dad, there he is."

At seventy-four, George Kaklis was a handsome man, tanned and fit from playing golf, and still with a full head of white hair. He'd always been particular about his dress, even after retiring from the car business. Today he wore a navy sport coat with a yellow tie and pocket square.

She stood to greet him with a kiss on the cheek. "You're looking dapper." It struck her too late as the wrong thing to say since he probably had an afternoon date with Lois Townes.

He paused to order a Chivas XV on the rocks, a top shelf scotch. "Just came from Dr. Adams's office. My annual checkup."

"Everything all right, George?" Hal asked.

"Eh, you know how these doctors are. If you hate something, you need more of it. But if you like it, well…you can't have it anymore."

"Let me guess," Anna said. "Exercise and salt, in that order."

"Same thing year after year, like a broken record. But you know me. I'll just go about my business and a year from now I'll pretend I got it backward." He slapped his chest. "Never felt better."

It was true what Kim and Lily had said. Her father was healthy and full of life. Fate had dealt him a cruel blow, taking first her mother and now Martine.

The waiter returned with his cocktail and took their lunch order.

"So what's this all about?" her father asked. "Before you answer, I'm *not* coming back to work, so forget it."

"Not that, Dad. I promise." Anna had pulled him out of retirement twice to take over struggling dealerships. "Hal and I have some pretty fantastic news, but you have to keep it under your hat until the press release tomorrow. I mean it or we'll all go to jail."

"Uh-oh, that can only mean…"

"It does. You're familiar with the Pinnacle Auto Corporation?"

"Pinnacle…sure, that's Doug Whatsizface. Nice guy."

Anna nodded. "Doug Marshall. He's made us an offer for Premier Motors. A very good offer."

"An *excellent* offer," Hal interjected.

"You mean all those dealerships you've been collecting like baseball cards? I assume you'll keep the main one. It was your grandfather's, you know. The first BMW dealership west of the Mississippi." It wasn't, but that brag had been part of his folklore for too long to overcome.

"It's for the whole company, Dad. All the dealerships, all the outstanding debt. It means us getting out of the car business."

He was clearly taken aback. "To do what?"

"I don't know yet. Thought I'd keep my options open."

"If you want my opinion—I assume that's why you asked me here—you're making a big mistake. The car business is in your blood, Anna." He glanced from her to Hal. "That goes for both of you. You'll go crazy inside a year. I did."

Anna nodded along to show she was listening, the least she could do since she'd asked him here. He didn't have an actual vote on the matter.

"I'm already crazy, George," Hal said, a timely rejoinder that kept the conversation light. "I'm Jonah's dad, remember?"

"All I'm saying is you'll be sorry. You won't know what to do with yourself."

Anna considered telling him of her opportunity to work with Helios but decided not to muddy the waters today. She told him instead of the agreement they had in place, whereby most of Premier's employees would hold onto their jobs and benefits. "I'm really proud of this deal, Dad. It does right by everyone."

"I knew when you bought Sweeney's VW dealership you were taking on too much." He raised his glass to signal the waiter for another Chivas.

While her father's head was turned, Anna and Hal traded indulgent looks. "I never felt like it was too much," she said, "even after we bought the Audi group. Thanks to Hal, we knew exactly what we were getting with every acquisition."

Hal spoke up, "We're printing money, George. Every single dealership we picked up saw a rise in profits after Anna took over. Wait till you hear what she's putting in her pocket." He paused for her nod, then whispered the number into her father's ear.

The shock on his face was priceless.

"That right there," Anna said as she smiled. "I believe that's the same look you had when we told you Lily was pregnant."

"I believe he's in shock, Anna. Makes me think of that time Martine donated his golf bag to the charity yard sale. Except it was the one Jack Nicklaus signed at Pebble Beach."

Anna savored the moment. Her success was so obvious, it hardly was necessary to rub his nose in the fact that he'd been wrong about Sweeney. Still, she deserved a victory lap. "What do you think of that, Dad?"

"I think"—the waiter interrupted with his drink, buying him time to respond—"I think there are lots of ways to measure success. The main one's being happy. If this makes you happy, then...I can be happy for you."

It was far from the ringing endorsement she'd hoped for but that wasn't a complete surprise. His emotions were clouding his business judgment, much as hers had. He didn't care one whit what she did with the dealerships she'd acquired, but it obviously bothered him that she was selling the one in Beverly Hills. Valued at almost forty million by itself, it was the crown jewel of the deal because it sat on a prime piece of commercial real estate.

The waiter brought their salads, a welcome distraction that eased some of the tension. It was a perfect window for changing the subject, but Anna had one more question. "Any ideas for how I break this news to Andy?"

He shook his head. "I don't envy you that one. Maybe you ought to buy him a car first."

Hal spurted his drink and said, "Great idea. Buy him a car he's not allowed to drive." He related to George the story of Andy's unfortunate accident on the Premier Motors lot. "Andy told Jonah they weren't letting him drive again till he was thirty."

Anna chimed in with how she and Lily were dealing with the aftermath. "If it hadn't been for Lily, I probably would have yanked his learner's permit for good and made him wait till he was eighteen to get his license. He was already on thin ice from his report card, and that sent me over the top. But Lily's right. He's doing better in school, so that's worth a reward. Once I cooled off, I decided to go ahead and let him get his practice hours in. He still needs about twenty more to qualify."

"There's a good time for you, George," Hal said. "You can teach the boys to drive a stick shift. Andy first, then Jonah."

"Why not? I've got plenty of Xanax. How about I swing by on Sunday, Anna? We'll take your car and head down the One to Palos Verdes…terrorize the neighborhood. That'll knock a good four hours off."

"Are you serious? He'd love that. So would I, as a matter of fact. You'd save me a patch of gray hairs."

George yanked his thumb at her and addressed Hal, "You should've seen this one when she was learning to drive. So precise about every little thing, holding her hands at ten and two on the wheel, five miles under the speed limit, complete stop, all that. Lasted about a week. Next thing you know she's whipping in and out of traffic on the freeway, swearing like an old pro."

"Oh come on, Dad. I only swore that one time when I thought we were going to die."

"The FedEx truck," she and her father shouted simultaneously.

Anna playfully glared as they laughed at her expense. "Promise me you won't let Andy drive like that. Any chance you could pick him up late in the afternoon? It gets dark around five thirty and he needs to get some nighttime driving in. He's still about seven or eight hours short."

"Your wish is my command." He sat back and shook his napkin as the waiter delivered their entrees. Then all too casually he continued, "And now I have a favor to ask of you, Anna. All of you, really."

Here it comes. The unavoidable conversation she'd been dreading. Lily and Kim had primed her to listen with an open heart. This was her father and she loved him.

"I suppose you've heard by now that I've been spending time with a new friend. Her name is Lois, she's a docent at the Getty. She's sixty-three, a widow." He briefly described the circumstances of their meeting and how their friendship had grown. "I figure it's time I put my cards on the table so we're all clear about what's going on—and what *isn't* going on. All right?"

Anna nodded, managing a stiff smile for all of three seconds.

"Lois and I have a special relationship. We share our thoughts and feelings, something I can't do with Martine anymore. I miss that. But Lois and I, we've agreed that sharing certain other things would be inappropriate at this time, so we've set some rather old-fashioned boundaries." His face reddened slightly and he cleared his throat. "A kiss on the cheek here and there. She takes my arm when we walk. I like that. Makes me feel manly, you know? And it's nice having someone to spruce up for, something to look forward to. I'm telling you this because I don't want you to think I'm sneaking around and doing something I'm ashamed of."

He made it sound quaint, like a bashful courtship from an 1880s costume drama. Put that way, Anna found herself strangely warming to the idea of her dad having a friend who could comfort him at this difficult time, especially if it wasn't the torrid affair she'd imagined.

She proffered a genuine smile and clasped his hand, a gesture he clearly relished. "It sounds nice, Dad. Thanks for telling me. I kind of knew but not the details. So what's the favor?"

"The favor is don't give me any grief about it. No more whispering behind my back. And whatever you think of all this, don't hold any of it against Lois. You might meet her one of these days and I don't want her to feel any resentment."

It briefly crossed her mind to needle him about his resentment of Lily when they first began seeing each other. She was a bigger person than that.

* * *

Lily breathed a sigh of relief as Anna entered the school office and took a seat beside her on the bench. "Thought for a minute there you weren't going to make it."

"Lunch with Dad was a real adventure. I'll tell you about it later."

Normally they took turns meeting with the kids' teachers, but Andy's guidance counselor had specifically asked both of them to attend so they could go over his achievement test scores and plan for his critical senior year. They already were on a first-name basis with Mark Harper, who'd kept them apprised not only of academic hurdles but also of problems with peers. Andy's small stature and Latino heritage occasionally made him the target of bullies.

Mark entered the room with a wide smile. "Mrs. and Mrs. Kaklis. I love saying that. How are you both?"

Lily liked knowing that students at Hills Academy, an exclusive private school for grades K-12, had such a great role model in Mark, a gay man in his late thirties. She wondered if Andy got special attention because he had two moms, but Anna guessed all the parents felt Mark cared especially for their kids.

After exchanging pleasantries, they followed him to his office, a spacious room that looked out on a beautifully landscaped courtyard. At Mark's invitation, they helped themselves to flavored coffees from a pod brewer and sat side by side in cushioned armchairs waiting anxiously for news about Andy's progress.

"Let me paint you the big picture which we can then discuss in more detail," he said, handing them a custom one-sheet with numbers and bullet points. "Andy is doing just fine, as you can see from his test scores. He scored above standard in both areas of the test, math and language arts. That's what we like to see, though I should tell you his math score was a real squeaker."

"I'm not all that surprised," Lily said. "He's always had a hard time with numbers. If you want to know the truth, I'm proud of him for doing as well as he did. He's been working much harder on all his subjects since that last report card." She looked to Anna for confirmation. "What do you think this means for the SAT, Mark? He's supposed to take that in April."

Andy had a B average overall in his coursework. He'd need a high score on the Scholastic Aptitude Test for acceptance into a good college.

"To be honest, I think he's going to struggle with it, which is one of the reasons I thought we should start strategizing about how we're going to help him reach his goals. The last time I had him in here, he was pretty set on going to work at Premier Motors. Said he planned on being the boss someday."

Anna's deep sigh gave away her frustration. "That could be a problem. Andy doesn't know about this yet, but I'm considering some big changes. I have a feeling he's not going to take it well."

Lily laid a hand on her shoulder. "One thing at a time, Anna. Let's hear what Mark thinks about Andy's academic plan. Once we settle on that, we'll have a better idea how to approach his future."

They returned to the one-sheet, which Mark used as talking points to describe Andy's aptitude across several areas of study. "Andy's definitely college material, although I don't see him qualifying for either of his dream schools, Cal Poly or UCLA."

"Those were our colleges," Lily said. From the first time Andy visited the BMW dealership, she had known he'd want to follow in Anna's footsteps at Cal Poly. She felt a small swell of pride to hear that he'd considered her alma mater too.

Mark went on, "Personally, I think Andy's better suited to a smaller school where he'll have more access to individualized instruction. Perhaps a liberal arts college like Pepperdine or Whittier. There's also Westmont in Santa Barbara. It's a Christian school, nondenominational."

"To study what?"

"Psychology? Business or communications? Andy has a real aptitude for sales, and I'm not just blowing smoke. After our last chat I came this close"—he pinched his forefinger and thumb—"to trading in my Nissan for a BMW. He rattled off all the features, the packages I could get. He even looked up my trade-in value right here in my office. I swear, if I'd had a couple thousand more to put down, I probably would have come in that day for a test drive—all on the strength of his sales pitch. He's a natural."

Lily had no trouble believing that. When something piqued Andy's interest, he explored every detail and committed it to memory. Just like someone else she knew.

Anna gave her a wink as if reading her mind. "Mark, you should know that Andy and I can put you in a BMW if you're still interested."

He smiled. "You never know."

* * *

Lily pulled the blanket up to Eleanor's chin and planted a kiss on her forehead. "Sweet dreams, Hedy."

Eleanor had been reading about Hedy Lamarr, the actress-turned-inventor credited with developing war-time technology that led to modern day Wi-Fi.

"Don't call me that. I'm saving it for my kitten's name."

"We haven't decided on a kitten yet. Georgie might be allergic."

"He's not allergic to Gracie. He petted her and didn't sneeze or anything."

"Hmm…we'll see."

Eleanor's face soured. "That always means no."

"Not *always*," Lily admonished. "Mom and I will talk it over, I promise. You should save the name, just in case."

Putting the twins to bed was normally Anna's job, but Lily was making herself scarce while Anna broke the news to Andy down in the family room. She'd stalled long enough though, so it was time to go down and help clean up the aftermath.

She arrived to find Andy sitting on the floor, his knees pulled to his chin. If the swollen eyes and red nose were any clue, he'd taken the news hard. A quick glance from Anna told her the situation had gotten testy.

"They're going to laugh their butts off at me," he groused.

"Who is?" Lily asked, taking a seat beside Anna on the sofa. While she didn't want Andy to feel ganged up on, they needed to present a united front so he wouldn't make Anna the "bad mom."

"The guys at school. Premier Motors was the one thing I had that made me halfway cool. I told them I was going to run it one day, that they could come to me when the new models came out and I'd hook them up. Now I've got nothing. They'll all be calling me Poco Niño again."

Little boy. Lily and Anna had spoken with his teachers about the bullying when he was younger, but after seventh grade he'd asked to handle it himself. He had, with a fistfight that got him and the other boy suspended for five days.

Anna shook her head. "Come on, pal. You're not a little boy. And that kind of name calling is third-grade stuff. It says way more about them than it does you."

"Easy for you to say. You aren't the one who has to deal with it."

"Andy, your mom's right. Besides, you can still be their go-to guy for cars. You don't need Premier Motors for that. You could start your own business one of these days. Think about it. High-end custom cars for serious drivers. With all you know about cars, you'd be an expert at something like that."

Anna cast her a dubious look out of Andy's line of sight. "Or who knows, pal? You might change your mind when you get to college and decide you want to do something else. Now you have a blank slate to recreate yourself. Anything you want."

His scowl grew even colder and he rose to go upstairs. "What's wrong with the way I am?"

Lily caught him by the sleeve. "Nothing, sweetheart. We didn't mean it that way. There's absolutely nothing wrong with you."

"That goes for me too, Andy," Anna said, sounding more than a little exasperated. "Your ma and I both believe you have a bright future. Whatever you want to do with your life, we'll help you get there."

They listened as his footsteps faded and his bedroom door closed.

"He'll be all right, won't he?" Lily asked.

"Eventually. But I have a feeling he's going to be mad at me for a very long time."

CHAPTER SEVEN

Lily looked down at the petitioner, whose brown sport coat had been brushed with dirt, perhaps to make it appear old and worn. "Mr. Seaver, I'm having some trouble with this. You've gone out and purchased a new car. And now based on those car payments, you're asking the court to have another look at your financial situation and reduce your child support payments accordingly. Do I have that right?"

"Yes, Your Honor."

"And then what? Will you buy a sailboat? A weekend house in Malibu?"

Wringing child support out of divorced fathers was notoriously difficult, especially with men who imagined their ex-wives living in luxury off what was meant for their children.

"I don't need any of those things, but I *do* need a car so I can keep my job. If I can't drive to work, I can't pay child support at all." He said it emphatically, as though he'd practiced in a bar to a chorus of "Hell, yeah!"

Lily held up the dealer's invoice, which he'd provided to document his claim. "Mr. Seaver, I happen to know a little bit about cars, so I looked into this. It says here you purchased a brand new Dodge Charger. Not the base model or even the GT, both of which would have gotten you to work just fine. No, you chose the R/T with the V8, which I'm sure is sweet. And I see that you even paid an extra thousand dollars for something called 'dual carbon stripes.' Seriously…a thousand bucks for decorative racing stripes. Everyone should drive to work in such style."

Seaver had pulled his head in like a turtle, obviously taken aback by her challenge.

"And now you come to my court asking me to take food off your children's plates and clothes off their backs in order to lessen the financial pinch you're feeling from lavishing such a gift upon yourself. That *deeply* offends me, Mr. Seaver." She shook her gavel at him.

By now his face was red, his predicament settling in.

"In fact, I'm tempted to order a review of your financials because it's clear to this court that you have extra money lying around. We should see if your children deserve more than you're currently giving them." She scowled at him to let him know she was serious. "You'd best think long and hard about what you choose to drive, sir. Not only will I *not* reduce your child support payments today, I'm putting a flag on this case. I intend to follow it closely until your youngest child turns eighteen. If I see so much as a late payment, you'll be right back here in front of me in contempt of court. Do I make myself clear?"

"Yes, ma'am."

Lily slapped her gavel and called for the next case, which she'd squeezed onto her docket at the last minute. Her annoyance immediately dissipated at the sight of Selena Cortes and her attorney, Linda Kovak, who had once worked with Lily at the legal aid clinic.

"Thank you both for coming back to the court on such short notice. Upon further consideration of your case, Ms. Cortes, I reached out to Sandra Henke in the Office of Child Protection and asked her to conduct a reassessment of your current home situation. She has assured me it is safe to suspend my ruling and allow your daughters to be returned to your home without delay. I've arranged for a caseworker to collect them after school today and deliver them to your apartment in time for dinner."

The surprise on Selena's face was one of the reasons Lily loved her job. After sharing an exuberant hug with Linda, Selena pulled herself together and faced Lily, wiping tears from her cheeks. "Thank you so much, Your Honor. My brother won't stay there ever again, I promise. I love my girls too much to let him."

"I'm glad to hear that you understand the seriousness of this, Ms. Cortes." Underneath her judicial veneer, Lily shared her happiness but didn't allow herself to show it. Drugs in the home of small children was an issue never to be taken lightly. "I'm providing your attorney with a set of strict guidelines, which I expect you to follow to the letter. Child Protection Services could turn up at any time to check."

"Yes, Your Honor. They won't find anything, not ever again."

Lily dismissed the case and exited through the side door as the bailiff ceremoniously held the courtroom at attention. Only then did she allow herself to grin.

* * *

With Hal and Holly in her office, Anna presided over a conference call on speaker phone with the general managers from all of her dealerships. "Pinnacle put out a press release about fifteen minutes ago, so there's no embargo on this information. You'll receive a letter shortly to share with your staff, and there's an FAQ on the employee website that covers the transfer of benefits. That should go a long way to calm anxieties, but I caution you not to make promises to anyone regarding the workforce. I have no reason to think Pinnacle is planning significant layoffs, but they'll probably want to bring Premier's workforce in line with their own. How they choose to do that is, of course, up to them."

"Anna, this is Mickey." Mickey Cheung, who managed the BMW dealership in Redondo Beach, asked the question on everyone's mind. "Do you have any idea how this deal will affect GMs such as myself…and everyone else on this call? Should we be worrying about our jobs?"

"I'll be honest with you, Mick. I can't promise anything. In any changeover, there's always a chance the new owners will want to put their own management team in place. Vivian Zhao has negotiated quite good severance packages for those who are let go. I'm sure Pinnacle has high standards for its leadership ranks. That being said, I believe *our* leadership standards are even higher, so I'll recommend each of you without reservation." It was the best she could do.

"This is Hal Phillips, everyone. We're turning the process over to an LA firm that specializes in mergers and acquisitions so we can get back to what we do best, which is to sell and service cars." He laid out the steps the firm would take to help complete the due diligence phase, including onsite visits by the Pinnacle brass to all the dealerships. "I don't need to tell you that's a great chance for you to make an impression."

Anna drew a deep breath and consciously relaxed the muscles in her neck and shoulders. As was often the case with Hal, his timely interjection had been deliberate, designed to take some of the heat off her. Her inner circle—Hal, Lupe and Vivian—had advised her earlier to try not to get caught up in a line of questions that might become confrontational. They knew her well enough to worry that she'd take her managers' concerns to heart and let emotions override the practical decision she'd painstakingly reached.

"If there's nothing else," Anna said, "I'll leave you to share this news with your staff. I know some of you have serious concerns. If you'd like to talk further, my door's always open."

When they ended the call, Anna's first impulse was to hole up in her office with Hal and get his take on how it went. The dejected look on Holly's face made her think again. "Hal, will you make sure that letter goes out right away? We can talk later."

"Sure thing, boss."

With a sheepish smile, Holly waited until he was gone before saying, "Do you mind if I'm first through that open door of yours?"

"Of course not." Among all the folks who worked at Premier Motors, Holly was her closest friend. In fact, their kids had played together as toddlers in this very room. Since making her general manager of the Beverly Hills dealership nine years ago, Anna had watched with pride as Holly stacked up accolades as one of BMW's best in service and sales. "How can I help?"

"Does our health insurance cover extensive therapy for depression?"

It surprised her that Holly, of *all* people, would be the one concerned about the fallout. "To be honest, I'll probably be the one needing therapy. This is all I've known since I was a child. But I'm convinced it's the right thing to do and the right time to do it. I'm ready for something new, whatever it turns out to be. One of these days you might be ready too."

"One of these days?" Her voice was heavy with sarcasm. "It's coming sooner than you think, Anna. There's no freaking way I'll keep this job once the sale goes through."

"Why on earth would you think that? Doug Marshall tried to poach you for his Lexus dealership three years ago. He's going to be thrilled to have you on his management team."

Her face softened, but her voice remained skeptical. "I guess what I meant was that my job won't be *here*."

"What do you mean, it won't be here? It'd be foolish for Doug to turn this dealership over to someone else after you've made it number one in Southern California."

"Maybe, but this place is an institution. I love that wall of photos down there, all those Hollywood stars coming here to buy their new BMW. But you've said it yourself, the land this dealership is sitting on is worth millions. Pinnacle will probably flip it to a developer and move us out to one of those auto rows next to the 405. Which would suck. I know this is just a building, but it's also our brand."

Holly was right about the importance of this location, which to Anna and her father captured the essence of Premier

Motors. *What you drive is who you are.* Luxury cars practically sold themselves in Beverly Hills, where the city's name on the license plate frame could be worth an extra thousand dollars. It was a perfect pairing, subliminal but deliberate.

"Sorry I'm dumping on you, Anna. It's totally selfish. I'm sure you're right about Pinnacle keeping me on somewhere, so I shouldn't be complaining at all. It's just that I'll miss working here…and especially working with you." Her voice cracked and Anna saw a swell of tears. "You've been so good to me, all the way back to when I was a green know-it-all who couldn't even fill out a simple form without screwing up."

"Because I believed in you even then." Anna came around her desk and wrapped Holly in a hug. "Whether you realize it or not, you've just hit on the two reasons I almost didn't do this—nostalgia and friendship. But here's what I think." She loosened her embrace to look Holly in the eye. "What matters is that we hold onto our memories and friends. You and Jai will always be dear to me, your kids too. We don't have to work together for that to be true."

"You'd better mean that." Holly hugged her harder.

"I do. We can be each other's therapy, save ourselves thousands of dollars. How about that?"

Anna managed to hold it together until Holly left. Then she closed the door, leaned against it and slid all the way to the floor fighting tears. Holly had owned up to her selfishness, but had she? She'd done this deal knowing it would break Andy's heart, and though convinced it was best for her family's future, the ripple effects could upend lives in ways she hadn't considered. People she cared about were anxious and distressed, and she was singularly responsible.

* * *

Lily was glad for the chance to finally accept their friends' dinner invitation, especially when Sandy called to say one of Suzanne's coworkers at the ER had gifted her a fresh catch of sea bass. She opened the sliding glass door to Suzanne, who carried her platter around the table depositing grilled kebobs on each plate of wild rice.

Anna rubbed her hands together. "This looks amazing. You'll have to give me the recipe"—Suzanne gaped at her incredulously—"so I can give it to Serafina."

"You had me worried for a minute there," Suzanne said. "I heard about your last adventure in the kitchen. Blackened oatmeal?"

"Hey, the top of it was edible."

Lily took her usual chair with her back to the door. "I threw the pan out so poor Serafina wouldn't spend two hours chiseling it. I bet we're the only ones in LA paying combat wages to our housekeeper."

Sandy joined them last, carrying a large wooden salad bowl. "Speaking of Serafina, any more word on her immigration status? I bet she's chewing her nails off. It's like the laws change every day."

"Tell me about it. Before I can rule on a case, I find myself looking up everyone's status so I can decide if whatever they did is bad enough to get deported. I can't stand seeing these families ripped apart."

"It's unbelievable what this administration is doing," Sandy said. "Snatching children from their mothers' arms. Lily, you know how hard it is on kids when we have to take them out of the home—it traumatizes them even when their parents are abusive. Can you just imagine how terrified these kids are down at the border?"

"I know, and some of them will suffer for years because of it."

"If you ask me," Anna said, "it's pure evil. I can't believe they call themselves the party of family values when they're breaking families up."

"It's not just happening to immigrants," Suzanne said, her voice dripping with scorn. "Families all over the country are being torn apart because of this president. Mine included."

Lily recalled that Suzanne's relationship with her family had always been strained, chiefly because they refused to accept her sexuality. Sandy had complained for years about feeling unwelcome at their holiday dinners in Bakersfield. She only went because of Suzanne's hope they would come around someday.

Lily leaned over and squeezed her shoulder. "It won't be like this forever, Suzanne. We just have to get out there and vote next year. I honestly don't think this is the real America."

"It's a lot more real than you think. Tell them, Sandy. You've seen how they are. The reason they love this president is because he hates all the same people they do. Mexicans, Blacks, Muslims, Asians—"

"Women," Sandy added. "She's right, I've been around them. It's always been iffy with Suzanne's family because of the gay thing, but it's way worse now. And there's no reasoning with them. Her brothers wouldn't know a fact if it bit them in the ass. They actually revel in their ignorance. It's nauseating."

"So yeah, we can vote this asshole out of power," Suzanne went on, "but we're never going to get rid of this shit stain. America knowingly elected a white supremacist who gave them permission to say all those hateful things they used to keep to themselves. Now that we've seen them without their masks, we won't ever be able forget what they look like."

From the corner of her eye, Lily saw Anna nodding along with every word. Anna knew this litany well, as it was something she repeated almost every time she watched the news.

"Anna and I are lucky that everyone in our family is on the same page," Lily said. "I honestly don't know how we'd handle it if they weren't."

"There's only one way to handle it—you write them off," Suzanne said as her voice began to shake. "Now that I know who they really are, I don't want them in my life anymore. They won't ever change. As far as I'm concerned, I no longer have a family."

Typical Suzanne, brash and resolute. Yet beneath her proud bravado, there was unmistakable anguish. Lily found that heartbreaking, but she didn't mind seeing this new sense of empowerment. After all this time of waiting for her family to accept her, Suzanne finally had freed herself from caring whether they did or not.

Anna abruptly pushed her chair back and walked around the table to hug Suzanne, who buried her face in Anna's side and held on. She probably hated the fact that she was crying.

"You absolutely have a family, Suzanne," Anna said. "You have two sisters right here at this table who love you very much."

Lily winked at Sandy and said, "She's right, sister. And whether you like it or not, that makes you and Sandy aunts to our children. Heck, if something ever happens to us, you might even have to raise them."

Suzanne's eyes got wide with exaggerated alarm. Then she clasped her hands in prayer and looked skyward. "Dear God, please don't let anything happen to Lily and Anna. Take good care of them...at least until all their kids grow up."

On the drive home, Lily replayed the emotional scene in her head. "That was really sweet what you said to Suzanne about family."

"It's true, isn't it? Friends that close are as good as family."

"They are." She trailed her fingertips along Anna's thigh. "I remember back when Mom died. Your father hugged me after the funeral and promised me you all would be my family. I believed him."

Anna caught her hand and raised it to her lips. "And here we are."

"And here we are," she repeated softly. Lily had never been a religious person, but in moments such as this one she liked to imagine that her mom was looking down from heaven, proud of the person she'd become and overjoyed at her happiness. "I'm the luckiest woman on earth."

"Pfft!" Anna gave her a sidelong look and shook her head. "You're not even the luckiest woman in this car."

CHAPTER EIGHT

Sitting casually on a desk in front of two dozen girls—Eleanor's STEM class—Anna advanced the screen to an animation of a four-stroke internal combustion engine. "As the piston rises, it compresses the air and fuel that's mixed into the top of the cylinder. Then the spark ignites it and forces it back down. That's what turns the drive shaft. Cars have multiple cylinders—usually four or six, sometimes more—and they fire in sequence to keep the shaft turning. Otherwise you'd get something like this."

Holding her hands as if on a steering wheel, she took halting steps across the room, triggering a wave of giggles.

"What do you think it means when they say a car has a one-point-six liter engine, or a four-point-four liter engine? Bigger is better, right?"

A few seconds of silence passed before Eleanor raised her hand.

Anna shook her head. "Not you, kiddo. I caught you looking at my slides this morning."

After another few seconds, one of Eleanor's friends, a girl of about twelve, spoke up. "Is that the size of the cylinder?"

"That's a very good guess, pretty close but not quite. What they're talking about is actually the amount of air that gets pushed out when the pistons go down. We call that engine displacement. The more air it pushes, the more force there is on the down stroke to the drive shaft. That makes it a rough indicator of a car's power. Here's what the physics looks like, for anyone who's interested in the technical aspects."

Her next slide displayed the corresponding mathematical formula, which prompted several of the girls to scribble notes. It thrilled her to see so many of them interested in what she thought of as the "greasy side" of the car business.

"All right, those are the basics of a combustion engine, which runs on gas. Let's see what happens when we add an electric motor to the works." She walked them through the mechanics of hybrid, plug-in hybrid, and electric engines before opening the floor to questions.

The first came from one of the older girls sitting at the back of the room. "I'm not trying to throw shade or anything, but… this isn't really STEM, is it? It's more for garage mechanics, not scientists."

The pushback came quickly, not from Anna but from another girl in the teenage clique. "It's mechanical engineering, Madison. We have to know how things work so we can improve on them, like they did when they turned the gas engines into hybrids."

"And it's not just cars either," another girl said. "They use engines like these in airplanes and rockets too."

Anna stayed out of the conversation as long as she could to let the group debate among themselves. Only when the discussion died down did she add her perspective. "If I can speak from personal experience, I first began to study the mechanics because I found it interesting. I was about Eleanor's age when I started going to Munich with my dad to visit the BMW design center, where we'd get to preview the new technology. I still go every year because there's always something new to learn. Last time I was there I saw a concept car that runs on hydrogen cells. Where do we get hydrogen?"

A chorus of voices answered, "Water."

"Right, so we're talking zero emissions and unlimited range. That would be a game changer." She returned to sit on the desk, letting her legs swing casually. "There's another reason I like knowing the details of how cars work, and it relates to this class. Selling cars is like the STEM fields in a way, because our culture assumes men know all about cars and women don't. I've always refused to accept that, and I bet you would too." There was no mistaking she had their full attention now. "When I'm doing business with someone, I want to be the expert in the room. Why? Because knowledge is power. At my company, the entire sales staff gets trained on how these cars work. All the men, all the women. I believe it levels the playing field and gives everyone the confidence they need to succeed."

She ended her presentation to polite applause and opened the floor to questions that allowed her to speculate about Helios and its solar cars. Judging from the girls' enthusiasm, she should have included this in her slideshow.

As the girls dispersed, Anna was approached by Dr. Leticia Johnson, one of the organizers of the STEM group. "You're a lifesaver, Anna. Thanks for jumping in on such short notice."

"You're very welcome. I enjoyed it."

"So did they." Lowering her voice, she added, "Don't worry about Madison. She challenges everyone."

"Good for her, I say. And I thought she had a point. A lot of what we covered today were the basics for fixing an engine that isn't firing the way it should. Lots of little boys learn this kind of stuff at their father's knee, but girls should know it too."

"I could tell they enjoyed hearing you talk about the business side of things. That's one thing we could emphasize more in our seminars, I think. Not everyone is heading for a career in the lab or the classroom. They'll have to learn to navigate the competitive side too."

"If you need help branching out, I have connections." She could assemble an army of women business leaders thanks to her stint as president of LA's Chamber of Commerce.

"Actually…" Leticia walked with her outside, where Eleanor was waiting in Anna's usual place. "I was wondering if you might consider having a conversation about joining our board. We could use more representation from the business community. I can have someone reach out if you're interested."

"I don't want to muscle in on Eleanor's turf, but I guess it wouldn't hurt to have a chat. You have my contact info."

Anna was definitely intrigued by the prospect. In her musings about what to do once Premier Motors was sold, she'd toyed with the notion of setting up a small foundation to benefit programs such as this one. But she also could make an impact by volunteering her leadership—especially if she found herself with time on her hands.

* * *

Lily sat with Andy on the bleachers, where they shared a bag of barbecued chips. "Your brother's really upped his game. See how deep he drives the ball? And he's hammering his backhands."

"He ought to be good. It's all he thinks about. I wonder if that other kid gets private tennis lessons every day."

"I think we can assume he does since he's also ranked in the top twenty. You don't get to be that good without private lessons and tons of practice."

Andy had been in a sullen mood since breakfast when Anna squelched his request to drive to Palm Springs and back. He then complained that his siblings monopolized every Saturday so he might as well stay in bed all day.

"Wonder how Georgie would feel if you and Mom sold all his racquets and told him he couldn't take lessons anymore."

"Andy…"

"Or if you pulled Ellie out of nerd class."

"Come on, why would we do something like that?"

"It's what Mom did to me. I go to Premier Motors every day after school, right? That's just like going to practice, and it's private lessons too if you count all the people there who teach me stuff."

Lily let him stew as she weighed whether or not to address his grievances. Was he jealous of his siblings or angry at Anna? He clearly blamed her for his troubles. The two of them often needed a mediator, someone who could head off the inevitable hurt feelings when their emotions boiled over.

"Andy, I remember back when you were little. Most days you and Jonah went to the Big House with Grandma and Grandpa after school, but your mom insisted on having you one day a week all to herself. She'd leave work and pick you up from school, then you'd go back with her and hang out at the dealership. It was the highlight of her week. She blocked it out on her day planner—no calls, no meetings. Did you know that?"

He mumbled, "That's what I was saying. I've been going there for eleven years."

"Right, so maybe it's a little unfair to complain about Georgie and Eleanor's activities, since you had lots of those yourself. And that's not including six years of Mighty Mite football."

"But that's the point. I don't have any now. I don't play sports anymore and Mom's selling the dealership right out from under me. I bet she wouldn't do it if it was Eleanor because she's her *real* daughter."

Lily was shocked he'd say such a thing. They'd put that issue to bed years ago. "Andy, I cannot believe you said that. You know darn good and well it isn't true. All three of you are precious to us, and it would destroy your mom to hear you say that. And for the record, it hurts me too."

He looked appropriately ashamed and mumbled an apology, but it wasn't the end of his complaints. "Sometimes I feel like Mom hates me. She's always getting mad at me for something."

The recent tension between Andy and Anna was undeniable. Lily found the best way to play peacemaker was to play both sides against the middle, push them to understand one another.

"Honey, you're allowed to feel sad about your mom selling the company, but you need to cut her some slack. I know for a fact that it breaks her heart to see you upset. She would never hurt you deliberately. That's not who she is."

His expression was hard to read through his sunglasses, but he had a habit of biting his lower lip when he was deep in thought. "That's what I don't understand. She knew how much it would hurt me and she did it anyway."

"Because this time it couldn't be helped. When it comes to business, your mom has to look at the big picture. She watches for warning signs about the economy, trade agreements, politics, driving trends...basically anything that might signal trouble for the car industry." In light of Anna's observations about Andy's limited interest in the inner workings of the business, it struck her that he might not fully grasp the seriousness of the potential risks. "Here's the deal, son. Our family is very lucky that Premier Motors has been successful, but practically *all* of our money is tied up in the business of German cars. From a financial standpoint, that's extremely risky. Mom's been worried the last couple of years about our trade agreements with the Europeans. If they were to blow up, it could literally wipe us out. If she thinks now's a good time to cash out, we should trust her judgment. She always puts us first, even if we can't see it."

The cluster of parents around them erupted in applause at the heroics on the court, which Lily had missed completely.

"What just happened?" Lily asked.

"Georgie won a point, I think. The other kid ran for it but didn't get there in time."

Lily tugged gently at his forearm to remind him not to bite his fingernails. One day he'd stop on his own, when he realized girls found it unattractive.

"Honey, I know this is hard, but your mom's right about the opportunities you're going to have. You've got your whole future in front of you. You might find something at college that excites you even more than selling cars. But if you finish your degree and still want to be in the car business, we'll help make it happen for you. That's an absolute promise you can take to the bank."

"At this rate, all I'll be taking is the bus."

She decided that was meant to be dark humor and laughed. "I don't think it'll come to that, sweetheart. You'll have your fifty hours in soon. As soon as we think you're ready, you can get your license."

He rolled his head and groaned. "But if I do one little thing wrong, Mom will say I'm not mature enough, that I'm not being responsible."

"Andy, please. She's not your enemy. She just wants you to do your best."

"She wants me to be just like her, perfect all the time."

Lily could hardly push back on that since she'd accused Anna of that very thing. It didn't make it true. "She's well aware she isn't perfect. In fact, didn't she come to your room last week and apologize for overreacting? When was the last time *you* apologized to her for something you did wrong?"

Every now and then, she got a glimpse of one of the traits that triggered Anna's frustration. The complaining, the blaming, the obfuscating. While his stubbornness seemed deliberate at times, Lily wondered if it somehow traced back to the insecurity of his early childhood. Foster kids faced constant upheaval, a lot of which happened without explanation, leaving kids to worry they were somehow to blame for being shuttled from one home to the next. Since joining their family, Andy had faced only one significant change—the arrival of his siblings. That had sparked a two-year stretch of jealousy, hoarding and acting out, which only abated after months of family therapy. She never wanted him to feel like that again.

"Why don't you talk this out with Mom while we're down in Los Cabos? Just tell her everything you're feeling and why."

"I have!"

"Do it again, but this time I want you to listen too. *Really* listen. I'll even sit her down ahead of time and tell her she has to listen to you also. She loves you, and there's nothing you could ever say or do to change that. If you accept that, it'll go a long way to helping you understand each other."

He took a long time to respond, so long that Lily wondered if he'd simply shut down. "Can I ask a favor? It's important."

"Of course."

"There's this cookout next Saturday at Brock's house. I'm invited."

"We're supposed to fly down to Los Cabos on Friday. If you're asking not to come with us on our family vacation, that's probably not going to happen."

"I'll come, just not on Friday. I want to stay here long enough to go to the party, and then fly down by myself the next day. I'd only miss two nights."

The likelihood of Anna agreeing to that was practically nil. "It's a pretty big ask, Andy. Spring break vacations are a family tradition, all of us together. Jonah, Alice, your grandpa. We've booked a huge villa right on the beach."

"How many times is somebody as cool as Brock going to invite me to a party at his house? With a DJ and everything."

Lily had to admit Andy's "pleading voice," as Anna called it, was world class.

"I have a note from Brock's mom telling all about it. It starts at one o'clock on Saturday. Evan said he'd pick me up and take me home. And then Serafina could take me to the airport on Sunday morning."

"We've given Serafina that whole week off. She may already have plans. It wouldn't be fair to expect her to change them."

"I can ask her though, can't I? Or maybe Evan will come over and give me a ride. Please, Ma. It's just this one party. I wouldn't ask if it wasn't important. All the kids will be there. It feels stupid to be left out when everybody's talking about it at school."

It was true that Andy didn't get many invitations to hang out with classmates at their homes. Brock Diedrich was an exemplary student at Hills Academy, smart and athletic, junior class president. More important to Lily was the fact that he'd stood up for Andy back in ninth grade when the others teased him about his height. Andy had sealed their friendship last summer by helping him select an X2, BMW's sporty compact SUV, a present from his father for his sixteenth birthday. Anna had even let Andy do the delivery spiel, as if he'd been the actual salesman.

"Let me talk it over with your mom." As he opened his mouth to object, she added, "And I'll make sure she *strongly* considers how important this is to you."

* * *

"No way, it's a family trip. Family means all of us."

Lily had known that would be Anna's first reaction. She clung stubbornly to traditions. "Please don't say no yet. Let's at least talk about it."

"*Eeeka brrr ownow*," she replied emphatically.

"Once more without the toothbrush."

Anna spat in the sink and wiped her face. "I said, he could burn the house down. Remember that time we let him stay home by himself for three hours while we took Eleanor and Georgie to see *Shaun the Sheep*? He left the stove burner on the whole time we were gone."

"Honey, he was twelve. I'm sure he knows to be a lot more careful now."

"Easy for you to say. He just rammed one of my brand new cars into a stack of tires."

"All I'm asking is that you consider what this party means to him. The poor guy's been teased for years by the cool kids and now all of a sudden here's a show of acceptance. And I bet you anything Vanessa McFarland's going to be there. That's the girl he likes. This is a huge deal for him."

"So are family traditions. This year's already going to be sad because Mom can't come with us. The rest of us need to be there for each other. Plus I don't want us to have to worry about him. It'll ruin the fun for everyone else if we have to keep checking on him."

Lily peered around Anna so she could see her face in the mirror. "He'll only miss a couple of days. Sixteen-year-olds are perfectly capable of staying home by themselves for two nights without being checked on a million times. Besides, I've already spoken with Serafina. There's an eight o'clock flight on Sunday morning and she's more than happy to take him to the airport. But there's a tradeoff for Andy—he has go with her on Saturday night to the Los Amigos Festival at Hollenbeck Park. That's her and Enzo's old neighborhood."

"I take it this means you're on Andy's side?" Anna's glum expression signaled her impending surrender.

"Yes, but I'm on your side too. That's why I'm letting you have the honor of going in there tonight to give him the good news. It'll mean a lot more coming from you because he's still upset over the dealership."

She threw the hand towel on the counter. "I wish you hadn't put it that way. Now it feels like emotional blackmail, like we *owe* him this. Especially after he tried to make us feel guilty this morning about Georgie and Eleanor. What's he going to ask for next?"

The last thing Lily wanted tonight was another parenting tiff, but it drove her nuts that Anna sometimes showed little empathy for Andy's feelings, as though she expected him to think and behave like a miniature adult. Clearly she couldn't relate to his ordinary teenage anxieties. She probably had floated through high school as the prettiest, smartest and most popular girl in her class, to say nothing of her family's wealth. How could she possibly understand Andy's insecurities and struggles with his peers?

"Honey, I don't think he's trying to manipulate us, but I can vouch for the fact that he feels let down about the sale. And he's super frustrated over not getting his driver's license. It may not seem like a big deal to us, but it's a lot for him to have on his plate. Why don't we give him a little freedom and let this be a chance for him to earn our trust?"

Anna pursed her lips pensively. "I sometimes get the feeling all of you are ganging up on me."

"Because we are." Lily stood on her tiptoes to nibble her ear. "Now go tell him. By the time you get back, I might just have a surprise waiting."

Anna tilted her head to open her neck for more kisses. "You should have led with that. I'd have said yes right away and saved us all this trouble."

CHAPTER NINE

"Wish I could've stayed home till Sunday too," Georgie grumbled from his window seat. By the line of lights below, they were flying just off the coast of the Baja Peninsula.

Anna brushed his wavy golden hair back with her fingertips. "And miss all the fun we're going to have at the beach tomorrow?"

"I've won five matches in a row. Coach Bobby says I'm in a super zone. I was supposed to play Lucas O'Brien tomorrow. He's ranked sixteen. I could've jumped two whole spots on the ladder. Instead I'll get dropped a spot for missing a match. Probably even two since we'll be gone next Saturday too."

Anna squeezed his shoulder. "Lucas will still be there when you get back, and I bet you'll still be in a super zone. Maybe you should consider taking a little break and resting those muscles. Instead of tennis, you can surf and snorkel with us."

"Coach always says to practice at least three times a week unless I'm sick, or my muscles can forget. A whole week and I'll be rusty. I'll probably lose my next match and drop some more on the ladder."

"Then I guess it's a good thing I booked you for three lessons with the resort's pro, huh?"

His mouth dropped open in surprise. "Awesome!"

"I thought you'd like that." She was proud of Georgie for his dedication to excelling in the sport. On the other hand, his competitiveness on the court often struck her as overly intense for a ten-year-old. "It's not all about winning, is it? Do you still enjoy it even if you lose?"

"Sometimes…but only if it's really close and the other guy beats me instead of me beating myself."

"You mean by making mistakes?"

He nodded. "Yeah, unforced errors. It means your opponent didn't hit a good shot and make you miss. You just flubbed it."

As they chatted, Anna was disappointed in herself to realize she hadn't had a real conversation with Georgie about his tennis in weeks. She couldn't blame that solely on the sale, since she'd found time for both Andy and Eleanor. "Ma says you get better every time you play. Tell me how it feels during a match when you know you're hitting the ball well."

He expressed a sense of accomplishment at being able to execute a new skill Coach Bobby had taught him. "Like backspin. You hit it at a downward angle"—he made a slicing motion with his hand and twirled a finger to emulate the spin—"and it makes the ball not bounce very high." He grew increasingly animated as he described techniques for topspin and slices.

"It's amazing how much you've learned, honey. You work so hard at practicing. All those hours just prove how dedicated you are." He probably was blushing, though she couldn't quite tell in the dim light of the cabin. "I'm so sorry I missed your match last week. It was my turn to come with you but that thing with Ellie's class came up at the last minute."

"I like it when you and Ma come watch me together because you both yell and clap. I pretend I'm at Wimbledon."

"Then we'll have to figure out how to do it more often."

The subtle drop in airspeed signaled their descent into Los Cabos. Across the aisle, Eleanor tapped furiously on her phone as her shoulders danced to something coming through her headphones. As if sensing Anna's eyes on her, she leaned forward so they could share a giggle over Lily, whose head had fallen to her chest in slumber.

"*Ladies and gentlemen, we've started our descent into San José del Cabo. At this time…*"

Anna touched Lily's hand, guaranteeing that her smile was the first thing she would see. "Have a nice nap?"

"Did I snore?"

"Yeah, I think that's why we're landing. Passengers were starting to panic. They thought all that noise might be engine trouble."

"Ha! At least I didn't do that other thing I sometimes do when I fall asleep."

Anna scrunched her nose. "For which we're all very grateful."

* * *

What made the Pedregal area of Cabo San Lucas special to Lily was its spectacular ocean view. There weren't many spots in the Western Hemisphere where she could watch a sunrise over the Pacific Ocean, and even fewer to watch a sunset from the same chair. From the veranda was a telescopic view of Lovers Beach, near the Arch of Cabo San Lucas, a natural rock formation at the southernmost tip of the Baja Peninsula.

Lily congratulated herself on getting up early to enjoy the tranquility. The traffic and bustle of LA seemed light years away.

Anna presented her with a steaming mug of coffee and stretched out on the adjacent chaise lounge. She was barefoot and wearing summer pajamas of soft blue cotton. "I looked out here and asked myself what could possibly make this picture more beautiful. It was caffeine."

"You read my mind."

"Does this mean I'm forgiven?"

"Pretty sure I forgave you last night…which is why your pants are on inside out."

"Details, details."

The airport limo company had lost their reservation, leaving them stranded until Anna found a driver who could handle the four of them with all their luggage. Everyone was tired and cranky by midnight when they finally arrived at the villa, prompting Lily to sound off about Anna's insistence on flying down on Friday night instead of Saturday morning.

"You were right about coming down a day early. I had no idea how much I needed to see a sunrise over the ocean." She almost added that she could get used to it, but then Anna might take her seriously and go buy a house with her newfound millions.

"For what it's worth, I laid awake till almost two o'clock thinking about Andy and I decided you were right after all, that we should have waited till this morning. He would have had only one night on his own, and we wouldn't have started off our vacation wanting to kill each other."

Lily was past caring about last night. If they'd waited a day, they'd never have gotten this peaceful moment to themselves. By midafternoon, the villa would be a hive of activity, with Kim and Hal's brood, and George, who'd decided only at the last minute to join them. Kaklis family vacations were always fun and exciting. What they weren't was relaxing.

"I had a couple of messages from Andy last night," Anna said. "The first came about twelve thirty. Said he was going to watch the first three *Fast & Furious* movies at one sitting, but then he wrote me back at one fifteen and said he was going to bed. Little wimp."

"I bet he's in heaven. The whole house to himself, and Serafina left an entire chocolate pie in the fridge."

"He's probably in a sugar coma."

Lily had no trouble envisioning Andy in his bed, the covers pulled over his head. He'd probably sleep till noon, waking just in time to shower and dress for the party at Brock's house. "I think we should call him."

"Now? It's ten after six. He's dead to the world."

"All the more reason," Lily replied, scrambling into the bedroom for her phone. By the time she returned to the veranda,

Andy had picked up and she put the call on speakerphone so Anna could hear.

"Hullo."

"Andy! Oh, thank goodness I caught you. I didn't know what time your party was."

"Whut? It's not till one o'clock, Ma. Geez…I'm still asleep."

Anna covered her mouth so Andy couldn't hear her snickering.

"Honey, I'm so sorry, but I need you to check something for me. I'd call back later but this can't wait. It's really important."

He groaned in protest, but after a few seconds replied, "Fine, what is it?"

"It's a huge favor, son. I need you to go down to the kitchen. Let me know when you're there."

They both rocked with silent laughter as he grudgingly followed Lily's instructions, even stubbing his toe on the door to his room.

"Okay, I'm here, what is it?"

"Honey, is the refrigerator running?"

"Yeah."

"You're sure?"

"Yeah!" he yelled.

"Then you better go catch it before it gets away!"

It was a full ten seconds before he put all the pieces together and realized he'd been pranked. "Aw, man! I can't believe…"

Lily and Anna squealed with laughter until tears leaked from their eyes.

"You both suck! I'm never speaking to either one of you again."

"You're so precious, pal," Anna said, gradually gaining control of herself. "I hope this proves you were the very first thing we thought about this morning. That's how much we love you."

"Yeah, you just wait. My payback is going to be epic."

Lily was glad to hear the playful revenge in his threat instead of genuine anger. "Fair is fair. We totally deserve it."

"You sure do."

"We love you bunches," Anna said, still laughing. "Can't wait to see you tomorrow."

"Yeah, don't bet on it. I'm changing my plane ticket and flying somewhere else." His voice faded sleepily until he suddenly shouted, "And I'm taking this stupid refrigerator with me!"

* * *

As Kim peeled and deveined a pile of raw shrimp for their Asian feast, Anna rhythmically tossed the chicken with vegetables in a wok. "I can't believe you trust me to do this. Lily won't let me anywhere near an open flame."

"I know, but chicken's not really my favorite. I don't care if you burn it."

"Should have known there was a catch. How do I know when this is done?"

"It is." Kim turned off the stove burner and lit another to sauté the shrimp. "I'll finish this. You get out the plates and silverware. Stack everything over there. I have to fix Jonah's plate or he'll scoop all the meat out before anyone else gets any. Selfish little prick. You'd think he was raised by wolves. Did I tell you he went apeshit when he found out Andy was staying over for that party? He was invited too, and now he's pissed he didn't get to stay home and go. No way are we leaving that kid at home by himself. I'm just not ready to see another house go up in flames."

"I'm not too worried about a house fire since Serafina's there. But man, Andy's been getting on my last nerve lately. How do you guys handle Jo-Jo when he's like that?"

"I drink wine. Lots of it."

"Not an option. We're a booze-free zone." Anna had given up alcohol fourteen years ago as a show of solidarity with Lily.

"I can't get totally shitfaced in case I need to jump in and save him and Hal from killing each other. Jonah's like a little needle, always poking him. Must be a testosterone thing. Sometimes I think Hal has too much." She cocked her head and laughed. "Bet you never thought you'd hear me say that."

Since college, Kim had unabashedly offered the lewd details of her extremely active sex life with Hal, though she admitted it wasn't as much fun to share once Anna stopped being shocked or embarrassed.

"It has to be something other than testosterone because I don't have any," Anna said. "I lose my shit with Andy too. Lily says I'm overreacting. She's like you, always there to smooth things over before they explode."

"It's the same principle. You're the alpha in the house. Boys are genetically wired to take you down."

Anna could picture that with a kid like Jonah, who'd asserted himself even as a baby. "I don't get that dominance vibe from Andy though. Deep down he's still that same shy kid he was when he first came to live with us. But he's chafing for independence. I know that's a normal teenage thing, but he isn't ready because he still makes stupid decisions." She told of the accident at the dealership. "And he could stand to work harder at school. I'm starting to think his lack of effort is my fault. I let him believe I was going to hand over Premier Motors just because he was my kid and he wanted it."

Kim snorted and rolled her eyes. "Call me crazy, but that sounds exactly like someone else I know."

"Yeah, but…" On second thought, there was no *but*. She'd always known the dealership would pass to her when her father thought she was ready. "The difference is I prepared myself to take it over. I got an engineering degree and an MBA, and I worked in every single department until I knew the guts of it. All Andy seems to care about is what's sitting in the showroom."

Kim reached out and tweaked her nose. "Now I get it. You're annoyed that he isn't more like you."

"God, you sound just like Lily."

"Because we're right? If you're waiting for him to reach your level of wizardry, I've got news for you—it's not going to happen."

"I don't expect Andy to do *everything* the way I'd do it. It's fine that he's no genius, but I think he could do better if he applied himself. I've worked with him at the kitchen table for hours, we've hired tutors. He does just enough to get by."

"Whereas you want him to 'reach for the stars.'" She punctuated the last bit with sarcastic finger quotes.

"I didn't realize ambition and initiative were such character flaws," she snapped, proving she could be sarcastic too. Kim never shied away from delivering blunt criticism when she thought it was needed, but Anna didn't feel she deserved it this time. "Come on, isn't the whole purpose of parenting supposed to be to raise kids who share our values? Hard work is a value I want him to have. And like I said, it's not really his fault he's coasting, it's mine. I haven't instilled in him the value of working hard for the things he wants. To be honest, that's why I'm still dragging my feet about letting him get his license, because it's the last leverage we'll have to get him to put out the effort."

"Give it up, Anna. It's not going to work. Andy's got you figured out and he's got his own way of dealing with it. Or at least that's what it sounds like to me."

"What are you—"

Kim shook her spatula for emphasis, as though she relished her chance to lecture. "Look, I don't mean this as an insult. It's just a fact. *You* are intimidating as all fuck. I'm not saying you're an asshole. You don't even do it on purpose. But you still have that effect on everyone. Me included, and Hal. And Lily too, most likely. It's just who you are."

"I have no idea what you're talking about."

"You take the wind out of other people's sails just by opening your mouth. Andy knows he'll never be as smart as you, that he isn't going to measure up on all those things you want him to learn. He's intimidated by that. So instead he focuses on something he thinks he's good at—like the cars, not the dealership. I've seen that up close and personal too, remember?"

Of course she remembered, but it peeved her that Kim would throw it in her face again after all these years. "How many more times do I have to apologize for that? I'll have it carved on my tombstone."

The incident in question happened thirty years ago when Kim showed off a set of house plans she'd drawn for a drafting class during her sophomore year at Berkeley. Anna spotted multiple miscalculations in a matter of seconds. Stung by the critique, Kim returned to school and promptly switched her major from architecture to art history.

"I never asked for an apology, Anna. All you did was accidentally point out that I couldn't be an architect if I couldn't grasp trigonometry. Not a crime, but like I said, intimidating."

"If I could go back in time, I'd keep my mouth shut. You'd have made a great architect."

"Nah, I'm happier selling someone else's house than I ever would have been sitting at a desk and designing my own. Let Andy find what makes him happy and support that." She bumped Anna playfully with her hip. "Speaking of houses, how about selling us yours when Mom's gone? You guys can move into the Big House with Dad and his new wife."

That was the worst idea Anna had ever heard.

* * *

Lily wiped down the wok with a tea towel and set it on the counter where it would stay until someone taller returned it to its place on the top shelf. Cleaning the kitchen wasn't her favorite chore, but she appreciated its solitude compared to the cacophony of TVs and computer games competing with multiple conversations from all corners of their villa.

Kim was sitting out on the veranda with Alice and Eleanor, all of them quizzing each other in Spanish. The guys were in the living room, where Hal and George were talking golf as Jonah and Georgie battled one another with paintballs in a video game called *Splatoon*.

Hal caught her arm as she walked behind the couch. "Thanks for cleaning up, Lil. I've got breakfast duty tomorrow and George is taking us all out for lunch."

"Did you guys volunteer, or were those your marching orders?"

He tipped his head toward the veranda. "What do you think?"

"Good on her."

Anna was in their bedroom with the door shut. Lily opened it gently on the off chance she'd gone to bed early. Instead, she found her propped up with pillows on the king-sized bed having a video conversation with Andy.

"Come say hi to your son, who looks very dope in his new rugby shirt."

Andy groaned. "Just say it looks cool, Mom."

Lily squirmed into the picture. "Did you just say Andy looks like a dope? I think he's very cute." She made a mental note to order him another but in a smaller size. This one hung off his shoulders.

He palmed his face. "Just so you both know, I still haven't forgiven you for dragging my butt out of bed this morning."

Anna's eyes went wide and she covered her mouth. "You said a bathroom word."

"Andy, what time are you and Serafina going to the festival?"

"She's supposed to text me when she's ready. Soon, I hope. I'm starving."

"Didn't you eat at the party?" Lily asked.

"I had chips and stuff, but I didn't want to mess up my shirt. I could murder a burrito. What did you guys have for dinner?"

"Chinese food," Anna replied. "Which you wouldn't have liked because it had lots of vegetables."

"You won't believe this, Andy—your mom helped cook. And she didn't even set off the fire alarms."

"Now *that's* dope."

"I'll be so glad to see you tomorrow, pal." Anna's tone was unmistakably sentimental. "I keep looking around for you, expecting you to be here. It just isn't the same without you."

"Me too," Lily said.

"It's only been a couple of days, you know. Not even that."

"I know, but it feels like a long time when you're missing somebody, and I'm missing the heck out of you. I can't imagine what I'll be like when you go off to college. Maybe I'll go with you. We could share a dorm room."

Seeing Andy's look of alarm, Lily shook her head. "I won't let her do that to you, son. But she's right, we miss you."

"Uh-oh, there's Serafina. I gotta go."

"Text us a picture from the festival," Lily said.

"I'll pick you up tomorrow morning outside customs, pal. Ten thirty."

"Okay, see ya then. Love you." His smile turned quickly to a sneer. "And don't either of you call me in the morning. I'll set my phone and get my own self up. If you do, paybacks are going to be double. No, triple."

When they ended the call, Anna tossed the phone aside and tugged Lily across her lap. "I love you."

"I'm lucky that way. Andy's in a good mood tonight. So are you."

"It's fun to see him so excited. This was a good idea, letting him stay home by himself a couple of days. You were right, I was wrong. As usual." Her voice held a hint of sadness. "When he gets here I'm going to tell him how proud I am that he's my son…something I don't say often enough. He's a good kid and I don't give him enough credit for that. I need to remind myself to say these things aloud, not just think them."

Lily would love to see Andy's face as he absorbed praise like that. She sometimes sensed that he was desperate for Anna's approval. "He's going to be a fine young man…and soon."

"Before we know it." Anna shifted on the bed until they were lying face-to-face. "Lily, am I a good mother?"

"Absolutely," she replied emphatically. "Where did that come from, sweetheart?"

"Something Kim said."

"Your sister"—she poked Anna in the chest—"is a troublemaker. What kind of nonsense is she spouting this time?"

Anna snickered. "The same nonsense you spouted. I guess that means you're a troublemaker too…which I already knew, by the way. We were comparing notes on raising teenagers and she said I expect too much of Andy, that I hold him up to myself at that age. Remember saying that?"

"I do, but it was in the heat of an argument. I've had a chance to think about it, and you were right. Or partly right. He deserved a bigger punishment for lying to us."

"But was I right to assume that his ambition in life stops at being a car salesman? And more important, did I use my disappointment about that to justify, as he put it, selling the business out from under him? Because if I did, then I didn't really give him a chance to prove he was capable of running it someday."

Lily started to answer but Anna cut her off.

"And if that's true, then Kim was right and so were you. I judged Andy against who I was at sixteen, not who he is."

"Honey, it's possible you did. It's also possible you weren't wrong. When I think about the blood, sweat and tears you've put into running that company—all those sleepless nights you worried about drowning in debt, personnel headaches, the recession—I admit I have trouble seeing Andy deal with all that too. But if he decides his life's passion is to sell BMWs to the whole world, you and I both know he'll do it."

"You're not wrong there." Anna sighed and allowed herself a flicker of a smile that quickly gave way to a look of alarm. "Please don't let me judge Eleanor that way too."

Lily laughed and squeezed her hip. "Something tells me you'll get the short end of that, Ms. Einstein. Our daughter's going to run circles around us both."

"You got that right. And we won't have to worry about Georgie at all. At the rate he's going, he'll be a playboy tennis pro in Monte Carlo someday." Her soft smile faded. "Stay on my case, Lily. I want to be a good mom. Whatever it takes, just don't let me fail my kids. I'd never be able to forgive myself."

Anna's wistful plea swelled her heart with love. "Sweetheart, you're not going to fail them, I promise."

"How can you be sure?"

"I just know. I deal with mothers all the time, and the bad ones never think to ask if they're good mothers."

CHAPTER TEN

"Keep watching for him, Dad. I'll try him again," Anna said, nodding toward the trickle of passengers emerging through the door from customs. The arrivals board showed the flight from LAX landing almost forty minutes ago. She'd texted Andy half a dozen times already with no response, and her call went straight to voice mail again. "I'm starting to think he's forgotten his phone."

"What's he wearing?"

"How should I know? He's sixteen. He dresses himself."

Anna darted toward a man who exited wearing a Dodgers cap. "Excuse me, were you on the Alaska Airlines flight from LA?"

He shook his head. "Sorry, Delta."

The Delta flight had landed twenty minutes later.

"You want me to call Lily, see if she's heard from him?"

She shook her head. "Not yet, she'll just worry. Go ask at the ticket counter if there was a problem in LA. Maybe he got bumped to another flight. Could be he's in the air and that's why his phone's off."

When a third call to Serafina also went unanswered, Anna scrolled through the contacts on her phone until she reached a neighbor who promised to send her husband to see if Serafina's SUV was in the driveway.

Her rational side assured her there was a simple explanation. The lost phone, the bumped flight. That wasn't enough to stop traumatic scenarios—the worst imaginable—from seeping into her consciousness. An accident on the freeway. A carjacking. A carbon monoxide leak at the house.

Suddenly it struck her and she broke into a grin. "Son of a—I'm going to wring his scrawny neck." *Epic paybacks!* She spun around, fully expecting to find him peeking around a corner, doubled over with laughter.

Instead, she saw her father striding toward her, his face grim. "They said he wasn't on the plane. Never checked in for his flight, never canceled."

She shuddered, a wave of panic rising as she began to give credence to her fears. "All right, that's it. Something's wrong, Dad. I don't know what, but I need to get back to LA right now and find out what's going on. Call Lily and—"

"I'm coming with you. We'll call her from the gate."

* * *

Kim joined Lily at the rail and handed her a bottle of sparkling water dripping with ice slivers. "What do you want to bet they passed each other in the air somewhere over Tijuana? Andy's going to call from the airport any minute now, probably on some total stranger's phone because he left his at home. And he'll say he missed the flight but Serafina helped him book another one."

"I'd be so happy if you were right," Lily said. But it strained credulity to think Serafina wouldn't have called to let them know. Unless she'd dropped him off and he'd gotten distracted in the airport, missed his flight and had no way of calling her. That's what she wanted to believe. She looked out from the veranda toward the pool where Hal had engaged the kids in a game of Marco Polo. What she wouldn't give to be so oblivious right now. "Kim, you wouldn't believe how hard it is not to be scared to death."

"Try not to be scared, sweetie. You're sure he's not just yanking your chain? He did promise to pay you back for that refrigerator-running prank. God, I still can't believe he fell for that."

If this was Andy's idea of payback, then Anna was right about his lack of maturity. Surely he wouldn't do something so outrageous.

"Hey, don't you have one of those trackers on his phone? We have that for our kids...except Jonah keeps turning his off, the little shit."

"That's exactly the problem. We have an app called Find My Family, but Andy disables it. He says he's old enough not to be watched all the time."

"Hal thinks they're creepy. Of course, that's because I sent him to the garden store for some potting soil and clocked him two hours at the marina on his boat. As if I needed a phone tracker to tell me that's where he'd be."

Though Lily appreciated Kim's valiant efforts to distract and reassure, there was no rationalizing Andy's inexplicable disappearance. "What really scares me is that Serafina's not picking up our calls either. I could see her playing along with a small prank but not something this serious. She'd know we'd be freaking out. And the odds of *both* of them losing their phones? I don't think so. Whatever's happened, it's happened to both of them."

"Chill! Nothing happened." Kim wrapped her in a hug. "You've already ruled out all the bad shit. No earthquakes, no fires. No hostage takers at the airport. If there'd been an accident on the 405, it would have shown up in the traffic report. I'm telling you, there has to be a simple explanation for all this. Once you find out what it is, you can whip his ass for not calling you."

Lily lunged toward her chirping cell phone. "Anna?"

"We just landed...coming into the gate right now. Any word?"

"No, and he hasn't posted anything on social media since that one picture from the party yesterday afternoon. I even got Jonah to check all the accounts we don't know about."

"And Serafina?"

"Nothing from her on Facebook, but she doesn't post much anyway. I'm here with Kim, putting you on speaker."

"The plan right now," Anna said, "is that Dad and I clear customs and swing by the ticket counter to see if anyone recognizes him. Maybe somebody will remember putting him on another plane. If they have access to other airlines' manifests, they can check and see if he rebooked somewhere else."

"Good idea. Let me text you the picture from the party. He might still be wearing that same shirt, the blue and white one." She scrolled through her phone to find the photo and send it through the message app. Another icon on her home screen caught her eye. "Hold on a sec… Anna, did you check the alarm at home to see what time they left the house?"

"It never crossed my mind."

The app took forever to load, and again to recognize her thumbprint in place of a password.

Anna got hers loaded first. "Never mind, Lily. I've got it. Status is armed."

"Scroll down. There's a history."

"Shit." A rare curse word from Anna, which made it ominous. "It says it was armed at a quarter to seven last night."

"Which would mean…"

"Andy and Serafina never made it home from the festival."

Lily sat down before her legs gave way. "Anna, go straight to the police station and file a report. I'm going to the airport right now and catch the next flight home."

* * *

"I'm under the Alaska Airlines sign," Lily said into her phone. "White shirt and jean jacket. Where are you?"

"I see you." Headlights flickered on Anna's dark car inching her way.

Lily tossed her shoulder bag into the back seat and leaned over the console for a quick kiss. It was after ten o'clock, the absolute soonest she could get back to LA from Los Cabos. "Tell me everything. What did the police say? I assume you went to the West LA station on Butler."

"Yeah, they took a missing persons report. But without any information on the circumstances, it automatically goes to the juvenile division to investigate as a runaway. That was even after I told them Serafina was missing too."

"Those lazy bastards. I hope you told them that was fucking moronic."

"Not as well as you would have." Anna sounded weary, probably more from stress than physical fatigue. "They asked if it was possible Serafina had taken him. You have no idea how close I came to saying yes so they'd get off their asses and do something."

"They'd have picked her up and deported her, no questions asked," Lily snarled. The ICE aggressions forced millions of hardworking immigrants to live in fear on a daily basis—even those like Serafina with resident status. "Jonah said he'd keep an eye on all of Andy's social media accounts in case he posts something."

"How are Georgie and Eleanor handling this?"

"I can tell they're worried." They'd agreed it was best for the twins to stay behind with Kim and Hal for now. "I told them we were going to find Andy as soon as possible so we could come back to finish our vacation. That's what I have to keep telling myself."

Her phone rang from her purse—a call from Kim—but then the Bluetooth in Anna's car picked it up and put it through the speaker. "Lily?"

"I just got here. I'm in the car with Anna. What's up?"

"Eleanor found something."

"Eleanor? She should be in bed by now."

"Sorry, that's what you get for raising a daughter with her own agency. Anyway, she's been noodling around on Hal's laptop trying to check some kind of doo-dad stuck up there on her cloud account. Here, you talk to her."

"Mom?"

"What is it, honey?" Lily asked.

"No, other Mom," she said. "Remember that STEM class I had with Kylie Redeker, the blogger who showed us how to make a data file from a phone app?"

Anna shook her head, flustered. "Ellie, unless this has something to do with finding your brother, it'll have to wait."

"I might know where they are. I got some data."

Lily's shoulder banged sharply against the window as Anna whipped the car off West Century Boulevard and into a deserted parking lot. "Ow! What's she talking about?"

"She built a data file to capture…you explain it, Ellie. What do you have?"

"Uncle Hal let me use his laptop and I made a data file for Find My Family."

Lily spoke up, "Sweetheart, we tried the phone app already. Andy disabled his and Serafina's phone is either turned off or the battery's dead."

"But Serafina's came on a little while ago. See, the file I programmed captures Find My Family locations every sixty seconds in case their phones turned on."

"Ellie, that's brilliant!" Anna said. "God, you're so smart. You're saying her phone turned on? Where was it?"

"It came on for about two minutes, then it went back off. I mapped the coordinates and it looks like it was at the King Taco in Maywood."

"Maywood." Anna closed her eyes as if trying to visualize. "That's near the river, isn't it?"

"Yeah, I used to have some clients there. It's a Latino neighborhood." This was a huge clue, Lily thought.

"But why would she be there? And why isn't she answering her phone?"

Lily could think of a few reasons, and she didn't like any of them. "Maybe she ran into someone she knew at the festival."

"I took a screenshot of the map on my phone, Ma. I can text it to you."

"Yes honey, do that."

"It doesn't make sense, Lily. I can see her leaving the festival with a friend, but she wouldn't overnight somewhere without Andy. And to not put him on the plane? It isn't like her."

Lily had to agree. Her phone dinged with the arrival of Eleanor's screenshot. "I got it, sweetie. Thanks."

"You should go to sleep now," Anna told Eleanor. "My genius daughter. We'll call tomorrow. It's all going to be okay."

The image wasn't as helpful as Lily would have liked. King Taco was labeled on the map, but the star marking the location of Serafina's phone overlapped also with nearby homes.

"Anna, I don't know what to make of this. It's Serafina's phone, but is it Serafina? I can't think of any reason she'd be in Maywood."

"Maybe her phone was stolen." Anna sat behind the wheel with her arms folded, in no apparent hurry to turn back onto the boulevard. "Maybe we should go back to the police station and show them this map. Not that I expect them to actually do anything, but they ought to add it to the report at least."

"Screw the Butler station. We need to go straight to LAPD headquarters." Her mind suddenly raced with a raft of frightening possibilities that could explain Andy and Serafina's disappearance. "I'm thinking we've got a sixteen-year-old kid who's never run off on his own before and a nanny who'd never go off script without calling us. And now they've both been missing for twenty-eight hours. This is definitely not a wait and see."

"Agreed."

Anna shoved her car in gear and roared out of the lot, turning toward the freeway that would take them downtown. "You know people at the station there, right? You can call in a favor."

"Tony can help if we need him," Lily said, thinking of her former boss at the Braxton Street Legal Aid Clinic. She'd visited the jail enough to know how such favors worked. "For now I vote we go down there and shake a few trees until a detective falls out."

* * *

The last place Anna ever expected to find herself on a Sunday night was at LAPD's Metro Detention Center. Yet here she was, in a waiting area that smelled of myriad bodily fluids, watching the fruits of a seedy weekend in LA parade by. Delirious drunks, bloodied brawlers, agitated addicts. Some on their way to booking, others dumped outdoors into the rain. None of it seemed to faze Lily.

"I guess you've seen all this before," Anna murmured, keeping her voice low so as not to draw attention.

"And then some. At least no one's vomited since we got here."

"That's good. Because when they start to vomit, so do I."

They'd been waiting more than an hour, since Lily had insisted on speaking to a detective. Apparently, all their detectives were out detecting.

"Are you sure they're going to send someone down for us? Looks to me like it's the troublemakers who get all the attention around here."

Lily squeezed her knee. "Relax, babe. I know how to make trouble too. Let's hope it doesn't come to that." She'd found a power outlet and was charging her phone as she scrolled through Twitter feeds from news outlets in case there was a clue she'd missed. "Weekends are always hellacious. Why don't you check that vending machine over there, fetch us a bottle of water."

As Anna tentatively crossed the waiting area, the elevator opened to a tall, powerfully built Black woman with a burgundy pixie cut and lipstick to match. She wore a crisp blue shirt and gray slacks, with a detective's shield affixed to her belt. Her eyes lit upon Anna and she smiled. "Are you Judge Kaklis?"

"That's me," Lily said, springing to her feet to join them. "Lilian Kaklis, and this is my wife, Anna. We're looking for information on our son Andy."

"And our housekeeper, Serafina Casillas," Anna added. "They went to the Los Amigos Festival last night in Hollenbeck

Park and no one's heard from them since. I filed a report this afternoon at the station in West LA."

"Yes, I've read your report. I'm Detective Tawna Cooper," she said, handing each of them a business card as she shook their hands. "Captain Shively assigned me this case. I take it he's a friend of yours?"

"A friend of *hers*," Anna said, nodding toward Lily as she gently freed her hand from the detective's crushing grip.

"Andrew Shively and I go way back," Lily said, ostensibly to impress upon the detective that she was well-connected in the department. As if being a Superior Court judge wasn't enough to command Cooper's full attention.

"Let's go upstairs and talk this over, see if we can find your boy."

Making mindless small talk, they rode in a secure elevator to an upper floor and followed the detective down an interior hallway with a flickering fluorescent light. Cooper led them into a small impersonal office she likely shared with others. On the desk was a phone and a computer monitor, and an open blue folder with Anna's form on top.

"All right, first things first," Detective Cooper said as she cleared her throat. "Is Andres's father in the picture?"

"We call him Andy."

While Lily explained the circumstances of Andy's adoption, Anna tried to get a peek at the contents of the folder. It was already several pages thick, which she found both encouraging and unsettling. "I see you've been looking through Andy's case. Have you found something?"

"Actually I did. It may or may not be relevant." Cooper paged through to what looked like a second police report. "There's nothing in our records for Andy or Andres Kaklis, but I got a hit on your housekeeper, a Serafina Casillas at your address. That's what all these papers are from. Apparently she was a key witness to a stabbing last night at the festival."

"Oh, my God! What about Andy?" Anna's heart hammered as she scooted to the edge of her seat. Several photos had scattered from the folder, including a mug shot of a man whose neck was colored with tattoos. Another was the apparent weapon, a rounded, talon-shaped dagger that looked especially vicious.

Lily patted her arm. "Just a witness, she said. I take it she wasn't directly involved in the incident?"

"No, ma'am. And there was no mention of your son anywhere in the report. These were gangbangers already known to the LAPD. We arrested four, including the victim. Right now he's hospitalized but he's expected to recover. There were several festival-goers who gave statements regarding the fight, but Ms. Casillas was the only one to have witnessed the actual stabbing. She identified the assailant."

"And now she's gone missing," Lily said, as though finishing the detective's thought.

"We can't automatically assume those two things are related, but it is a disturbing coincidence. I'll bring the arresting officers in on this investigation. We'll need to speak to all the parties again and see if we can identify anyone else who might have gotten involved after the fact."

"After the fact?" Anna shuddered at the implications while her mind worked to fill in the pieces. "Are you suggesting Serafina and Andy might have been taken by someone to shut them up?"

The detective pursed her lips. "It's not something we usually see with gang-related incidents. Involving so-called civilians, that is. Mostly they fight amongst themselves. But it's definitely something we'll look into. If there's a reason to suspect they've been taken by a gang, we'll get warrants to search all the places they frequent."

Anna liked Cooper's straightforward manner. She was forthcoming about the facts, and she seemed to grasp that Andy and Serafina's disappearance was highly unusual, unlike the officers at the West LA station.

Lily drew out her phone. "Here's something that might help. Our daughter—she's good with computers and apps— she sent us this a little while ago. It's an app we use to keep up with our family. It lets us check where everyone's phone is. We couldn't locate either of them—I guess their phones were off—but then Eleanor wrote a program to record their whereabouts every sixty seconds in case they turned them on. Serafina's phone popped up a little while ago. Nine thirty-two, to be exact. Just for a couple of minutes, like it was turned on and off." She showed Cooper the map. "It's in the Maywood area, possibly King Taco."

"Send me that. I can pull their surveillance video."

Anna was terrified to think Andy and Serafina were being held somewhere by a violent gang. Or even worse—she shook the horror from her mind. It worried her that Andy might lose his temper. Surely he'd know better than to mouth off to someone who posed a genuine threat. Serafina would keep him calm. "I know my son. If he's being held somewhere, he'll try to talk his way out of it."

Lily nodded. "She's right. He'll tell them his ma's a judge. If that doesn't work, he might even offer them money. Andy knows how to make a deal and he won't take no for answer."

"Okay, that's good. Before you think the worst, keep in mind this is all still speculation. There could be another explanation that doesn't involve anyone being threatened. We just haven't found it yet." She scribbled notes on a legal pad. "By the way, I ran a check on the hospitals and didn't find anything relevant. That's good news. There's nothing yet on the vehicle. I put out an ATL—attempt to locate. It's possible one of our patrols will pick it up tonight."

"My father and I drove through all the parking areas around the park this afternoon," Anna said. "The signs say no overnight parking, that violators will be towed."

"Right, we also check all the impound lots. If it was left there, one of our enterprising tow services would have collected it by now."

If Serafina's car had been abandoned or impounded, it could only mean they'd been taken by force from the park. Anna couldn't fathom a single harmless explanation for why that would be. "What does your experience tell you, Detective?"

"Sometimes people just go off. They get drawn into an adventure and turn up later, oblivious to the fact that everyone's out looking for them." Her grave expression suggested otherwise. "I'm not saying that's what happened here. Andy and Serafina sound like they're responsible people. Would you agree?"

"Definitely. Andy wouldn't go off like that, and even if he had, Serafina would have called us."

"How long will it take you to check the impound lots?" Lily asked.

"I should have it by morning. It'll take a day or two at least to reinterview our suspects with their attorneys."

"That's a long time for a kid if he's being held against his will."

"I understand. We'll cover all the bases, but there's another scenario I think we should look at in this case. I did some background on the two of you. You're both in the public eye, not famous by LA standards but certainly prominent. Am I right that you have substantial means?"

"You think this could be a kidnapping?" Lily asked, then shook her head. "I can't see it. I mean, think about all the rich celebrities in LA. Why would they pick us?"

Anna's heart began to pound as she suddenly considered the thousands of employees who knew Andy from their visits to the dealerships. "Because I just struck a deal to sell my company for half a billion dollars."

Several seconds passed before Cooper spoke. "I wasn't aware of that. Is this information widely known?"

Anna described how she'd informed her staff in a conference call barely a week ago. Yes, some of her employees were anxious, but she couldn't imagine anyone was angry or desperate enough to do something like this.

"We can't necessarily assume it was someone you know. It could be one of their family members."

"Or practically anyone," Lily said. "They put out a press release so the news is all over town. What doesn't make sense though…we were all supposed to be in Los Cabos. Andy staying home was a last-minute thing. How would they have known he'd be at the festival?"

Cooper flipped her notepad to a new page. "Could be they were watching your house waiting for their chance. Again, we're only speculating, but this is an avenue we need to pursue." She scribbled again on her pad. "I'll have someone check street cameras to see if there was a vehicle following them from the house to the festival."

Anna was able to provide the precise time they left the house based on the alarm. While it frightened her to think someone was holding them for ransom, it was better than them being in the hands of violent gang members trying to shut them up permanently.

"I'd like to get our technicians inside your house first thing tomorrow to set up phone tracing on all your lines and accounts in case you get a ransom call. And just to be on the safe side, they should look through everyone's computers to see who you've been talking to. I suggest for now you go home and get some sleep. Frankly you both look whipped, and it could be a long few days." She closed her folder and stood, signaling an end to their meeting. As she escorted them down the hallway, she calmly assured them of the steps she'd take to follow up with the arresting officers and others at the scene. "I can only imagine what you're going through. But this case is mine now and I promise it'll get all the attention it deserves."

As they walked through the parking garage to their car, Lily said, "I feel like we've been dropped into someone's idea of a horror film."

Anna stopped and grabbed her by the shoulders. "If there's a ransom, we pay it. I don't care if it takes everything we have."

CHAPTER ELEVEN

The gangbanger raised his weapon, a hook-shaped dagger. Anna shouted, "Andy, I love you!"

He looked back with narrowed eyes, his lips pressed tightly together—refusing to answer.

"I love you, pal. I love you."

"*Anna!*"

She went limp as Tawna grabbed her by the shoulders and shook her hard.

"*Anna!* Anna…wake up, sweetheart. It's just a dream."

Breathless and shaking, she opened her eyes to find Lily looming over her in their bed. "A dream…"

Was she awake for real now? She sat up and looked around the room. The bed, the alcove, the clock.

"Honey, are you okay?"

"How am I supposed to be okay when we don't know where our son is?" She regretted the sharpness of her reply and planted a light kiss on Lily's cheek. "Sorry. I dreamed they were holding Andy in a basement, some gangbanger with a knife and one of my GMs. They wanted a million dollars in ransom, but Hal was trying to negotiate a better deal."

"It's no wonder, what with all those things bombarding your head."

She threw back the covers and swung her feet to the floor. "I'm surprised no one called me a cunt."

They'd arrived home last night to find *JUDGE CUNT* spray-painted across their front door, raising the specter of yet another potential threat—Claré Zepeda's rabid fanbase. Their doorbell camera had caught a clear image of the vandals, a young male with a spray can and two women who cheered him on. Lily had sent the video to Detective Cooper and also to the security team at the courthouse.

They'd barely dressed and made it downstairs before Cooper showed up with Peter Nguyen, a police technician. He set up his computer gear on the dining room table and went to work right away linking their devices to a program that let him monitor their communications.

Cooper followed them into the kitchen, quietly assuring them Peter was a trained police officer and not to be put off by his worn jeans and sneakers, or the headphones that were a permanent fixture around his neck. "He ID'd your vandals already, caught them on street cameras pulling onto Wilshire Boulevard and ran their license tag. Patrol officers dragged them out of bed at four this morning. I seriously doubt they had anything to do with Andy, but I guarantee you they're going to be very sorry they messed with a judge."

As Lily passed her a mug of coffee, Anna said, "I never saw a need for a gated driveway, but now that you're a judge I'm calling Samuel to put one in this week."

"Probably a good idea." Lily stifled a yawn before addressing the detective, "Any news on Serafina's car?"

"As a matter of fact"—she paged through her notes—"it was located in the impound lot at Pepe's, not far from Hollenbeck Park. They towed it at three a.m. on Sunday. We're running some prints, but there was nothing unusual in the search."

"Your guys have been busy," Lily said.

Cooper held up a hand. "That's not all. Those street cameras they used to track your vandals? They also tracked Serafina's vehicle on Saturday night, and it doesn't appear that anyone was following from the house...which makes it more likely their contact was at the festival."

"That means it probably wasn't one of Anna's employees either, because they had no way of knowing Andy would be there. Same with Claré fans."

Anna shuddered at the implication. It was looking more and more as if someone from the gang had taken Serafina and Andy to keep them from talking. If so, how could they ever let them go? "It *has* to be something else. What if Andy told a friend at Brock's house where he was going? They could have met him there. Or...or maybe we've got it completely wrong. Say it has nothing to do with Andy. What if it's someone Serafina knows? A stalker or something like that."

The detective nodded, albeit indulgently. "If she has an admirer, there's probably a record of it on her computer. Peter will check that out."

"Detective Cooper, you need to see this," Peter called from the dining room, where he was scrolling through what looked like a series of messages. "Looks like you guys were doxed last Tuesday on *Claré-2-Z*. This is a forum run by fans, basically a free-for-all. No moderators that I can see."

"What does doxed mean?" Anna asked.

"They posted your home address and both of your work phone numbers. Also the Premier Motors website...and your email at work," he added with a nod to Lily. "This post also mentions Andy, with a link to an article in *LABizMag*. Looks like a profile of Anna."

Anna rushed around to have a look. "That's an interview I did eleven years ago when I became president of the chamber of commerce. We'd just adopted Andy and they asked me about balancing work and home. I had no idea it was still out there."

"The internet's forever," Peter said glumly.

Cooper sighed. "We should at least find out if any of these fans are here in LA and keep that line of inquiry open for now."

After living her entire life in LA, Anna was mostly numb to its celebrity culture. Premier Motors drew a steady stream of actors, singers and sports stars in search of a stylish BMW to fit their upscale image. Plus she and Lily were on a first-name basis with several stars whose kids attended Hills Academy. But this side—an army of fanatics willing to do harm to those who dissed their idol—was something she couldn't fathom.

She couldn't stand around and wait for some computer geek to trace a number to a whacko fan. "I'm going to the dealership to go through my mail. Call me if you hear something."

Lily walked her to the door. "I take it you need some head space, right?"

"That's part of it. The other is if they're sending stuff to work, I'm the best person to go through it. The sooner I do that, the sooner we can focus somewhere else."

"Okay…" Lily tugged the lapel of her sweater. "But don't be gone long. I need you here."

Anna crushed her with a hug meant to hide her tears. "We'll get him back. We have to."

* * *

With the couch throw wrapped snugly around her shoulders, Lily paced the pool deck watching for Anna's return. The police had given them prepaid cell phones so they could keep the other lines open. She was talking to Kim, who'd called to say they all were booked on a midday flight that would have them back in LA by two thirty.

"Anna's a wreck, Kim."

"We're all zombies here too. Your kids were up at five o'clock begging to come home. Eleanor already had her suitcase packed. That kid…I tell you. She knows what she wants and she won't take no for an answer."

"Hmm…remind you of anyone?"

"No shit. Who all's there?"

"George is on the way over, but right now it's just the detective and a technician. Officers keep coming in and out with reports. They've set up in the dining room. It looks like command central for a space launch. They've got all our phones wired into a computer program that records and traces. The good news is they've checked all the hospitals and didn't find anything."

"That's one thing off the list to worry about."

Hearing her children's voices in the background made Lily glad they were coming home. "Sorry about ruining everyone's trip, Kim. I know you guys have been looking forward to it."

"You're fucking kidding, right? We're *all* scared to death, Lily. Even Jonah. He's trying to pretend it's no big deal, but I see him checking his phone every fifteen seconds to see if Andy's posted somewhere. We're all in this together."

Lily sighed. "I know and we appreciate it. You and Hal…we owe you big time."

"Sell us your house and we'll call it even."

"Sorry, you'll have to take that up with the boss."

Moments after they ended the call, she heard the garage door go up, signaling Anna's return. Lily met her at the back gate. "Anything?"

She shook her head. "No mail, no packages. A couple of crank calls over the weekend, Trina said, but she blocked them from calling back. I texted the numbers to Peter."

Inside at the kitchen bar, Lily shed her blanket and shared the update from Kim. "She's worried about Eleanor and Georgie. They're both anxious. I asked if she'd mind keeping them at the Big House for a few days. I don't want them here with all these cops in and out. We can't leave them by themselves if we have to run out in a hurry."

Anna grunted her disapproval.

"You disagree?"

"I think there's something to be said for all of us being together."

Lily recognized the impulse. Anna wanted her family under her protective wing. "Okay, how about we ask George to stay with us? He's on his way over now."

"Fine." Her tone was sullen. "We never should have let Andy stay home by himself."

"If you feel that way, then I have to assume you're blaming *me* because I'm the one who sided with Andy. Do you?"

Anna angrily pounded her fist on the bar. "Of course not. I just wish we hadn't is all. What bothers me most though"—her eyes suddenly filled with tears—"when we were hanging up the other night, Andy said he loved us. I don't remember saying it back."

"But Anna—"

"No, it's true. He already believes I try to hurt him on purpose…selling the company, not letting him get his driver's license. It kills me that wherever he is right now he could be remembering the last time we talked. He might think I refused to say it because he hadn't measured up in my so-called perfectionist eyes. Isn't that what you said?"

"Don't go putting words like that in my mouth. Besides, it's utter bullshit. Andy knows you love him. I was on that call too. If he's thinking about it, he's remembering how the three of us laughed and teased each other. And how we couldn't wait to see him."

"I know, but it was those three words that mattered and I choked."

"Judge Kaklis?" Detective Cooper appeared in the doorway with her keys in her hand. "We just caught a break. Peter was able to crack Serafina's phone code and turn it on remotely. We tracked it to an address in Huntingdon Park and I've got two squads on their way to intercept. I'm heading over there now."

Anna bolted around the bar. "Can we come?"

"No, I need you to sit tight here with Peter. There's still an outside chance you'll get a call." With a promise to keep them in the loop, she raced off, blue lights flashing from the grill of her unmarked car.

* * *

Anna couldn't take her eyes off the clock. The family would be landing soon. They'd see this through together, comforting and leaning on one another for support. With every passing minute, Andy was either closer to coming home—or further away.

Her father stretched across the kitchen table to give her forearm a gentle squeeze. "You can't keep your kids in a bubble, you know. Especially when they get to be sixteen."

She released a ragged breath. "I know, Dad. It's just hard to think about my son needing me, and me not being there. Isn't that the very definition of failing as a parent?" She couldn't stop agonizing over her nightmare.

"We've all been there, darling. There are so many bastards in this world, crawling around like vermin in the dark. Whoever's behind this business with Andy and Serafina, they better hope they're never left alone in a room with me."

Anna loved his bravado but she couldn't imagine her father raising a hand to anyone. He'd always possessed such a kind and nurturing manner, a trait she'd sought to strengthen in herself as a parent. She'd fallen short so many times, especially with Andy. If only she could take back those times she'd lost her temper. Andy wanted so badly to please. All he'd ever needed from her was a gentle word of encouragement and a hug.

"Sweetheart."

As he nudged his handkerchief across the table, she realized she was crying. "I'm worried about him, Dad. I just want him to know how much I love him."

"He knows. He's always known. I'll never forget how he clung to you and Lily when he first came here to live."

"Mostly Lily, but then one night we clicked and it was me too. He was scared to death at first."

"Yeah, until he wasn't. I never saw a happier kid in my life than that first year we had his birthday party out at the pool. And I guarantee you there's not a day that goes by that he doesn't think about how lucky he is to have you two as his moms."

"You wouldn't say that if you'd seen me over these last few months. I've been hard on him. Too hard. Just ask Lily and Kim. Hell, ask Andy. His grades, his attitude." The night they'd fought at this very table had seared her heart. "To top it all off, I'm selling the one thing he cares about most. He practically accused me of doing it just to hurt him."

"Which isn't true," Lily said from the doorway. Fresh from a shower, her hair dripped around her collar. She slid into the breakfast nook and took Anna's hand beneath the table. "If anything, you did it to keep from hurting him."

George cocked his head. "How's that?"

Filled with shame, Anna couldn't bring herself to repeat it.

Lily said, "Unfortunately, Andy just doesn't show the kind of aptitude it takes to run a business like Premier Motors, no matter how much he wants to. He'd need a whole team around him to take care of things that are over his head."

"Isn't that how we've always done it? You get somebody who knows parts, somebody else who knows service, a finance guy, a sales manager. Anna's the only one who thought she had to do it all." He shook his head. "Not me. I liked selling cars, period. The rest was somebody else's headache."

"That might have been true with one dealership, George. Now it's twenty-two. She was afraid she'd be setting him up to fail."

Anna swallowed hard, the lump in her throat threatening to choke her. Every word was one more indictment of how she'd wronged her son. "Which takes us back to where this whole miserable conversation started. I didn't have confidence in my own kid."

And if that weren't bad enough, she hadn't told him she loved him.

* * *

Lily delivered a sandwich to Peter just as Detective Cooper returned from chasing down Serafina's phone. "Did you find it? Come to the kitchen. We have fresh coffee. You must be dead on your feet."

Cooper joined them at the table and laid a mugshot of a young Latino man on the table. "Do you recognize this guy?"

"Never seen him before in my life." Lily would have remembered his round face, distinctive with its wispy goatee and the heavy pewter stud drooping from his brow. "What do you think, Anna? Look familiar?"

"Mmm…no." She held a hand over her stomach, as if her anxiety was making her sick.

"His name's Bobby Gutierrez. No gang affiliations. His friends call him Banco because he sometimes lends them a little cash from his job stocking shelves. Strictly small change, but he makes like he's some badass loan shark. Honestly, I don't even think he knows what that means."

"What's he doing with Serafina's phone?"

"He claimed someone gave it to him to settle a forty-dollar debt. He didn't want to tell us who it was at first. That's what took so long. He's got a court date coming up for food stamp fraud and his public defender wanted us to make that go away."

Lily threw up her hands. "Food stamp fraud for a potential kidnapper? Sounds like a no-brainer to me."

"We had to get it through the DA's office and make peace with the fraud squad, since they're giving up a collar. So he gives us a name—Angel Martinez." She snorted softly. "Any guesses how many Angel Martinezes there are in Greater LA?"

"A couple of thousand," Lily said.

"At least. No address, no phone. Barely a description, except late teens and a Pitbull tattoo on his forearm. The rapper, not the dog. No joy from the photo lineup either, so this Angel's not on our gang squad's radar. I've got five patrols fanning out in Huntington Park and Maywood looking for him."

Lily let out a frustrated sigh. "Even if you find him, it sounds like a dead end."

"How do you figure?" Anna asked.

"If Andy and Serafina were taken, it wasn't by a petty criminal who sells food stamps."

The detective pursed her lips as if to concede the point. "But there's always brothers and cousins and sisters' boyfriends they look out for. We still need to untangle it and find out how Angel got his hands on that phone."

Lily hadn't meant to step on the detective's toes. She knew from her own work that even the thinnest of threads could tie a case together—or unravel it completely.

* * *

The kids were surprisingly chill considering everyone's stress levels were off the chart. Jonah, Alice and Georgie were in the family room mouthing the lines of a Jim Carrey movie they'd seen at least a dozen times. Eleanor was hanging out with Peter, who had shown her some of his technology tricks, including how he'd managed to turn on Serafina's phone.

Though Lily had initially dreaded the chaos, she found herself glad to have the family back together. Sitting in the formal living room, she and Anna updated the others on all the avenues the police had pursued. They were on pins and needles awaiting word from Detective Cooper, who'd called earlier to say police had identified Angel Martinez and were staked out waiting for him to return home.

"These have been the longest two days of my entire life," Anna said. "The only thing keeping me sane is knowing wherever they are, they're together. Serafina's always shown good judgment. She'll make sure Andy does whatever he needs to do to stay safe."

Everyone seemed to know intrinsically that worst-case scenarios were not to be discussed, not even in a whisper.

"I wish we'd hear something," Kim said. "It's been hours since she called. What the fuck have they been doing all this time?"

"Ma?" Heads turned to see Georgie in the doorway, looking sheepish.

Hal pulled out his wallet. "Sorry, bud. Here's five bucks for the swear jar."

"It's ten for the F-word," he stated firmly, holding his hand out for more. "Can we get some pizza, Ma?"

Lily had lost track of the time. "Of course! You and Grandpa find out what everyone wants and order from Johnnie's. Be sure to ask Peter too."

Anna hung her head. "Some parents we are, forgetting to feed our kids."

"I can let you have Jonah," Kim said. "He'll remind you every thirty minutes that he needs to eat. But you have a teenager… you already know how that works."

It was jarring to suddenly wonder what Andy was eating. His list of favorite foods was short—pizza, burritos, chips and mozzarella sticks—and he'd sooner starve than eat a vegetable. What would he do in the hands of captors?

"Mom!" Eleanor screamed from the top of the stairs. "Come see."

Anna looked annoyed. "What's she doing up there? I thought she was with Peter."

"Mom!"

"I'll go," Lily said. She trudged upstairs to find Eleanor sitting on her bed with an iPad on her lap. "What is it, honey?"

"I did it. I turned on Andy's phone like Peter showed me."

"Oh my God, is that Andy's iPad?"

"No, it's mine but he borrowed it last week when his ran out of juice. He saved his password. And look, right here's where his phone is. Alameda Street and…East Aliso Street."

Lily snatched the device. With her heart pounding, she enlarged the map to show an entire city block downtown that included the Edward R. Roybal Federal Building, which housed the federal courthouse. She'd argued a handful of cases there and happened to know it was connected via underground garages and tunnels to every building on the block.

This entire corner of downtown LA was the exclusive domain of the federal government. For the past several years, its plaza had been a frequent site of protest aimed at its most controversial tenant—Immigration and Customs Enforcement. Better known as ICE.

CHAPTER TWELVE

"*Puedo tener esto?*" a girl of about twelve asked, reaching for the tiny box of raisins from Andy's brownbag dinner. She must have noticed that he never ate them. They reminded him of dead bugs. Her brother though, who was only four or five, apparently loved them.

"*Esto tambien*," he said, handing her the packaged cookie for her toddler sister, whose face lit up with a smile. He didn't much like cinnamon, though he would have eaten it anyway had he not felt bad for the little girl. Surely he wouldn't have to spend another night in this shithole, though it was already pretty late in the day. By now these ICE morons had to have realized they'd practically kidnapped a US citizen. What a story he'd have.

The man who'd delivered their dinner reappeared with a plastic bag and walked through the room to collect everyone's trash. The meal itself was trash, Andy thought as he tossed his remnants in the bag. A baloney sandwich on stale white bread without even a drop of mustard or mayonnaise. There also was a bitter celery stalk, plus the raisins and cookie, all washed down with a tepid bottle of water. Same as yesterday, and probably tomorrow too if he was still here. The first thing he planned to do when he got out was order an extra-large all-meat pizza from Johnnie's and eat every bite himself.

He'd tried to tell the officers at the park they were making a mistake, only to be told, "Shut the fuck up, José." They'd sprung suddenly, dressed like Ninja Turtles and shouting in English and Spanish, demanding proof of residency from everyone there. In the ensuing scramble, Serafina had been knocked down and lost her purse with her green card. All Andy had was his learner's permit, which was deemed "proof of jack shit," since legal residence wasn't required to drive in California. If only they'd allowed him a call before bagging his phone. Surely his moms would be working to get him out of here by now. One group of kids had been freed yesterday, but then six more had arrived last night. That made twenty-four in a cage with benches for half that many and flimsy mats on the floor.

"Eat it now or throw it in the bag," the man barked, shaking the bag as he circled the room.

"*Cómelo ahora*," he whispered to the children. *Eat it now.* His Spanish vocabulary was okay—reading and speaking—but his ear for it sucked. He barely understood a word of what the others around him were saying.

He'd counted fifty-one others on the windowless bus that brought them from the festival to this place after the stabbing on Saturday night. He'd been mostly chill on the short ride, thinking they'd straighten out who he and Serafina were once they got here and allowed them a phone call. That chill turned to panic upon arrival when the officers separated them, taking the men one way, and the women and infants another. Andy was sent with the other minors, a third group that included several teens with younger siblings, some of them still in diapers. Three guys in his group were apparent friends, close to Andy in age but with swagger that made them seem older. The only other kid on his own was a little boy named Ruben who'd cried and screamed pitifully as his father was led away. He'd continued to sob that first night until one of the teens invited him to sit with her siblings. Andy felt guilty he hadn't done that, but he always expected to be released any minute.

As anxious as he was for his own wellbeing, he was physically sickened to see Ruben so upset. The poor boy was alone in a strange place with people he didn't know or trust, and clearly gripped with fear over what would happen to him and his father. Andy didn't have a lot of specific memories of his time in foster care, but he'd never forgotten those fretful feelings when he was moved to a new home. Ruben probably felt the same way.

"Casillas!" a gruff voice called out from the doorway. "Andres Casillas."

When no one else moved, Andy realized the guard was calling for him. *Finally*. "It's Kaklis. I'm Andres Kaklis. I was brought here with a woman named Serafina Casillas, but she's not my mom."

"Grab your gear and line up here." From this man's graying beard, Andy guessed him to be Hal's age, maybe older. Like the others, he wore a black polo shirt and tactical vest with a patch identifying him as ICE Police.

Relieved at last to be getting out, Andy collected his meager "gear" and hurried to the door. He couldn't imagine needing the cheap toothbrush, plastic comb and flimsy foil blanket ever again, unless it was to toss them in a bin on his way out.

"Ruben Ibarra," the guard called next.

The boy eyed him warily, then looked to the girl who'd taken him in. "*Esta bien*," she said.

"Let's go...*rápido, chico!*" Most of the guards spoke only in English, leaving some of the kids at the mercy of someone who could translate. He then called Lucía, the girl who'd asked for his raisins, and ordered her to collect her siblings too. Last was a guy named Santos, one of the three friends.

At Andy's count, that left eighteen in the small room to fight over whatever space his group had freed. Any minute they'd probably bring in six or eight more who were unlucky enough to have been in the wrong place at the wrong time.

"Here we go, single file." The guard motioned with his arm to keep the line straight.

Stepping into the hallway, Andy blew out a triumphant breath. Which of his moms would be waiting on the other side of the door? Ma might have used her pull as a judge to get him out, but heaven help the poor sucker who'd had to tangle with Mom. She never took prisoners. Laughing to himself, he imagined their faces, their look of relief. They probably had freaked right out when he didn't show up in Los Cabos. At least he'd paid them back for that refrigerator prank.

Expecting to retrace their steps from two nights ago, Andy was taken aback when the guard led them into a stairwell… and *down*. The reason became clear when they exited into an underground parking garage, where a white GMC van waited, its side door standing open.

"In you go, all the way to the back."

Andy wondered if the others understood his commands. It made no difference, since the guard steered each one aboard and into an assigned seat. Andy and Ruben had the back row to themselves, Lucía and her siblings had the center, and Santos sat alone in the row behind the driver.

Several guards playfully chatted outside the van until one came out and stowed a duffle bag in the back. Andy sifted through the gear they'd been issued. Where were their personal belongings? His phone, his wallet?

"*A dónde vamos?*" Lucía wondered aloud. Where were they going?

Santos shrugged in response. Away from his friends, he seemed less sure of himself.

The door rolled shut as the driver boarded and another guard slid into the passenger seat. They were young, in their twenties, but starkly different. The driver was boyish, with curly red hair and a face full of freckles. The other had a shaved head and full beard. "Buckle up," the driver said. "*Cinturón.*"

When they rolled out of the garage onto a dark street, Andy realized they were downtown, just a few blocks from the courthouse where his ma worked. After a couple of turns they entered a freeway, the 101 according to the sign. The exits weren't street names he recognized. The reason for that soon became clear—they were going in the opposite direction from Beverly Hills and Brentwood, heading east toward San Bernardino.

"Where are we going?" he called out.

The driver casually replied, "Relax, man. You're going home."

"I don't think so…'cause my house is in the other direction."

The guards shared a laugh, then the driver answered back in a mocking voice, "What, you thought this was an Uber?"

Andy drew a deep breath and felt his chest tighten, a reminder that getting excited or panicked could lead to an asthma attack. He needed to stay calm. On the other hand, if he didn't speak up soon he'd be halfway to Mexico before somebody figured out he wasn't even supposed to be there. "Look, there's been a mix-up or something. I'm a US citizen. My mom's a judge, I swear. Her name's Lilian Kaklis. She works back there at the courthouse. You can look it up."

They ignored him, continuing to joke with one another. Even Santos seemed to find his predicament funny. All the while Andy grew increasingly desperate.

"Come on, guys. This is fucked up. I was born in Oakland. All you have to do is call my mom. I can give you her number."

The bearded man turned in his seat and aimed his flashlight across the two rows directly into Andy's face. "My friend here told you to relax, didn't he?"

Andy bit his lip and tried to shield his eyes from the light.

"Didn't he?" he barked, causing Lucía and her siblings to flinch.

"Yes."

"Then I suggest you shut the fuck up, amigo."

The light bored into him for another few seconds as the van went dead quiet. When the guard turned away Andy's eyes slowly adjusted to the darkness, stinging with unshed tears.

* * *

Anna wrapped up the leftovers from five different pizzas, thinking Andy would eat it all when he got home. Whatever he wanted—pizza, chips, milkshakes—anything to help put this traumatic ordeal behind him.

"I vote we drive downtown right now and bust him out of there," George said. "Poor kid's probably scared half to death."

"It wouldn't do us any good, George," Lily said. "That place is a fortress in normal hours. Even attorneys have to go through one of the federal offices to get access to their clients. This time of night, there's no one to ask but the janitor."

"Yeah, well…I've got a thousand bucks for a janitor who'll go in there and sneak him out."

Anna was simmering with anger but resigned to the fact that their son wasn't coming home tonight. "I'd settle for a janitor who'd go in there and tell him we love him and that we're out here working our tails off to get him out. I can't stand the thought of him feeling like we're just letting him sit there."

"I'm sure he knows we're trying, honey," Lily said.

They were waiting in the kitchen for further word from Detective Cooper, who was on the phone in the dining room trying to track down someone from the Department of Homeland Security who could get them access to the detention center. Unfortunately, she said, ICE usually bristled at cooperating with law enforcement in LA, since the city had declared itself a sanctuary for immigrants. Whether they'd make an exception for the child of a sitting judge remained to be seen.

"We don't even know for sure if he's still being held there," Lily added. "I worked a couple of immigration cases with Tony, and they move people around a lot. And fast. Plus there's a paperwork lag, so the records might have them in one place but they're actually somewhere else. Frankly, I think the assholes do it on purpose to inconvenience the families. By the time we get Andy released, we might even have to go all the way up to Oregon to pick him up. That's one of the places they take teenagers."

While Anna was relieved to know Andy hadn't been kidnapped by a ruthless gang, she wasn't going to celebrate until he was home. She'd heard the horror stories, detainees piled on top of one another in dirty, lice-infested quarters.

Older children forced to take care of toddlers separated from their parents and left to fend for themselves. The idea that Andy had already spent two nights in a place like that made her sick to her stomach. Their sweet, sensitive son locked in a cage. It was all she could do not to cry.

"Penny for your thoughts," Lily said as she tugged Anna onto the bench of their breakfast nook.

"I'm just trying to manage my expectations. Finding his phone down there isn't the same as finding him."

"No, but at least now we know where to look."

The officers Cooper had sent to canvass for witnesses had confirmed that ICE agents came through the festival after the stabbing and rounded up dozens of people. But why Andy and Serafina?

"This makes no sense, Lily. Serafina has a green card, and Andy…sure, he looks Latino but Christ, his last name's Greek. It's right there on his license."

"It's obviously a screwup. I've read how they raid these events, scooping up everyone and asking questions later."

George snorted. "Or not asking questions at all. These macho jerks act like they're working on a quota system. End of the month, they still need a couple thousand bodies. Any bodies will do."

A movement caught Anna's eye, Eleanor leaning against the doorjamb. Her arms hung loosely at her sides as a yawn escaped her mouth. "Come over here, sweetie." She folded her daughter in her arms and kissed her head. "You've had a really long day. Maybe you and your brother should go on up to bed."

"Can I sleep with you and Ma? Grandpa's sleeping in Georgie's room."

It was rare for the children to ask to join them in bed. Even when they did, Anna usually carried them back to their room in the night. This, however, was not an ordinary plea. The kids were genuinely stressed out. "Do you promise not to snore and kick and steal all the covers?"

Eleanor laughed. "Are you talking to me or Ma?"

Lily sneered and rose to steer her out. "Come on, kiddo. Let's go up and get you and Georgie to bed."

As their steps faded on the stairs, Anna said to her father, "Thanks for being here, Dad. I didn't realize how much I needed the kids with us."

"They needed it too. They're as worried as we are."

Detective Cooper entered from the dining room. Behind her, Peter was packing up his equipment. "The good news is patrol picked up Angel Martinez an hour ago trying to buy baby stuff at Target with Serafina's credit card. Said he picked up her purse off the ground when everyone scattered. Her green card was still in her wallet, which explains why ICE took her in."

Anna blew out an exasperated breath. "Baby stuff. Could we have been more wrong about these guys?" She had half a mind to track Martinez down and hand him a check to make up for her horrible thoughts. "You said good news. Is there bad news?"

"We haven't been able to locate Andy. They won't talk to us through official channels, but a friend of a friend unofficially reported that Serafina was bused out yesterday morning to the processing center at Adelanto. That's up near Victorville, San Bernardino County. However, he said Andy wasn't with her."

"They were separated?" The idea that Andy had weathered this alone pierced Anna's heart. "He's just a kid. Why wouldn't they keep him with his guardian?"

"Because they're sadistic bastards," George spat. "Cruelty's a feature, not a bug."

"I'm afraid he's right," Cooper said. "Splitting up families is meant to be a deterrent. The current administration believes immigrants will think twice about coming to America if they know their children will be taken from them."

"So that has to mean he's still downtown."

Cooper's face fell. "I wish I could tell you that. Unfortunately, ICE's juvenile detention is notoriously difficult to navigate. Sometimes it's four or five days before minors even appear in the system." Sheepishly, she added, "Which is a roundabout way of saying that as of right now Andy hasn't shown up on the detainee list. Until he does, getting him released is going to take some tenacious lawyering."

Anna could hardly stand to think of her son spending another night in that place. She'd never felt so helpless. "Fortunately,

I'm married to a tenacious lawyer. I guarantee you she'll be in their faces first thing tomorrow morning."

"Oh, I believe you." Cooper strolled toward the door. "All right then, I guess that pretty much gets the LAPD out of your hair. I can get one of the officers to drop off Serafina's bag."

"Good, it'll help to get her green card back." Anna walked her out, where they started with a handshake that gave way to a hug. "Thanks for everything, Tawna. You were great."

"You have my number. Give me a call when you get your boy back, okay?"

Anna turned out the lights one by one and trudged upstairs to share the news. She found Eleanor tucked beneath the covers in the center of the bed. Lily, still fully dressed, was wrapped around her—sound asleep.

CHAPTER THIRTEEN

Andy's stomach growled with envy as the bearded guard returned to the van with a bag that smelled of Canadian bacon and hash browns. There had been no such breakfast for Andy and his fellow passengers. *Detainees*, the driver had called them. They'd been handed gooey breakfast bars and warm bottles of water from a bag in the cargo compartment. That was an hour and a half ago at a rest area on I-10.

They'd driven all night, ending here at sunrise in Phoenix, Arizona. Fifty-two degrees according to the digital sign they'd passed before pulling off the freeway. Andy was stiff from the ride and tired from lack of sleep. When was this nightmare going to end?

The guards finished their breakfast and tossed the trash out the window as they got underway again. To Andy's surprise, they didn't turn back toward the freeway. Instead, they crossed the intersection and entered a complex of office buildings marked only with numbers. The parking lot was empty at this early hour but for a small cluster of vehicles at a brick and glass building that topped out at six floors, identified as Building 250.

"End of the line, amigos. We know you have a choice in security escorts and we appreciate you choosing ICE Tours for your travels back to May-hee-co." The driver guffawed at his lame joke as he pulled into a parking space next to a van identical to theirs. "They're all yours, Berman."

The bearded guard slid the door open and directed Lucía and her siblings out to stand beside the van. Then he motioned for Ruben to join them. Santos was ordered to sit in the van's doorway while they wrapped him in a chain belt attached to both handcuffs and shackles for his feet.

"Your turn, José. Oh, wait...you want us to call your mommy, the judge? I can do that for ya." He took out his phone and pretended to dial as the driver burst into laughter. "Sorry, she's not answering. Looks like I'll have to hand you off to a *real* judge."

Though he burned with anger and humiliation, Andy knew it was no use to argue. If anything, they'd probably treat him worse, as evidenced by how tightly they'd pinched his wrists and ankles in the cuffs. At least they were taking him to see a judge. He'd been to the courthouse a few times to watch his ma argue cases, and once right after she became a judge. He recalled that defendants always got the chance to speak. He would explain how this was all one big mistake.

He fell into line with baby steps, noticing Santos was far more adept at walking with his feet tied together, as though he'd done it before. The first floor of the building was empty and dark. No wonder, since the clock on the wall said it was only twenty after six. On the second floor, Berman led them into Courtroom 5 and steered them to the back two rows. Several children and teens—that's who was in the other van, Andy realized—sat near the front, where the parties stood before a judge on a large TV screen.

An attorney was presenting her case for one of the children. "Your Honor, Eduardo García has family in Las Vegas who are willing to post bond and take him in while his request for asylum is being adjudicated. One call and they can be here to pick him up by lunchtime, relieving the American taxpayer of the burden of his care for what could very well be the next two and a half years." She sounded sure of herself. "I know my esteemed colleague would agree that would be preferable to relegating Eduardo to custody in a detention facility to the tune of nearly eight hundred dollars a day."

Andy watched with both fear and fascination. Poor Eduardo was Georgie and Eleanor's age. He looked scared until the woman gave him a wink. Maybe she was the designated attorney for all the kids. Andy hoped so. She was younger than both his moms but sounded like she knew what she was doing. Her confident smile and dark-rimmed glasses instantly reminded him of his seventh-grade math teacher, the only one who'd ever made math fun. Best of all, she had a snappy way of talking the judge seemed to listen to.

The other attorney, with his buzzcut and stiff black suit, looked as if he'd never had a day of fun in his life. "If it please the court, Eduardo García's father resides in Honduras. I'm sure Your Honor would agree that it's best for Eduardo to remain in his home country with his family."

"Counselor?"

"Your Honor, Mr. McInnis knows very well Eduardo's *mother* is currently being held at Eloy Detention Center. And his father likely doesn't *reside* in Honduras, or anywhere else. He disappeared eight months ago after being threatened by drug gangs. Fearing the same would happen to her and Eduardo, his mother has requested US asylum and is likely to be released soon to live with these same relatives in Las Vegas."

"Objection, calls for speculation," McInnis said. "Such an outcome for Mrs. García is far from assured. If anything—"

"That'll do." The judge raised his hands to silence them both, then ruled matter-of-factly that Eduardo would be handed over to his relatives.

Victorious and smiling, the woman briefly hugged the boy before nudging him toward a clerk who guided him out. As the next case was called, she pushed her file into an overstuffed leather satchel and turned to leave.

Andy then watched in horror as a pair of children, the oldest of whom was Ruben's age, approached the TV without an attorney. Who was going to speak for them?

He swiveled in his chair, shifting his shackled feet into the aisle to get the attorney's attention as she walked past. "Excuse me, ma'am," he whispered. "I need a lawyer too. My moms can pay, I promise."

"No talking, Casillas!" the bearded guard hissed as he sprang toward them.

Andy kept his voice low. "Please, there's been a mistake. I'm an American. My ma's a judge in LA. Her name's Lilian Kaklis. K-A-K-L-I-S."

She gave him a pained look. "Sorry kid, there's no time to file. But call me at this number and I'll try to hook you up with someone who can help." She handed him a business card, which the guard snatched immediately.

"This detainee is not authorized to engage legal services at this time."

"Are you prepared to back that up in a court of law, officer?" She peered closely at his ICE vest. "Badge number six-one-one-five-two."

"I think his name's Berman," Andy offered meekly, earning himself a steely glare. Probably not a good idea to call out the guy who decided how tight his handcuffs and shackles would be.

The door opened suddenly to a larger group of detainees, all of them children and teens. As they were guided into the rows opposite Andy's, the attorney snagged three of them, saying they were her clients. She left Andy with a pat on the shoulder. "Good luck, kid."

* * *

Dozens of cylindrical concrete pylons formed a blockade around the federal plaza, their purpose to prevent a vehicle attack like the one that had destroyed the Alfred P. Murrah Federal Building in Oklahoma City in 1995. Lily perched on one as Anna paced.

"I can't believe we live in a country where they can snatch *children* off the street and lock them up," Anna fumed. "And feel absolutely no obligation to call their parents. When did the US turn into a fascist state?"

"I assume that's a rhetorical question."

Anna had been ranting nonstop since waking at four fifteen. She'd taken Eleanor back to her own room and returned wide awake, all but pushing Lily out of bed so they could be at the federal building when it opened.

Lily shielded her eyes from the morning sun as she eyed a familiar figure at the crosswalk heading in their direction. Tall and balding, he had an easy smile she could see from almost a block away. "Here comes Tony."

As the head of the legal aid clinic where Lily had worked for over fifteen years before her appointment to the bench, Tony had personally handled the lion's share of their firm's cases involving immigration. He was just the one to guide them through this federal maze.

"He looks happy," Anna said. "It must be good news. Maybe he's talked to someone already."

"Nah, he's been like that ever since he married Colleen. You couldn't break his face with a sledgehammer." She greeted Tony with a warm hug. "Thanks for being here, Tony. Trust me, we'll make it worth your time. Billable hours, my friend. We need someone who knows what they're doing."

"Happy to help get the ball rolling. Immigration's more than half our caseload these days." He gestured toward the entrance to the federal building. "I made us an appointment with Randall Thorn at Homeland Security. If anyone can cut through the red tape, it's Ran. Did you bring the paperwork?"

One by one, she made a stack in his hand. "His birth certificate, my sister's birth certificate, her death certificate, my birth certificate and Anna's, the adoption decree with his name change, his passport, our passports. There's never been an American citizen with more documentation than Andy Kaklis."

She also provided the paperwork they filed each year to keep Serafina in their employ, including her A-number, which would identify her as a permanent resident. Once they finished with Thorn, Tony would be off to Adelanto to try to arrange for Serafina's release.

Feeling upbeat for the first time in three days, Lily squeezed Anna's hand and followed Tony inside, waiting while he cleared their visit with security. With visitor passes pinned to their chests, they were escorted to a third floor office where Tony made the introductions.

Randall Thorn was straight out of central casting for a paper-pushing bureaucrat. Mid-fifties, silver crewcut, with a short-sleeved shirt and what looked like a clip-on tie. He was affable, and it was clear he and Tony were friends.

"First off, let me apologize for this mix-up. I know you must be worried sick. Any given day we've got about fifty-four thousand detainees in federal custody. We're bound to have a handful of honest mistakes here and there." He tipped his head back to peer through his glasses at the computer monitor. "I'm not seeing Andres Kaklis on our list of detainees…but that doesn't mean we don't have him. I always said we could have a nuclear strike on LA and it wouldn't show up in the system till next week."

Lily found his explanations far from reassuring. "Is there any way we could do an in-person check? It's just that it's been three days since he was picked up and I'm worried because he doesn't have his asthma medicine. If he were to have an attack…"

Andy had mostly outgrown his asthma, but she wasn't above playing up the threat if it helped their case. Besides, stress could cause him to start wheezing, and it had to be stressful to be held in detention.

"I'm afraid that area's closed to unauthorized personnel," Thorn said, but then he squinted at Tony as if hatching a plan. "They sometimes let the lawyers in though. You know what this kid looks like?"

"Andy? Sure, I've known him since he was four years old."

As he made copies of Andy's documents, Thorn expressed confidence in a fairly quick release, given that Andy wasn't even in the system yet. Then for security purposes, he escorted them back to the first-floor lobby to wait while he and Tony walked the paperwork over to the detention center.

After an hour, Anna began to pace the marble floor. "What's taking so long? He made it sound like they were going to just walk over there and yank him out."

"It's a big place. Who knows how many floors they have to check?"

"Common sense says there's only one place a sixteen-year-old boy would be, and that's with other teenage boys."

While that was the logical assumption, Lily actually hoped it wasn't the case, since the raid at the festival had targeted gang members. Andy wasn't equipped to deal with street-savvy teens. They'd have a field day with someone so naive, especially if they learned he was from a well-to-do family.

Anna suddenly broke for the elevators where Tony and Thorn were exiting—without Andy. And also without Tony's famous smile. The men shook hands and Thorn departed.

Lily caught up in time to see him hand Andy's phone and wallet to Anna.

"They had his stuff but they can't say for sure they had him. He definitely isn't in there now."

"What the hell? How can they not know, Tony?" The exasperation in Anna's voice quickly turned to anger. "He's a child! If they're going to snatch him off the streets, they're supposed to be responsible for him. They'd better not touch a hair on his head."

Lily did her best to remain calm, though her temper was rising too. It wouldn't do for both of them to lose it. "Tell me what they said, Tony."

"I showed Andy's picture to a guard who said he looked familiar—he specifically remembered the rugby shirt—but they've taken five or six van loads of minors out for processing since Saturday. Trouble is, he checked all the manifests and Andy's name doesn't show up on any of them."

"That makes no sense," Lily said. "He was here. How else would they have gotten his phone and wallet?"

"Randall says they confiscate this stuff the moment they pick somebody up, so if they had his phone, they must have had him too."

"Then where the fuck is he?" Anna demanded. "Did they take him to Adelanto for processing too?"

"No, that's just for adults. The immigration courts for kids are all over the place. Oregon, Pennsylvania, Texas, Florida. They don't advertise. Some of these kids are in custody for a week or more before their families are notified."

"How can they be so goddamned incompetent!"

"Easy, babe." Lily took her arm to try to calm her down. "What's it like in there, Tony? Did you see any of the kids?"

He described a grim setting, a cage-like room with kids sitting on hard benches and mats on the floor. The younger ones were crying and several called out as they walked by.

Lily shuddered. "I'd have nightmares if I had to work in a place like that. How do these assholes sleep at night? It's inhumane."

"What happens now?" Anna asked, this time more evenly. "They know they've made a mistake, right? Please tell me it's somebody's job to track him down and fix this."

"Randall put an alert in the system so he'll get flagged the minute Andy gets entered into the database."

"He's just going to sit on his ass and wait for an alert? That's not good enough. As long as Andy's in custody, anything could happen. He's a nice kid and he's in there with gang members. Who's going to look out for him?"

"I hear you, Anna. I think your best play right now is to hire an attorney—"

"You're an attorney. We'll pay whatever you ask, Tony. You said yourself half your caseload is immigration."

"I can make a case in court, but right now you need a firm that can dedicate resources to tracking Andy down. We just don't have the manpower for that."

"He's right, Anna. We should reach out to Walter Shapiro's firm. They'll put someone on it today."

Walter was George's best friend and longtime family attorney. Though he'd retired from practice years ago, his firm still handled lots of legal work for the Kaklis family and Premier Motors.

"I'll call him right now."

Once Anna stepped away, Lily dropped her facade and let Tony see her fear. "What's it going to take, Tony? Assuming we can even find him, how do we get him released?"

He blew out a breath and shook his head. "There's no universal playbook for getting someone out of ICE detention, but just having an attorney makes all the difference in the world at a hearing. As soon as you find him, get somebody local lined up so they can get in to see him and file an emergency petition. Whoever it is, they have to be ready to go to court at a moment's notice."

"If I thought I could handle it, I'd resign my judgeship and take on Andy's case myself."

"And have a fool for a client, as the saying goes." He offered a hug, as he'd done so many times over the years when she needed it most. "He'll be okay, Lil. He's resilient, and probably a lot tougher than you realize."

For Andy's sake, she hoped he was right.

* * *

Andy strained to follow each case, hoping to pick up a hint of what the judge wanted to hear. So far he'd ruled only three times in favor of kids being released to their families, and those cases had been represented by the woman, the only attorney present besides the government's Mr. McInnis. Her remaining clients were two boys who looked like brothers, waiting their turn on the opposite side of the room. Andy had tried to no avail to catch her attention so he could ask again for her help.

Poor Ruben. His father had been transferred to jail on a charge of assaulting the ICE officer who'd taken them into custody. According to the government's attorney, he had a green card and was working legally as a landscaper. But now he was facing trial and perhaps prison, after which he likely would be deported. There was no record of family in the US, so Ruben was to be held until ICE made contact with his grandmother in Mexico.

Lucía and her siblings were being sent to live with a cousin in Honduras, despite her telling the judge through an interpreter that the cousin was involved with criminal gangs. Their family had overstayed a tourist visa and lived under the radar for the past two years in defiance of a deportation order. Even now, their parents were in hiding with their new baby somewhere in LA. The government lawyer argued that sending these children back would encourage the rest of the family to self-deport.

"Santos Aguilar," the court's bailiff called.

Santos rose and shuffled to the defendant's table at the front. His jeans bunched around his ankles and his oversized white T-shirt hung loosely to his thighs. For the first time, Andy noticed that Santos was a skinny kid like him, though he was taller. There was no fear in his eyes, only defiance.

"Your Honor, Santos Aguilar is a citizen of Mexico. His mother, also a Mexican national, is a permanent resident of the US currently serving in the armed forces in Germany. He resides with his mother's brother, a permanent resident who is married to a US citizen. Santos is known to law enforcement as a member of the Los Angeles street gang Florencia Thirteen." McInnis held up what looked like a mug shot for the judge to see. "Florencia is part of the Sureños syndicate, which is associated with the Mexican Mafia. Its activities include drugs and arms trafficking, robbery, extortion, and murder."

Andy was mildly aware of the Latino street gangs, but only because some of his tormentors at school thought it fun to accuse him of being in a gang. Not just any gang—the notorious MS-13, a violent, merciless criminal enterprise from El Salvador known for their facial tattoos.

"Santos Aguilar has been arrested twice for gang activity, including possession of a knife, for which he served four months in juvenile detention. We ask the court to consider the danger this detainee poses to the community, and permit us to hold him in detention until his eighteenth birthday on June fourth of this year, when he shall be deported to Mexico."

"Mr. Aguilar, would you like to respond?"

"It was just a stupid pocketknife on a keychain, that long," he said, holding up his fingers to show the size. "I didn't do nothing wrong since I got out of juvie. I don't hang with F-Thirteen no more. My probation officer say I gotta stay away so that's what I do."

"Your Honor, Mr. Aguilar was in the company of other gang members when he was picked up. It's clear that he's not adhering to the terms of—"

"Because they on probation too. We stick together but we don't hang no more with the gang, none of us."

Andy had no sympathy for anyone who'd joined a gang. Besides all the crimes they committed fighting with one another, they made it hard for Latinos to be accepted. It was fine by him for the judge to kick Santos out.

"The court orders Mr. Aguilar held, during which time he may petition for release."

As Santos returned to his seat, it was clear he was fighting back tears. He couldn't wipe his face because his hands were chained to his waist.

"Andres Casillas."

Andy sighed and hobbled to the front, throwing one last desperate glance toward the attorney. She gave him a slight nod, which he didn't understand at all.

"Your Honor, Andres Casillas is a citizen of Guatemala, brought to this country at the age of two by his mother, who is currently serving a four-year sentence for elder financial abuse at the California women's prison in Corona. Andres currently resides with his mother's boyfriend, who is a US citizen. Andres is fourteen years of age and known to Los Angeles law enforcement as a member of the street gang White Fence. They are affiliated with the Sureños syndicate, which as you know is—"

"That's not true! I'm sixteen and I've never been in a gang. Casillas isn't even my name."

McInnis held up a photograph that even Andy had to admit looked a lot like him. "Andres Casillas was identified by *two* confidential informants following a sweep that also netted Victor Alvarez, a White Fence member who is currently in the custody of the Los Angeles Sheriff's Department, accused of the murder of a nine-year-old girl in a drive-by shooting. It is believed Mr. Casillas serves as a courier for Alvarez, carrying contraband such as drugs and weapons."

"I'm telling you, that's not me! My name is Andres *Kaklis*, not Casillas. I'm an American."

"Control yourself, young man," the judge said sternly.

"Your Honor, I'd also like to point out the shirt Mr. Casillas is currently wearing. Blue and white are colors common to many of Southern California's street gangs, including White Fence members. We believe it's in the interest of the United States to detain Mr. Casillas until his mother is released from prison—possibly as early as next year—when their deportation to Guatemala can be arranged."

"All right, Mr. Casillas. It's your turn to speak."

"There's been a mistake. My name is Andres Kaklis." He pointed toward the photo, aware that his hand was shaking. "Whoever that is, it's not me. I was born in Oakland. My parents died and I was adopted when I was five years old by my aunt, Lilian Kaklis. She's a judge in LA—you can look it up. My other mom, her name's Anna Kaklis. She owns Premier Motors. It's twenty-two car dealerships all over Southern California. German cars. BMWs and Volkswagens and Audis. They'd kill me if I ever joined a gang."

"Counselor, could this be a case of mistaken identity?"

"Your Honor, as I said earlier, this detainee's identity has been confirmed by not one but two informants, independent of one another. It isn't unusual for illegal immigrants to insist they are citizens with different names." After a brief pause to review his notes, he added, "Also, Officers McKay and Berman, who escorted Mr. Casillas from Los Angeles, investigated his claim of mistaken identity. They found no record of his mother being a judge, nor of a company by that name. They're here in the courtroom if you'd like to question them."

Those lying dicks!

"Just call my ma on the phone. Please!" Andy recited the phone number. "Or call the dealership in Beverly Hills. They'll tell you who I am."

The judge was silent for several seconds, and when he finally spoke his voice seemed heavy with concern. "Counselor, I don't mind saying that I have some serious doubts about the identity of this detainee. However, I will grant your request for continued detention on the condition that he be given access to an attorney, followed by another status hearing within forty-eight hours where he will be allowed to present evidence. Is that understood?"

"Yes, Your Honor."

Forty-eight hours! That was two more days of hell. And if the guards were willing to lie to a judge, they'd probably ignore his deadline too. It could be days—weeks even—before he got to talk to an attorney. What he needed was a way to get a message to his moms about where he was. They'd make sure the judge saw his birth certificate. As he returned to his seat, Andy made eye contact once again with the woman attorney. Then for good measure, he yelled out his ma's phone number again, while Berman manhandled him out the door.

CHAPTER FOURTEEN

They had the observation room to themselves at the indoor tennis center where Georgie was taking a private lesson with the assistant pro. Anything to kill time as they waited to hear from Tony, who'd gone to Adelanto in search of Serafina, or the attorney from Walter's office, who was looking into Andy's whereabouts.

"Georgie seems off a bit today," Anna said. "Not surprising considering his brother's been kidnapped by ICE."

"It takes him a while to warm up. But yeah, he's off a little."

"I'm worried about them, like Eleanor coming to bed with us. We should sit down as a family and talk this out, find out where their heads are. What do you think they need from us?"

Lily's first thought was they needed to see their moms projecting calm and certainty that everything would turn out all right. The kids would feed off their emotions, and Anna was winding herself into a knot of anxiety and anger. Saying so might make it worse.

"Georgie needed *this*. You were right to call and set it up. This is how he lets go of stress. And he loves it when both of us are watching."

"Yeah, we talked about it on the plane. I haven't paid enough attention to his game, what with Eleanor's STEM camp. I plan on fixing that."

"How, by cutting yourself in two? We can't be everywhere all at once."

"No, but I can do better. And I will."

They'd dropped Eleanor at the Big House to hang out with Alice. Lily had a pretty good idea how she was dealing with stress. "What do you want to bet Eleanor's got Gracie in her lap right now? Nothing like a kitten to soothe your nerves. I'm coming around, by the way. We should all go together to the shelter when Andy gets home."

"Absolutely. I want the kids to be happy. I don't mean spoil them, but I've begun to realize that I always say no first when they want something. Like with Andy getting his license, and Eleanor getting a kitten. I need to break that habit and start listening more."

"Cut yourself some slack, sweetheart. We made those decisions together, and we had good reasons for saying no at the time." She clasped Anna's hand. "None of this is your fault."

"No, but it's my fault Andy feels like I'm ruining his life."

"All kids feel that way at one time or another." Lily laughed, imagining once again Anna's teen years. "Okay, so not you. But most of them only see what's right in front of them. They can't grasp what's down the road in a month, let alone a few years."

Lily's cell phone chirped—*finally*—with the call they'd been expecting from Tony. "Hey, I'm here with Anna. Did you get to see Serafina?" She switched it to speakerphone and held it between them.

"I did, and she's a wreck. All she cares about is Andy. She was in tears the whole time, saying how sorry she was for letting this happen."

"Why? She's not to blame, is she?" Anna asked.

"Of course not. What happened was ICE swarmed in out of nowhere as soon as the cops cleared the scene from the stabbing."

"In other words, some asshole in the LAPD tipped them off," Lily snarled.

"That'd be my guess too. It happens pretty much every time there's a gang bust. People get scooped up. Anyone who's not a citizen is a potential target for deportation if they're involved in a crime. That's what they're looking for."

"What crime, Tony? Serafina was helping the police."

"She said they came on real aggressive, yelling for everybody to get down on the ground and standing over them with rifles while they were being searched. One guy confiscated all the phones before anyone had a chance to call for help."

Bastards. Not that Lily was surprised. She'd once represented a client who was picked up by ICE at the courthouse only moments after he testified for the state against a drug-dealing neighbor. That was his thanks for doing his civic duty.

"She dropped her purse trying to get away, which you know about already. That's why she didn't have her green card. She tried to give them her A-number but they refused to look it up."

"Such bastards," Anna said. "They could have cleared it up right there on the spot. Why wouldn't they do something so simple?"

Lily saw it through a cynical lens. "Because this administration's real goal is to detain as many immigrants as possible and find a reason to deport them."

"It feels that way sometimes," Tony said. "Serafina was worried about Andy because the agent who detained him accused him of having a fake driver's license. Apparently that was the basis for their arrest."

Her fists curled with anger at the notion that ICE was free to make stupid mistakes all day because they knew damn good and well the DHS put the burden on immigrants to prove they had a right to be in this country.

Tony continued, "At least Randall's on the case now. Once Andy gets into the system, things will start to happen."

"What about Serafina?" Anna asked.

"I got her scheduled for a hearing tomorrow morning. I should be able to get her released then, unless…"

"Unless what?"

"That's the other problem. I'll have to wait till her paperwork comes through to know for sure, but a lot of these detainees get charged with a criminal offense, like resisting arrest or disorderly conduct. Some of these ICE guys, that's part of their MO. They try to pin a charge on people they pick up, especially if they have legal resident status. Nine times out of ten it's just a pretext to deport. All they need is a conviction."

Anna shook her head. "Serafina wouldn't have done anything like that."

Unfortunately, Lily knew it wasn't that simple. ICE officers didn't use body cameras to document their interactions with detainees. If they said Serafina resisted arrest, she was as good as guilty.

"Whatever it is, I'll try to sort it out," Tony said. "I'll give you a call tomorrow as soon as we're done. Maybe you'll get lucky in the meantime and hear from Andy. All it takes is one officer who'll listen to him and check out what he says."

"Yeah, let's hope." She dropped her phone in her bag and said to Anna, "It's pretty hard to expect compassion from people who keep children in cages."

"It's like the whole system is designed to inflict maximum cruelty."

"However bad you think it is, I promise it's even worse. I worked with Tony on some of those cases. You wouldn't believe all the roadblocks they throw up. It's like gambling—the house always wins."

Down on the tennis court, as Georgie's hour-long lesson wound down, the pro ran him ragged on the baseline. Now red-faced, sweaty and gasping for breath, he dragged himself into the observation room. "That was awesome."

"You're on fire, kiddo," Anna said as she ruffled his matted hair. "Whoever draws you next better look out."

Lily passed him his duffle bag. "Go shower and get changed. We'll meet you in the car and grab some In-N-Out burgers for lunch."

In the parking lot, Anna stepped in front to take the driver's seat even though it was Lily's SUV. "You don't mind if I drive, do you?"

"Since when do you have to ask? I only married you because you promised I'd never have to deal with LA traffic again."

"So that's what sealed it. I always wondered."

Lily glanced around to make sure no one was within earshot. "There was also that flicking thing you do with your tongue. I like that a lot."

"Mmm, I'll take that under advisement." Anna started the car and began adjusting the seat and mirrors. "I need to do that flicking thing more often…keep my flicker in shape."

It felt good to lighten up, if only for a moment. "Anna, when this ordeal is over, I vote we try the whole family vacation thing again. Just the five of us, off the grid for real. How about a long weekend in a tent right on the beach at Laguna? Or by the lake at Point Mogu?"

"Sounds tempting…except for the part where we have to sleep on the actual ground and pick bugs out of our food."

"Come on, the kids love it. We haven't been camping in ages." Her cell phone rang through the car's audio system, posting the caller info in the dashboard display. "Who do I know in Phoenix?"

"Probably someone who wants to know if you're tired of paying too much for life insurance. Don't hang up!"

Lily laughed. "Let's see if you're right."

"Hello, is this Judge Lilian Kaklis?" a woman's voice asked.

"Yes, it is."

"My name is Shelynn Kelly. I'm an immigration attorney in Phoenix. A young man claiming to be your son asked me to call you."

* * *

The afternoon sun cast long shadows across the tarmac at Gateway Airport in Mesa, Arizona, an overflow airport just outside Phoenix. Shelynn Kelly had urged one of them to get here as quickly as possible. For Anna, that meant a private jet out of Santa Monica's executive airport.

After a heated, tearful debate, Lily had reluctantly agreed that it was best for Anna to go alone to meet the attorney. Somebody was going to get an earful for not bothering to check Andy's story, but that couldn't come from Lily. As an officer of the court, she couldn't risk losing her temper in front of a federal judge. An ethics complaint would surely follow.

As they taxied from the runway, Anna called home. "Hey, we just landed. Any more news?"

"Tony checked out this attorney. He says we can definitely trust her. She gets most of her funding from human rights groups, so she's been vetted."

Anna recalled Lily saying their legal aid clinic had gotten a surge of funding from foundations and nongovernmental organizations to fight the administration's aggressive stance on immigration. "Let's just hope this woman's good at what she does."

"She was good enough to track us down. Call me as soon as you know something."

The copilot of the small jet emerged from the cockpit as they rolled to a stop. "We'll be on the ground here until about seven fifteen if that's relevant to your plans this evening."

"There's nothing I'd like better than to fly back to LA with you guys tonight. Especially if I can fly back with my son."

Generally speaking, she thought of private jets as a wasteful extravagance. Not today. Any price was worth it if it meant bringing Andy home.

She ducked through the doorway and stepped carefully down the steep, narrow stairs. A dotted line marked the path to the gate. Carrying only her handbag and a zippered folio with Andy's vital papers, she bypassed baggage claim and texted Kelly that she was ready for pickup.

"Mazda CX-5, brown."

Anna spotted the compact SUV right away and waved. The woman behind the wheel had short brown hair and glasses framing a heart-shaped face, but Anna instantly drew comparisons with Lily based on the condition of her vehicle. File folders were scattered on every seat, and brightly colored sticky notes adorned the console and dashboard.

"Sorry," Kelly said as she moved a stack of files from the passenger seat. "You can't tell it from here, but I actually have a real office somewhere with a desk and everything."

"No worries. Lily's car used to look like this too. She worked for years as a legal aid attorney."

"Then you know what it's like." Kelly drove past the airport exit and turned onto a service road. "Did you bring the documents? I need to be absolutely certain we're talking about the same Andres I saw in court this morning."

Anna patted her folio. "We call him Andy. He's half Latino, which is why his biological mother named him Andres. In fact, social services told us his father was killed in a gang fight. How's that for irony?"

"Whatever you do, don't tell them that. ICE already considers him guilty by association. You too, probably. And your dog."

"What's the plan?"

"We need to try to get the judge to look at this evidence and rescind his order sending Andy to a detention center. I don't want you to get your hopes up though. This is a Hail Mary. I'm not even sure I can get through to him this late in the day. Most of our immigration judges are teleconferenced from New Mexico."

A sturdy chain-link fence divided the service road from the tarmac. At the end was a gate that allowed vehicle access, and beyond, two midsized passenger jets emblazoned with the word *Swiftair*. Each had a staircase at the forward door.

"Swiftair, better known around here as ICE Air. Gateway's their hub, which is why so many detainees are brought to Phoenix for their hearing. We get them every day by the busload from all over the Southwest. LA, San Diego, Vegas. This way they can bus the Mexicans straight from the courthouse down to Nogales and dump them across the border. The others get put on a plane back to their home country. Or if they're really lucky, they go to one of our shithole detention centers."

"That's disgusting. Lily says some of these ICE agents actually relish the misery they cause."

"I think it's fair to say nobody dreams of becoming an ICE agent so they can help people." Kelly parked and began to peruse the documents, taking photos of each with her phone.

"I made two sets of copies," Anna said.

"Good thinking. Oh yeah, this is definitely the kid who was in court this morning. Looks like you brought everything I need to prove he's not their Andres Casillas. I wish all my clients came so prepared."

"Thank my wife. She's the attorney."

"I have a confession," Kelly said sheepishly. "The main reason I took up Andy's case was because it was obvious he was telling the truth and the ICE agents were lying *pricks*. The other reason is I felt a kinship with him when he mentioned his moms, *plural*. That makes us family."

Anna laughed and sealed it with a fist bump. "Andy's a good kid, the complete opposite of who ICE thinks he is. He goes to a private school in Beverly Hills and he gets teased for his size and for being half Latino. He deals with it, but I know it hurts his feelings. It's killing me to think what it must be like for him in there."

"If we can get him out right away, he should be okay. It's the ones who are held for weeks on end that I worry about. Or the little ones. It's a real SOB who takes pleasure in locking up toddlers. A lot of these kids have never been in trouble a day in their life. Now all of a sudden they're treated the same as hardened criminals."

Anna hoped Andy could keep his head down and do as he was told. Staying safe was the priority. He had to know they were working like mad to get him out.

"Whoa, look at this." Kelly nodded toward the gate, which opened for a white van with US government plates, then closed once it was inside.

The van pulled in front of one of the planes and deposited five adults, all dressed in orange jumpsuits, with one wearing chains that bound his feet and hands. Two guards got out and flanked them as they climbed the staircase and boarded.

"That plane must be the one going to Honduras," Kelly said. "That's where today's deportees were headed. Either there or on the bus to Mexico."

"What about the other plane?"

"Hard to say exactly, but I'd bet money Andy's on that one. They don't usually file a flight plan till the doors close, so we won't know for sure where it's going till it takes off. That's part of their game, spreading detainees all through the system and making them hard to track. I'm telling you, they get off on being sick bastards."

The van circled and stopped in front of the second plane. This time four children got out, including a girl no bigger than Georgie carrying a toddler on her hip.

"Oh, my God." The sight made Anna physically ill.

"Yeah, that's the kiddie plane. Can you imagine what it sounds like in there, all those terrified children?" Kelly nodded toward the gate. "Okay, let's go see if we can fix this mess."

As Anna climbed out of the car, it occurred to her that Andy might be able to see her through the window. The thought pleased her so much that she couldn't resist a small wave. "What do we do?"

"First, I need to make this call." Kelly adjusted her earbuds and scrolled through her phone for a number. "Yes, this is Shelynn Kelly. I'm an attorney in Phoenix. I represented eleven clients in Judge Pruitt's court today. I've tracked down some information he wanted on a case he was concerned about, and I've just emailed it to your office." She briefly summarized the issue of Andy's mistaken identity. To Anna, she said, "Okay, I'm on hold. Just follow my lead."

They approached the gate, where a uniformed ICE officer brandished a rifle and told them the area was closed to civilians.

"We're here to pick up one of your passengers, Andres Casillas. He's a minor, so I've brought his mother and legal guardian to take custody. She's a US citizen and so is he. He was picked up by mistake. His name is actually Andres Kaklis and these are his relevant documents." She passed them through the gate, having placed the passport on top, opened to Andy's photo.

"Yes, I'll continue to hold." To the officer, she explained, "I'm on the phone right now with Judge Pruitt's office. He presided over Andres's hearing this morning, and he was concerned this might be a case of mistaken identity. Turns out he was right."

The officer was clearly skeptical, but he examined the papers. As he did, he haphazardly dangled his rifle over one arm so that it pointed toward Anna's chest.

Shuffling to Kelly's opposite side, Anna motioned for him to secure his rifle. "Excuse me, would you mind not…"

"Do you want me to read this or not?" he gruffly asked.

"Yes, of course." *Idiot*. As if it were necessary to hold her at gunpoint while he did.

The attorney pressed on with her call, making sure the officer was aware she was speaking with someone in the judge's office. "Yes, I understand…No, I don't mind continuing to hold for Judge Pruitt. This is extremely urgent." She covered the phone and said to the guard, "She's asking the bailiff to pass him a message. I can't believe he's still in court. We started at six o'clock this morning. He'll be so glad to see this dealt with. One less headache for him. Would you be able to call Andres down here while we wait? The judge may want to speak to him before his release…probably to apologize."

"Which plane is he on?"

"He's being detained, not deported. Does that narrow it down?"

He grudgingly activated his radio. "This is Fagan. There's a lawyer down here at the gate who says one of the detainees isn't who he says he is. His real name is Andres…*Cackles*. That's K-A-K-L-I-S. She's on the phone with the judge now."

Anna felt like snatching his phone and shouting to the person on the plane to bring Andy to the gate. "Kaklis wouldn't be on your list. The agents who picked him up mistakenly believed he was someone named Andres *Casillas*. It wasn't their fault. Someone gave them bad information." She added the last bit to soothe their overblown egos.

"Try Andres Casillas."

"Thank you, I'll continue to hold," Kelly said. To the guard, she added, "I should have the judge on the line in a couple of minutes."

"I need to take these papers to my sergeant. He's on the plane."

Kelly reached through the gate and grabbed the folio. "No, no. You take the copies. I'll hold on to the originals."

"I love how you've got everyone believing you're here doing what the judge ordered," Anna said when he'd gone. "That's brilliant."

"Me? What about you. That was a stroke of genius telling him it wasn't their fault. Now they have an excuse to fall back on. And we're going to need it"—she waggled her phone—" since Pruitt's secretary hung up about two seconds after I asked to speak to him. But at least she promised me he'd look at the documents."

The news was like a gut punch. "And all this time, even *I* believed you were on hold for him. That means Andy's basically screwed."

"Not necessarily. ICE arrested him, ICE can release him, even without a court order. I can't imagine they'd want the PR shitstorm that would follow if they knowingly detained a minor when they had proof it was the wrong person."

Anna wanted to believe that but she'd seen too much evidence of ICE acting with impunity and not giving a damn what anyone thought. If they couldn't be shamed about putting toddlers in cages without anyone to answer their screams, it was hard to imagine them having compassion about anything.

They looked up as Fagan emerged and started down the stairs—without Andy, but with considerably more spring in his step than when he'd gone up.

Anna didn't know what to make of it. "He looks happy. Let's hope he's bringing us good news."

Fagan never even looked their way. Instead, he methodically released the brakes on the stairs and rolled them away as another guard reached out and closed the plane's door.

Kelly stamped her foot. "Those bastards! They don't give a shit whether Andy's a citizen or not. He's Latino. As far as they're concerned, he's just another beaner who doesn't deserve to live in *their* country."

* * *

Andy's stomach roiled as they hit another pocket of turbulence. The flight was a lot rougher than what he was used to, probably because he was seated at the back of the plane. He normally flew first class with his moms, but even for their flights in coach they paid extra to get seats close to the front. It was a lot smoother up there.

He gently rubbed the blister on his ankle, the result of a too-tight leg cuff that had caused the seam of his jeans to chafe his skin. Were these ass clowns actually stupid enough to think he'd make a run for it? No, they were just dicks who thought they were badass for treating kids like shit.

At least they'd taken the chains off when he boarded the plane. That was roughly ten hours ago. He'd spent the entire day crammed in the window seat of the last row, with nothing to read or watch, and only Ruben to talk to. Their only reprieve had been three bathroom breaks, the last one about two hours ago, just before they took off. Without his phone he had no idea of the time.

"I'm hungry," Ruben said.

"Yeah, me too," Andy replied. They both had picked at their food earlier, which was crappier than usual and that was saying a lot. Before takeoff they'd been given exactly the same meal for dinner as they'd had for lunch—a cheese sandwich with a limp lettuce leaf and a slice of tomato thin enough to see through. A little mayo would have been nice, but apparently there was a rule that all sandwiches had to be dry and tasteless. Today's fruit was a *disgusting* clump of dried apples and apricots wrapped in cellophane, and there was a crumbly white cookie that smelled of coconut, which he hated. "If I'd known I was

going to be this hungry, I'd have eaten everything in the bag…
and probably the bag too."

"Those apples were gross."

Upon being seated next to Ruben on the plane, Andy
discovered to his surprise that the boy spoke perfect English. A
second grader, he lived near Hollenbeck Park with his dad and
his dad's new girlfriend Liza, an "American" who didn't like
him very much. His Aunt Carla was in LA too, and married to
a US citizen. Liza didn't like her either so he didn't get to see
Carla very much. It scared him to realize that with his father
locked up there probably wasn't anyone looking for him right
now.

"Where do you think they're taking us?"

Andy looked up as a guard exited the lavatory and hitched
his pants before walking back up to the front of the plane.
"Not sure exactly but I heard one of them say something about
Louisiana."

"Where's that?"

"It's between Texas and Florida. And a heck of a long way
from California." He didn't want to swear in front of a kid only
seven years old.

"Why do they gots to take us so far? They should have let us
stay at the place they took us to first."

"Because nothing they do makes any sense."

"It's not fair. I don't know anybody in Luciana." The poor
kid looked seconds away from bursting into tears, which Andy
wanted to head off because one of the asshole guards was walking
up and down the aisle making fun of the kids who cried, calling
them babies and telling them to suck their thumb.

"Have you ever been on a plane before?"

Ruben shook his head. "I don't like it. It's scary."

"Nah, it's really safe." He repeated some of the things his
mom had told him when he'd gotten nervous flying over the
ocean to Germany, how people were far more likely to die in
cars and on bicycles. "My mom and me, we fly lots of places,
like to Germany. I was supposed to fly to Mexico all by myself
last weekend, but this happened."

"We never get to go to Mexico. That's where my *abuela* lives, but my dad's afraid to visit because they might not let us come back."

"Does she ever come visit you at your house?"

"She maybe came once when I was little. I don't remember."

Andy had learned in the courtroom that visitors to the US needed a visa, which was how the government knew Ruben had relatives in Mexico. Whereas Andres Casillas—the real one—had no record of visiting his mother in Guatemala, or of her visiting anyone who lived there. Whatever status his mother had, it was lost. She'd be deported as soon as she got out of prison.

"I want to go back home!" Ruben said, his voice quivering as if the dam were about to burst. "I hate planes. I hate the stupid food. I hate everything."

From the row ahead, Santos rose up and leaned menacingly over his seat. "Nobody gives a shit what you hate, you big baby. Shut the fuck up." His message delivered, he turned and slid back down.

Ruben wasn't the least bit intimidated. He kicked the back of Santos's chair and yelled, "I hate *you*. Why don't you shut the fuck up, you dog dick."

Wow. It took a lot of guts—or a lot of stupidity—for a seven-year-old kid to call a gang member like Santos a dog dick. While Andy was impressed, he was also worried about what might happen to Ruben if Santos ever got him alone.

"He's just tired," Andy said to Santos. "Everybody's tired."

Santos answered without turning around. "You need to keep his whiny ass out of my face."

"Maybe we should try to get some sleep, Ruben. Come on, you can lean against my shoulder if you want to."

Defeated, the boy swung his feet again, but deliberately missed the seat in front. Then he fell across Andy's lap as much as his seat belt would allow. "Wake me up if they start handing out snacks."

CHAPTER FIFTEEN

"There they are!" Georgie shouted, prompting Eleanor to squeal with excitement. They'd been watching at the window in the living room for Tony and Serafina. Tony had called earlier to report that the government hadn't contested her release.

Lily tugged Anna by the hand from the kitchen. "Let's go meet her, make sure she knows we don't blame her for what happened."

They walked out the side door from the family room to find Serafina tearfully hugging the twins. Eleanor, also in tears, stood on tiptoes with her arms around Serafina's neck while Georgie hugged her waist.

"Cue the waterworks," Anna said as she wiped her eyes.

"You and me both," Lily replied. She waited her turn as Anna drew Serafina into a hug, holding her for a long moment as they cried together. When Serafina turned to her, she managed a feeble "Welcome home" as her voice cracked. Hers were tears of joy, sadness and relief, acknowledging their shared trauma and the fact that it wasn't yet over.

"I'm so sorry, Lily. This is all my fault. I never should have asked him to go with me. He only said yes so you'd let him stay and go to the party with his friends."

Taking her face in both hands, Lily wiped Serafina's tears with her thumbs. "We do *not* blame you for this. They had no right to take either one of you. Believe me, we've seen these thugs for exactly who they are. ICE gives them license to do whatever they want—"

"And then lie about it to a judge," Anna added. She held out an arm. "Come into the kitchen so Lily can fix you a nice lunch. I'd offer to do it but you deserve better than that. I bet you haven't had a decent meal since you got picked up."

As they walked inside together, Lily hooked her arm through Tony's. "Thank you, my friend. Will she have to go back to court?"

"No, everything's dismissed. They say there's no record, but I don't trust those goons as far as I can throw them."

"I'm just worried this will come back to bite her in the ass once she's eligible for her naturalization interview." As soon as she said it, she felt Eleanor's eyes on her. "I know, that's a dollar in the bad word jar."

Tony laughed. "I bet that jar's seen a lot of action these last few days."

"Seriously, is this going to screw up her citizenship application? Her five years are up in October." All she needed now was to take the citizenship test. "Just please promise me she won't get denied because of this."

"I'm pretty sure this won't even show up in her file. But I'll make it a point to keep checking all summer so there won't be any surprises."

"Did Anna tell you we think Andy is in Louisiana? That's where his plane was headed when it left Phoenix last night. He probably won't stay there long though. They don't have any detention facilities for unaccompanied minors."

"If he headed east, he's probably on his way to Homestead but it could be Berks. Both are lockdown. Homestead's where they send suspected gang members."

Lily had read all she could find on ICE's detention of minors. Berks was a former juvenile detention facility in Pennsylvania repurposed for detention of immigrant families and youth. Kids sent there typically had longer stays. The Homestead center was like a sprawling child prison, housing up to two thousand minors at any given time. Most of the children had been separated from their families at border crossings but if they had any family members in the US, they were usually released to their care within a few weeks.

They caught up with the others in the kitchen, where Lily immediately went to work preparing Serafina's favorite breakfast burrito. Tony leaned against the counter as she whisked the eggs in a skillet, and said, "I was talking with Monique Johnson at the Legal Aid Foundation. She said this push to pick up gang members is a relatively new initiative. They used to wait until there was an arrest for gang-related crimes. Now they're just doing random street sweeps. Arrest first, ask questions later... if at all."

"A class action suit waiting to happen." In theory, anyway. Private law firms had little hope of a payday from the federal government because of sovereign immunity, so it probably would take a years-long suit from the ACLU to force changes at the policy level.

Meanwhile, it was attorneys like Tony and Shelynn who were fighting on the front lines of the immigration wars. Lily and Anna were now convinced they should hire someone from the trenches like those two instead of a Brooks Brothers suit from a firm like Walter's who didn't know how the games were played. In fact, Anna was disappointed they couldn't simply hire Shelynn to dog Andy's case through the system. She knew all the tricks, like the one about how to track detainee flights, but she said she had her hands full with cases in Arizona.

Lily delivered the fresh hot burrito to Serafina and joined them at the table. "Tell me everything. Start at the beginning, at the festival."

Between bites, Serafina recounted the events surrounding the stabbing, how the paramedics had tended to the victim while the police interviewed witnesses. "I wish we'd moved on, but it just wasn't right. A poor man was stabbed and his family deserved to know who did it, so I told them what I saw. Andy didn't even see it—he was buying a drink, but he came back while I was talking with the officer."

Lily was troubled by Serafina's gaunt look. If she'd struggled to get enough to eat in detention, Andy would be struggling too, especially since he was a picky eater to begin with.

"When the police officer finished, people all of a sudden started pushing and shoving, yelling at everyone to run. I fell and Andy helped me up, but someone picked up my bag and ran away." Her voice shook with anger as she complained of the officers' refusal to look up her green card information. "They came because of the gang members but they took everybody. There's even a name for all the extra people they pick up. They call us collaterals."

"Like collateral damage," Anna said with disgust.

"I thought they'd let Andy go," she went on, taking a few seconds to check her tears. "This one officer, he kept asking me my name, then asking Andy his. He did it three times, like he didn't believe us. The whole time he was taking videos of Andy and talking to somebody on his phone. Then he yelled for somebody to arrest us both."

Tony nodded slowly. "This is finally starting to make sense. That officer had an informant on the phone doing live IDs. That's who pegged Andy as Andres Casillas."

Serafina raised a hand to her mouth. "So that's why he kept saying Andy's driver's license was fake. He thought Andy was someone else."

"Not just someone else," Anna said. "An errand boy for a gang member who murdered a nine-year-old girl."

"Allegedly," Lily said. She was no longer taking ICE's word for anything. "How did Andy seem the last time you saw him? Was he scared?"

"More than anything he was angry. I warned him to keep his head down, to stay out of trouble. He knew you would come for him. He said he couldn't wait for his mom to get hold of those"—she made sure the twins weren't listening—"we say *los carajos*."

Lily met Anna's questioning look. "That means dicks. Andy's right, I'd love to get those dicks in my courtroom."

"Oh, he didn't mean you." Serafina pointed to Anna. "He said she was going to tear off their arm and beat them with the bloody end."

Anna slapped the table. "Well, he certainly read my mind. From what Shelynn Kelly said, there's not much else you can do to these bastards. Absolutely no one holds them accountable for anything. I can't believe what they do to people—especially women and kids—at these detention facilities. Every inch of those places ought to be covered with CCTV."

Serafina visibly shuddered. "A lot of them are. There were even cameras in the showers at Adelanto."

Lily couldn't stand to hear another word. She rose and carried the plate to the sink.

"Leave it, Lily. This is my kitchen again." Serafina shooed them toward the family room. "It feels good to be home. Now if we could just get Andy back."

Eleanor met them in the doorway holding Anna's phone. "Mom, you just got a text." By the expectant look on her face, she'd already read it. "It's from Shelynn Kelly."

"Hmm…she says a Swiftair flight left Louisiana at four fifteen this morning headed for Homestead." Anna whirled and bounded up the stairs, yelling, "Looks like I'm going to Miami."

* * *

Two large ceiling fans stirred the air in the windowless room, the only relief from the muggy heat that had hit Andy the moment he stepped off the plane. This was Florida. He'd never been here before and hoped never to come again.

"Let's go! Grab your size and keep the line moving," a guard bellowed, gesturing to a table piled with clothing. In a stark contrast to the ICE police, this one wore blue cargos and a yellow polo shirt with a chest logo that read CHS… whatever that meant. "Do not touch *anyone*. Not your brother, not your sister, not your best amigo. If you touch anyone while you're here in this tropical paradise, you will immediately be sent back to whatever shithole country you came from."

Andy looked around, wondering how many of the boys from his plane spoke only Spanish. "*No tocar los otros*," he said. Probably wrong but close enough.

"Zip it!"

Thank God Andy understood both the command and its crabby tone. In a prison full of Spanish speakers, the least they could do was have a translator. Then again, it probably was hard to find Latinos willing to treat other Latinos like shit.

He had no idea what size underwear he wore. He'd switched from regular briefs to Calvin Klein boxer briefs a year ago but had never bought them for himself. New ones magically appeared in three-packs on his bed, gifts from the laundry fairy.

Armed with this embarrassing ignorance, he was to choose a pair of white jockey shorts from the long table, where piles were loosely grouped by size. Most were kids' sizes, he realized, which was stupid since the guard on the plane said this place was for teenagers only, thirteen to seventeen. The younger ones, including Ruben, had remained on the plane to go elsewhere.

A pair of jockeys marked large looked as if it might be too small. After a few tense seconds of searching as the guard badgered them to hurry, he located what he thought might be the last extra-large on the table. Santos, who was behind him in line, was going to be pissed.

Andy already missed Ruben, who had cried and hugged him when he left the plane. Wherever the plane had gone from here, he hoped someone would take Ruben under their wing and keep him calm. The boy's temper could get him into lots of trouble.

The next table was dark green gym shorts, stamped on the leg with a white logo that read ICE. As if anyone here needed a reminder. He selected a pair and moved on to a third table of white T-shirts in adult and child sizes, then a fourth table with white crew socks.

"Next stop, bug check," the guard said, pointing a thumb over his shoulder. "No critters allowed."

Third in line for the head check, he noted that the checker was a female guard, the first one he'd seen since his arrest. She wore blue gloves and had her hair pulled into a tight bun. "Got another live one here, Jimmy! Coming your way." She directed the teen across the hall, where Jimmy awaited with clippers.

Andy's stomach dropped as he recalled how Ruben had leaned against his shoulder on the flight. Kids that age got head lice all the time. A couple of years ago Georgie and Eleanor had brought them home three times in one month. They all had to use a special shampoo, but that obviously wasn't how they dealt with lice here. He'd die of shame if he had to go back to school with a buzzcut.

It was the first time he'd thought of school since this ordeal began. What would he tell people when they asked what he'd done over spring break? By now he should have been posting photos from Los Cabos. Julian was probably sharing some from his dad's movie set in Tokyo, Jackson from skiing in Vail, and Albany from frickin' Paris.

I spent my spring break in an ICE shithole wearing shackles and handcuffs, getting my head shaved on account of lice.

"Clean," the guard declared after fluffing his hair with a pencil. "Straight to the showers."

Relieved, he hustled back to the hallway. A shower sounded fantastic, his first one in four days. Judging from the smell on the airplane, he wasn't the only one in need of a good scrubbing.

A male guard at the end of the hall, blond with pasty white skin, handed him a small red belt with clips. "This here's a laundry loop. You know how to use it?"

Andy shook his head.

"You run it through your shirt, your tighty-whiteys, and one of your belt loops. Then clip your socks here. Make sure it's tight or you'll never see those rags again. And write your name on the tag part," he said, handing Andy a black sharpie.

His name. Should he write Andres Casillas? That would be like admitting he was the gang member they thought he was.

But if he wrote Andy Kaklis, they might throw his clothes away. In the end, he compromised, writing small to fit it all on the tag: *Andres Kaklis (Casillas)*.

The shower room had twelve stalls with curtains, and a shelf outside each one where he could leave his fresh clothes and dirty laundry. He took a folded towel from a shelf and entered the farthest stall, where he stripped and looped the belt through his clothes. The water was tepid and the pressure was low, but he couldn't have cared less—he was finally getting clean.

"*Prisa!*" a boy's voice yelled. Hurry up.

Andy peeked through the curtain and saw four guys lined up against the wall waiting for a turn. He quickly rinsed the soap from his hair and toweled off. The briefs looked smaller than before… and the label said large, not extra-large. That was weird. He'd have to find a way to cut the elastic. At least the shorts and T-shirt fit okay.

With his socks and shoes in hand, he exited the shower and reached for his laundry loop. Suddenly he understood about the underwear. Someone had swapped them—and they'd also taken his rugby shirt.

* * *

Before leaving the parking garage at Miami International Airport, Anna entered the address Lily had texted her into the car's navigation system. It would take her to a hotel only a few blocks from the detention center at Homestead.

Once she entered the Florida Turnpike for the half-hour drive, she called home. "Any news?"

"I'm full of it," Lily said. "News, that is. Andy's new attorney is a man by the name of Arturo Gil-Torres. Tony found him and Shelynn gave him a big thumbs up. He works for a firm in Coral Gables where both his parents are partners. He's young— like fresh out of Miami Law School young—but he knows what he's doing. Ninety percent of his caseload is immigration. He's represented loads of kids at Homestead."

"Sounds like exactly who we need."

"He wants to meet first thing tomorrow at Starbucks, six thirty a.m. I'll text you the address."

"That's three thirty Pacific Time. I hope my brain's awake."

"Sorry about that," Lily said. "It has to be early because he starts seeing clients inside at seven thirty."

"Did he say anything about the case?"

"Just that he was going to submit the paperwork to be Andy's attorney and put in a request for a hearing. I assume he did that late today."

"Why would he have to request a hearing? The court ordered one within forty-eight hours. It should be scheduled automatically for tomorrow." The sound of Eleanor and Georgie talking and laughing in the background triggered a small wave of homesickness. "Sounds like the kids are in a good mood."

"They're happy to have Serafina back. She ate dinner with us and we had a serious talk about what Andy's going through. Georgie wanted to know what kind of food they served in detention so Eleanor looked it up. It was horrible, Anna. White bread and cold cuts, maybe a piece of fruit if they're lucky. This is coming from kids who were held in detention at Homestead. They say the bread sometimes has mold on it, or the fruit's gone bad. Instant oatmeal, instant ramen noodles. Or they heat up frozen burritos in the microwave and they're still frozen in the middle."

"Poor kid. We need to get him out of there right now. I don't care if we have to bust down the door to do it."

"That's the Anna I know and love. Take no prisoners." Lily laughed. "Better yet, take *all* the prisoners and set them free."

"I love you too. Thanks for being there for Eleanor and Georgie. That had to be a tough conversation, and there's no one in the world I'd rather have handling it than you."

"You're sweet. Give Andy a huge hug from me...from all of us."

Anna blinked back tears as she ended the call. She'd caught herself crying on the plane when she imagined the horror Andy was feeling—and the pain he might feel for a long time even after he was released. To this day, it broke her heart to remember how he struggled to feel secure when he first came to live with them, hiding his toys and growing anxious those first few times Lily packed his suitcase. The worst was after the twins were born when he began to feel "less than" because he was adopted.

It had taken years of steady nurturing to overcome his insecurities. What if he was sitting in there now doubting their determination to get him out? For all he knew they were still living it up in Los Cabos, reluctant to cut their vacation short, assuming the DHS would eventually discover its mistake. He had no way of knowing how difficult this was, how ICE was throwing up roadblocks at every turn.

Anna needed so much to see his face, to hold him and tell him how much he was loved. She promised herself that he'd never doubt it again.

* * *

"Positions!"

Andy emerged from beneath his blanket and squinted at the overhead lights, which had been left on even after everyone had gone to bed. His T-shirt was wet with sweat.

"Let's go! Positions." The guard casually knocked a stick against the metal frames of bunkbeds as he walked between the rows. Four rows, twenty-five beds each. If all the beds were full—and it appeared they were—that was two hundred detainees in a room half the size of a gymnasium.

The boys, most of them wearing only briefs, tumbled from their beds to stand at the foot as the guard began counting them off.

"Are you fucking kidding me?" Andy grumbled as he climbed down from his top bunk and stood across from Santos. The clock above the door said two fifteen. It had taken him over an hour to get to sleep the first time. Now his fury would keep him up even longer.

Not only did the asshole yell out every single number, he stopped from time to time to make crude remarks about how they looked in their underwear. "Sixty-six B," he said, referring to Andy by his bed number. "I see somebody took it literally when Gerald said to grab some tighty-whiteys."

Santos snorted and covered his face to hide his grin. Andy noticed that his briefs were larger, which likely meant he was the one who'd switched. He'd probably swiped the rugby shirt too.

Why the heck would they have bed checks in the middle of the night when there were guards right outside the door? The answer was obvious—because they were assholes. Bored and on a power trip.

Stewing with resentment, Andy crossed the vast dormitory to a corner room where the toilets and urinals were located. Dozens of others had the same idea, so he took his place in line against the wall. Closing his eyes briefly, he decided he could easily fall back to sleep after all.

The line moved fast enough that he was able to claim a urinal after only a couple of minutes. When he went to wash his hands he noticed three guys crowded around the door of one of the stalls. When a fourth one exited, two of them grabbed and held his arms while the third slapped his cheeks and jabbed him, counting each strike aloud until he reached thirteen. "*Trece! Trece de Sureños.*"

Thirteen from Sureños. Andy recognized the gang name as the one used by the government's attorney to describe Andres Casillas. And Santos as well, who'd appointed himself lookout at the door.

Andy felt sorry for the one they'd bullied but he knew better than to involve himself in their fight, not even to help the poor guy off the floor. He was humiliated but clearly not hurt.

He returned to his bed to find Santos waiting. He'd pulled off his shirt to reveal the number *13* tattooed just above his heart. "Out there you White Fence. In here you Sureños. We *all* Sureños. Thirteen."

"What's thirteen?"

"It means M—the Mexican Mafia." Santos eyed him with suspicion. "I bet you Norteños. Yeah, that's right. You told that judge you from Oakland. That makes you Norteños."

"I don't even know what that is."

"It's north. Sureños is south…LA. We enemies so you need to side up, *niño*. One or the other."

At least he hadn't said *poco niño*. "Look, I don't know how many times I have to say this. I'm not in a gang. I'm not who they say I am. They made a mistake."

"It don't matter. You in here now. You don't side up, everybody think you in the other gang. That's the way it is."

Andy slowly grasped what Santos was saying. If he didn't join a gang at all, Sureños would think it was because he was Norteños while Norteños would assume the opposite. "Why would they think anything? Are you telling me all these guys"—he waved his hand around the vast hall—"are in a gang? I don't think so. Most of them just mind their own business. That's what I'm going to do. You should too. You told that judge you quit the gang."

"A lot of good it did me," he groused. "They pick you up even if you ain't doing nothing. At least Sureños watch my back in here."

"Stay away from them and maybe your back won't need watching."

Santos sneered and shook his head, as if to say Andy didn't know what he was talking about.

And maybe he didn't. Seeing that poor kid smacked around in the bathroom showed Andy the appeal of a gang in a way he hadn't understood before. If that boy's gang had been there, it wouldn't have happened.

He suddenly felt sorry for Santos. He probably joined that gang in the first place because he felt scared. Maybe his was a tough 'hood where he needed allies. And now with his mother deployed, there likely was no one working to get him released. His future was shit. He'd be locked up here till June, then deported.

"Look, what I said in court was true, Santos. My mom's a judge, a real one. She can prove I'm not that gang member, Andres Casillas. She'll get me out of here."

"If you still alive," Santos snarled, though it sounded more like an attempt to shock than a threat.

"They promised me an attorney by tomorrow, and another hearing. I can try to help you when I get out…if you want me to. Tell me who to call. Maybe my mom can find you a lawyer."

Santos gave him a skeptical look, turned to walk away, and abruptly came back. "Why would you do that? You don't know shit about me."

"I know you're trying to stay out of trouble. I know your mom's in the army and they're disrespecting her by picking you up. It's not fair they don't even give us lawyers. That woman lawyer yesterday, she got all her clients released. Every single one. Let me see if my mom can help."

A tense moment of silence ended when Santos pulled his shirt back on and gave Andy a clap on the shoulder. "You might be all right, Casillas."

Andy heaved a sigh. "For the thousandth time…it's Kaklis."

CHAPTER SIXTEEN

Arturo Gil-Torres looked the part of a junior associate at a prestigious law firm. Clean-shaven with designer eyeglasses, he wore a smart gray suit with a white shirt and yellow striped tie. His briefcase was a high-end Montblanc like the one Anna had given Hal for Christmas a few years ago, except Arturo's was stuffed so full it wouldn't latch.

"Do you always start your days so early?" Anna asked. Lily would call this the ass-crack of dawn.

He smiled and gestured to his briefcase. "I need to see five clients inside the center before their hearings, which start at nine o'clock. I was able to get Andres on the client list, so I can see him first and push to have his hearing today," he said before pausing to sip his double espresso. "Nothing happens until we get him in front of a judge."

"His hearing *has* to be today, right? The other judge's order said forty-eight hours."

"Theoretically,"—he winced, telegraphing bad news—"but they miss a lot of deadlines when it comes to immigration and the judges are usually forgiving. The government will simply argue that it made a good faith effort but he hadn't been processed, the docket was full, he's getting a medical assessment…basically whatever excuse they want."

Anna pressed two fingers against her brow and reminded herself not to lash out at Arturo. He wasn't to blame for the way detainees were treated. "These people we're dealing with, they're real bastards, aren't they?"

"I'm afraid a lot of them are, Ms. Kaklis."

"Please, call me Anna. What's it like in there? Is Andy safe?"

"He should be. Don't get me wrong, all of these youth detention facilities have problems, but Homestead has a fair bit of structured time for classes and recreation. It's run by a private contractor, Comprehensive Health Services—CHS. They have strict procedures for everything. Kids are escorted everywhere they go in groups of twelve."

"Are there problems with gangs? Because Andy's been mistaken for a gang member. That's how he ended up there in the first place."

Arturo conceded with a slight nod. "There have been reports of gang fights but nothing serious. All the detainees are under constant surveillance or supervision. Skirmishes are broken up quickly. Are you worried about Andy fighting?"

"I'm worried about him getting picked on. He's small for his age and not at all street savvy. We tried to teach him to solve problems without fighting, but that's going to leave him vulnerable if he's in there with a bunch of gangbangers."

"I understand. I can speak to the officials inside the center and make sure they're aware of his situation." He took a legal pad from his briefcase and began to make notes. "What I'd like you to do is call this number at nine o'clock and ask to speak to Superintendent Vogler. He probably won't be available, but tell whoever answers that you've come to Homestead to pick up your sixteen-year-old son, that he was arrested by ICE agents in Los Angeles who mistakenly believed he was someone else. Tell them you have documents proving your son's identity and citizenship. Ask if you can meet with him right away, preferably in the next hour."

"Should I mention the judge's order that he's to have a hearing today?"

"It wouldn't hurt. At the end of the call, ask when they expect Vogler to pick up his messages. No matter what they say, if you haven't heard from him by ten, call him back. And again at eleven. If you still don't hear from him, text me at this number and I'll set up an interview with Channel Six. Then I'll call Vogler's office and give them a heads up that you're planning to talk to the media. CHS's board of directors doesn't want that kind of publicity." He checked his phone. "Time to go. I'm going to ask to see Andy first thing when I get there. Is there anything you want me to tell him?"

"Yes, of course. Tell him we love him, that we can't wait to have him come home." She thought again of her fear that he might have felt abandoned. "And tell him we've been frantic this whole time, that the reason we haven't gotten him out is because we didn't even know where he was till yesterday."

Anna watched him go, trying to hold her optimism in check. She'd gotten her hopes up twice before, once with Tony and his friend at the federal building, and again with Shelynn Kelly on the tarmac. This time felt different. Arturo was on his way inside where he would see Andy face-to-face and deliver their message of love and support.

She returned to her car and checked one of the airline apps on her phone. With the info in hand, she weighed whether or not to call Lily at her four a.m. "Oh, what the hell."

"Anna?" By her anxious voice, Lily was clearly startled by the call.

"Hi, sweetheart. Sorry to call so early, but there's a flight out of LAX at six o'clock, gets into Miami at two this afternoon. I know I said I'd handle this but I'd really like to have you here with me. Can you come? Please?"

"All you had to do was ask."

* * *

Andy shuffled into the small room to find a well-dressed young man sitting behind a table. His smile was the first one Andy had seen from an adult since the night he was arrested… not counting the shit-eating grins from Berman.

The man gestured at Andy's chains and addressed the guard, "Are those really necessary? My client is neither dangerous nor a threat to run away."

The guard merely grunted and closed the door on his way out.

"God, you must be a lawyer. Finally! I was beginning to think the whole world had forgotten I existed."

"Arturo Gil-Torres. And you're right, I'm an attorney." He smiled and offered a handshake before remembering Andy's hands were bound. "Oops, sorry. Believe me, no one's forgotten you. Your moms are going crazy out there trying to get you out. I just had coffee with one of them."

"Which one?"

"Anna. She's followed you here to Miami, staying at a hotel just a few blocks from here in fact. I'm sure she's usually a nice person, but right now she's pretty salty about ICE kidnapping her son. I would never want to get on her bad side."

"Tell me about it," Andy said, realizing that he too was smiling. The fact that his mom was so close had to mean he was getting out soon.

"It was your other mom Lily who hired me. She's back in LA with Georgie and…"

"Ellie…Eleanor. They're twins."

"Yes, and I'm supposed to tell you everyone sends you lots of love. They can't wait to have you back home. How are you doing? Any problems?"

"You mean besides how they make us go to sleep with the lights on and wake us up for a bed check at two o'clock? The food's gross. Last night for dinner they gave us burritos that were frozen solid. Like, you could knock 'em on the table. They don't even get thawed before time's up. And since you can't take food out, you just have to throw it away."

Arturo shook his head with a look of disgust. "Amazing how these people can screw up something as basic as a burrito. Any other problems I need to know about? Do you feel safe?"

"Yeah, I…I guess." If he was getting out soon, there was no point bringing up the gang activity. Arturo might think he was involved. "Some guys fight with each other but it doesn't concern me."

"That's good. Stay clear of all that. Whatever you do, don't take sides."

He knew that already, regardless of what Santos had said. "How soon can you get me out?"

Arturo opened his folder, signaling an end to their get-to-know-you chat. "I wish I could say for sure but these guys don't make it easy."

"That's because they're dickwads, all of them," Andy snapped, figuring he didn't have to watch his language with a cool guy like Arturo. "They do whatever they want. I showed them my driver's license when they first stopped us and they arrested me anyway. Said it was fake. The whole time they kept calling me Andres Casillas. They told the judge I was in a gang."

"I bet you were furious." He patted the stack of papers in front of him. "But don't worry, I have proof of who you are right here. Your passport, your birth certificate, your adoption papers."

"Wha—you mean I'm adopted?" The sudden look of horror on Arturo's face was priceless. "Just kidding. I know, I was there."

"Whew!" Arturo glared at him before bursting into laughter. "Man, you just about gave me a heart attack."

"Sorry…I sometimes play around when I'm nervous. I'd give anything if you could get me out of here today."

Arturo smiled weakly but Andy could tell he had doubts. "That's my goal, but only if I can convince the judge to give you a hearing. That's what I need to talk to you about. I want you to be ready at a moment's notice in case I send for you because we won't have much time. So don't get caught in the shower."

"No chance of that. I had a shower yesterday when I got here. I heard one of the other guys say you only get one a week."

"We're going to get you out of here, Andy. I promise, but I can't guarantee it'll be today." Arturo stretched across the table to squeeze his shoulder. "However long it takes, I want you to keep your head down. You see any fights, you turn and go the other way. Okay, pal?"

Andy grinned. "My mom calls me that. Tell her I'm okay, I'm staying out of trouble. And when I get out I'm not eating anything but pizza for a whole month. Even for breakfast."

The guard removed Andy's chains almost as soon as he exited the room, proving they weren't at all necessary. Did they seriously think he'd attack the one person who was trying to get him out of this hellhole?

He arrived back in his dormitory as a woman was delivering their laundry loops. Someone had replaced his missing rugby shirt with a plain white T-shirt. As he'd suspected, the rugby shirt was attached to Santos's loop.

Santos eyed him sheepishly, clearly feeling guilty for stealing it. "Looks like they made a mistake. They accidentally gave me your shirt."

"It's a little big for me anyway," Andy said. "Try it on. If it fits, it's yours."

The shirt fit Santos perfectly and he lit up once he had it on. "How's it look?"

"Yeah, that works. Take it. I just met with my lawyer so I should be getting out soon. I'll get another one."

"Thanks, man." Santos returned to his bunk for a slip of paper. "You still want to help me when you get out? This my probation officer, Gladys Segura. I don't know her phone number but she in the office at Belvedere. And the other number's my Uncle Hugo. That's where I been staying since my ma left. He live on Percy Street. He don't even know where I am."

Andy changed back into his jeans and tucked the slip of paper in the hip pocket. "We'll find them. I'll get my moms to help."

Santos, the tough guy. His family didn't know where he was and probably wasn't even looking for him. Andy wasn't intimidated by him anymore. He just felt sorry for the guy.

* * *

A satellite news truck dominated the grassy lot opposite a brick marker that identified the detention center as Homestead Branch. Protesters lined the road for a hundred yards, many of them sitting in lawn chairs and holding signs. *Homes Not Cages. Free the Children. Shut It Down.* The entry to the center was enclosed by a solid green fence that blocked the view inside.

"What a zoo," Lily said. Zoo or not, she was already considering joining the protests at the federal plaza in LA once this ordeal was over. ICE was beyond reform—for all its abuses, it deserved to be abolished.

Anna turned down a side road looking for a parking space. "Arturo says the weekends down here are really crazy. Hundreds of people show up, including most of the Democrats running for office. They set up speakers to blast messages and music into the center, make speeches using bullhorns…all to let the kids inside know they haven't been forgotten."

"Did you like him?"

"Arturo? Very much. He seems to be on top of things and he knows a lot of people inside, even the superintendent."

"It's nice to see somebody from a top-notch law firm doing work like this. Usually it's just bleeding hearts like Tony and Shelynn cobbling together enough grants to keep the lights on."

Anna smiled as she pulled off into the grass. "It's obvious when you see the way he's dressed that he has plenty of family money. If you ask me, he's doing this to rack up his progressive bona fides. Mark my word, he's headed for a career in politics."

"Just tell me where to send the check." Lily was pleased to find Anna in such a good mood, almost giddy at the prospect of getting Andy released. "What's the plan here? Do you know who it is he wants you to meet?"

"Her name's Isabel Fuentes. She's supposed to be at the Channel Six truck. Speaking of that…I was thinking it might be better if you did the interview. You're used to making arguments and I know you'll watch what you say. I'm afraid I'll slander somebody and get sued."

"You're better at arguing than you think. I should know, since I'm usually the one you argue with." Lily leaned over for a kiss that turned deep when Anna cradled her head.

"Thank you for listening to your crazy wife this morning and flying all the way across the country to hold her hand while she tries not to have a meltdown."

"Anything for you, babe. You should know that by now." She stole one more kiss before opening the door. "Let's go give 'em hell."

Lily walked ahead a few paces while Anna stopped to take a call.

Anna shrieked with excitement. "Are you kidding? That's fantastic! What should we do about the interview?" She held up a finger to finish the call. "That was Arturo. He got the judge to agree to hear Andy's case when all the others are done today, but he wants us to go ahead with the interview. He says it'll help show how unfair the system is and make people think it could happen to them."

"That's a good sign. Most judges won't add cases to their docket unless they believe there's an injustice. It's the old 'justice delayed is justice denied' argument. Arturo must have convinced him."

"I told you he was good."

Isabel Fuentes was easy to spot. A young Latina with long dark hair and ruby red lips, she had a look that was made for television. Reading from her notes, she prompted their remarks for the camera with prepared questions.

Lily held up Andy's school photo from last fall. He was handsome in his tuxedo despite his refusal to smile, since he still had his braces at the time.

"This is our son Andy Kaklis. He's sixteen years old. His birth certificate"—which she also held up—"proves he was born in Oakland, California, making him an American citizen. He was swept up last Saturday in Los Angeles during an ICE raid that targeted a Latino festival. According to witnesses, Andy showed the officers his government-issued driver's license proving who he was, but they arrested him anyway." She stopped herself from calling the arrest arbitrary and capricious, which was a legal term for abuse of discretion, though it clearly was. She was here as a mom, not a judge. "Over the weekend Andy was held in a cage in LA with other teens and children. He then was moved to Phoenix, and from Phoenix to here. In all that time my wife and I have yet to receive an official notification from the Department of Homeland Security that our son is in custody. Not one word. He wasn't even allowed a call to let us know where he was."

"But you were able to track him."

"That was pure luck. He had a hearing in Phoenix that we only found out about because an attorney who was present in the courtroom phoned us and said he'd pleaded with the judge to give us a call. One simple gesture could have ended this but the judge denied that request. Andy wasn't even given access to his own attorney until this morning."

Though Anna stood silently by, Isabel directed a question her way. "Have you spoken with your son at all?"

"Not even once," Anna replied, "but we finally were able to send him a message through the attorney this morning. I want to emphasize what my wife just said—there are children going to court with no adult representation." She pointed over her shoulder toward the detention center. "How many others are in there cut off completely from their loved ones, left to worry that no one's coming for them? What they're doing to these people—especially the children—is unconscionable. America's supposed to be better than this."

Lily suppressed a smile but inside felt a swell of pride. The fire in Anna's voice was exactly what she'd wanted to avoid when she'd asked Lily to do the talking. But this moment called for anger like Anna's.

Isabel checked her notes. "Most of the children here were taken into custody at the border, but not your son. He was out for an evening with friends. How do you feel about that?"

"That's something else people need to understand," Lily said. "This could happen to *your* child if they're in the wrong place at the wrong time. ICE officers do whatever they want because they know they won't be held accountable. They're carrying out policies that are deliberately cruel with no regard for those they hurt."

Anna added, "Every day that we keep children locked up in detention without care, we do lasting harm to their emotional and physical well-being. The protesters here are absolutely right—we need to shut these places down."

Isabel signaled to a camerawoman to stop filming and stowed the microphone in a bag at her feet. "That was fantastic. This is going to go straight to air at five o'clock." She thanked them and excused herself to record her intro and sign-off.

"You totally killed that, Anna. I can't believe you were worried."

"Are you mad at me?"

"For what, making me fly three thousand miles and then not letting me get in a word edgewise?" She snaked her arm around Anna's and entwined their fingers. "I forgive you. Seeing you get all righteous up close and in person was worth it. What time's Andy's hearing? Did Arturo say?"

"Just that it would be at the end of the day. Probably soon."

Above the chants of the protesters was the unmistakable sound of an emergency siren in the distance.

"Sounds close," Lily said.

The exit side of the center's gate suddenly opened for a line of cars, one of which crossed the intersection and headed down the side road where the protesters had parked.

"Hey, there goes Arturo!" Anna pulled Lily along in pursuit as the siren grew louder. They caught up just as the young man climbed out of his car. "Arturo, what's going on?"

He nodded behind them, where an EMT truck was driving through the gate. "They won't say. All I know is they went to lockdown and made all visitors leave the premises."

"What about Andy's hearing?"

"Court was adjourned." He kicked wildly at a discarded water bottle, sending it clanking into the road. "We were *so* close. I'd already sent the bailiff to bring him to the courtroom. His case would have been up next and the judge was ready to release him. I'm so sorry. All we can do is try again tomorrow— assuming they let us back in—but we'll probably get a different judge, so I'll have to start over trying to get him on the docket."

At the moment Lily was far more concerned about the EMTs. She held out her hand to Arturo. "Hi, I'm Lily. Thanks for all you're doing. What do you think's going on in there?"

"If I had to guess, I'd say a fight of some sort. You can't lock up thousands of stressed-out teenagers with nothing to do and expect all of them to get along."

Lily knew that all too well from her work with the juvenile court. She also knew there were nurses on staff, and paramedics weren't called to jail unless there were serious injuries.

Anna must have read her concern. Squeezing her hand, she said, "You heard Arturo. He was with the bailiff on his way to the courtroom."

"Right." So why did she feel like throwing up?

* * *

Andy's legs shook so hard he thought they'd give out. Using the wall for support, he slid to the floor, discovering he'd somehow smeared blood all over himself. Santos's blood.

"What the fuck happened here?" a voice boomed. A man Andy hadn't seen before stalked into the restroom and looked over the shoulders of the two medical staff who were tending to Santos. "How bad is it?"

"A lot of bleeding but we've got it under control."

The man grunted and whirled around to take in the scene in the restroom. Though he was dressed like the others in a yellow polo shirt, his command of the room made it clear he was the boss. "Who's the fucking moron that let somebody in here wearing gang colors? What's the manual say about that, huh?

No red, no blue." The veins of his neck bulged and his shaved head dripped with sweat. "Do we have a weapon? A witness?"

The guard who'd come to take Andy to court cleared his throat. "This kid found him, Mr. Vogler...sir."

Vogler bent down and sneered. "And how do we know you weren't the one who cut him?"

Shocked and intimidated, Andy tried to answer, only to have his mind go utterly blank. Did they seriously think he was responsible?

The guard spoke up again. "I was escorting him to court, sir. He stopped to hit the can and came right back out to get me. It wasn't enough time for him to do it."

"He was my friend," Andy finally said. "Why would I hurt him?"

"Your friend, huh?" Vogler drew to his full height, towering over Andy with his hands on his hips. "Do you know who did this?"

Andy grasped the mistake he'd made by linking himself to a gang member. He had a *very* good idea who was behind it—the Norteño who'd gotten smacked around last night—but he didn't want to end up with a hole in his gut like Santos.

"Coming through!" A team of paramedics rolled in a stretcher. "Let's have a look. How ya doing, kid?"

"It hurts like a motherfucker," Santos grunted.

Andy could have cried with relief to hear him speak so clearly. When he first saw all that blood, he was sure Santos was a goner.

"What's your friend's name?" Vogler asked.

"Santos Aguilar. And we aren't friends, not really. We came here together from LA is all. I promised him I'd call his probation officer when I got out. Can I go to my hearing now? I need to see the judge."

"Hearings are canceled. This facility's on lockdown. No one's—hold on, did you say you came from LA?"

"Yes sir, I got here yesterday. Santos too."

"Oh, fuck me," he muttered, almost under his breath. "Please tell me you're not that kid they've been calling about all day. Andres something or other."

"Andres Kaklis. My attorney brought my passport to show the judge, and my birth certificate. I'm a US citizen. I'm not supposed to be here."

Vogler made a sound like a whimper and bit his fist. "Christ almighty. They aren't going to hang this bullshit on me. Get this boy cleaned up and ready to go."

CHAPTER SEVENTEEN

The restaurant at Gilbert's Resort overlooked Blackwater Sound, a shallow harbor off US-1 near Key Largo and less than thirty minutes from Homestead. Arturo had recommended it for breakfast at sunrise, when a dockside table granted a comical view of hungry pelicans stalking fishermen for chum.

Arturo had promised to call once he confirmed Andy's place on today's docket. Until then, Lily was determined to keep Anna's mind occupied with fun memories.

"I'll never forget that time you called me in San Francisco and told me Andy had dumped a whole jug of bubble bath in the hot tub and turned it on. I had to put the phone down and walk away so you wouldn't hear me cracking up."

Anna laughed heartily. "Oh my God, the whole back yard was a mountain of white foam. And on my way to turn it off I—"

"Fell into the pool!" they shrieked simultaneously.

"He was the funniest kid," Anna said wistfully. "Except that time he spilled an entire chocolate milkshake down the console of my Z8. That wasn't funny at all." Anna still called that sleek roadster her all-time favorite car. She'd been stubborn about trading it when the twins came along, but then a gang of car thieves took the decision out of her hands.

"Your precious Z8…in all the years we've been married, the only time I ever worried you might divorce me was over that milkshake. I even told Kim to find me a house just in case Andy and I needed to make a run for it."

"But then I realized I loved that little boy more than I could ever love a car." Even behind her sunglasses, Anna's gorgeous blue eyes were smiling. "And for the record, there's nothing you could do to make me want to leave you."

"Hmm…am I supposed to take that as a challenge?"

"I'd rather you didn't." Anna grasped her hand and brought it to her lips for a soft kiss. "You're the love of my life, Lily. You and our children. I don't know what I'd do if I ever lost any of you."

Lily took note of the serious turn. It was almost as if Anna couldn't give herself permission to truly let go and have fun until they were all back together again.

"This will pass, sweetheart. Today, if we're lucky."

"I thought Arturo would have called us by now," Anna said as she signed the check.

"Remember, he's not allowed to take his phone inside. We might not hear anything until he takes a lunch break."

Anna groaned. "You know, if I were going to design a program to torture families of ICE detainees, it would look a lot like this. I can't stand not being told anything."

Lily took consolation in the fact that they knew how Andy's story would end, unlike the thousands of less fortunate kids behind those walls. If they were released at all, it would be to a life with the threat of family separation or deportation hanging over their head at every turn. Or worse, a life of terror amid violent drug lords back in their home country.

"That's really something about us making the national news, huh?" Anna said. They each had gotten dozens of texts and emails from friends in California who'd seen their interview on the evening news as part of the network's story on children held in detention centers. "I've got about ten requests for comment from other reporters, including one at the *LA Times*."

"Wait till they hear that the center had to shut down. I wonder if Arturo will be able to tell us what that was all about."

As they headed back to Homestead, Arturo called. Anna answered the call through the car's audio system. "Arturo, we're in the car about twenty minutes away. What's happening?"

"I don't know how to tell you this. He's gone. Andy's gone. Vogler put him on a plane last night to Berks. It's in Pennsylvania. It's a detention center for families and unaccompanied minors."

"What the fuck?" Lily screamed. "Why would they do that? Are you telling me after all this that they still don't realize they have the wrong kid? I mean, what the actual fuck is wrong with these people?"

"It's complicated. I'll fill you in when you get here. But there's good news. We've got our hearing today. Wait for me at the gate. I'll be out there in twenty minutes and explain everything."

Despite Lily's caution to watch her speed, Anna made the thirty-minute trip in twenty. They waited in the shade among the protestors until Arturo jogged through the gate.

Anna demanded, "How did this happen? They knew damn good and well this was a case of mistaken identity. Why would they ship him to Berks?"

"It's because of yesterday's lockdown."

Lily listened in horror as Arturo described a stabbing incident in which Andy found the victim in the bathroom and then put himself in danger by fingering the gang member thought to be behind the attack.

"That's the *official* reason he was moved, because they were worried about retaliation."

"Those bastards," Anna grumbled. "If they were so worried, why didn't they just release him? They had my number. All they had to do was call and I'd have picked him up."

"That's the *unofficial* part. Vogler realized who Andy was because he'd picked up Anna's messages. In fact, he'd already called Homeland Security to get the okay to release him without a hearing but he hadn't heard back. Then after the stabbing, CHS corporate didn't want to take responsibility in case Andy was involved, so it was their decision to ship him out to Berks."

"Because Berks belongs to the feds," Lily said. "Now these private contractors get to wash their hands of it."

"Yeah, they'll probably end up moving the kid who got stabbed too. He spent the night in the infirmary but it looks like he's going to be okay."

Anna's face reddened with fury as she glared in the direction of the gate. "Is there no one inside this whole craven shit show with the guts to just do the right thing?"

"For what it's worth, it was Vogler who personally called a DHS attorney and got us in front of a judge today. I called Andy a little while ago to let him know what's happening. We've got a three-way teleconference hearing at ten thirty, after which I can almost guarantee he'll be released."

Lily took out her phone—it was twelve minutes after eight—and opened a ticketing app. "Let's go, Anna. We need to get to Berks. What airport is that?"

"Philly," Arturo said. "Or if you don't mind connecting, Allentown is closer, or Reading. Oh, and one more thing… Andy passed on some information on the other kid, the one who got stabbed. His name's Santos Aguilar. They were picked up together in LA, and I guess they got to be friends."

"What's his situation?" Lily asked.

"I'm not sure yet, but I'll make some calls when it gets to be business hours on the West Coast. But here's the thing: Andy promised him you guys would help find an attorney to take his case. I won't hold you to that part—I'm on it already. I'm only letting you know in case you want to be in the loop. Santos will never have more leverage for being released than he does right now."

Lily was reluctant to agree without knowing who this kid was and what he'd done to get picked up in the first place, especially since the ICE raid had targeted gang members. Her experience with clients in juvenile detention raised suspicions of extortion or intimidation. A naive kid like Andy would make an easy mark. "Is Santos in a gang?"

"Andy says he used to be but he did some time in juvie and now he's clean. I've got the name of his probation officer in LA. I'll call her later on and get the lowdown."

"What does it matter?" Anna said. "Andy wants us to help him. We should do it."

"Anna…" She gave her a stern look. "I'm a judge. I have to be careful about who I get involved with."

"Oh, right." Addressing Arturo, she said, "We'll talk it over on the plane. Maybe you can just send the bill to me at my office. I'll text you the address. And could you let Berks know that we're on our way?"

* * *

Andy's eyes roamed the cinderblock wall above his sink, taking note of several small crayon scrawls, most of which were swear words. *FuckU, Carajo. Motherfuckers.* Reading someone else's frustration made him want to add his own. Dickheads. Ass clowns. Clusterfuck. If only he had a crayon.

Every time he thought his ordeal couldn't get any crazier, ICE proved him wrong. Two nights on the floor in LA. One night across the desert in a van, then another one on a plane. One more in a massive room with hundreds of other boys. And now Berks, an honest-to-God jail. This wasn't a room—it was a cell.

On the plus side, they turned the lights out at night. And he'd picked up new underwear that actually fit, along with a pullover hoodie, since it was cold in Pennsylvania. In fact, there were patches of snow all around the building.

He definitely liked having the whole cell to himself, but he could have done without the obnoxious six thirty wakeup call. Especially since it was one o'clock in the morning before he got to bed, after another lice check and shower. What difference did it make what time he got up anyway? Those nasty breakfast bars were going to be just as stale and gross if they were handed out at nine instead of seven. He might never recover from that disgusting sour milk they'd served the day before at Homestead.

A pair of voices—an adult and a child—grew louder as they approached his cell. "We got a new kid in here last night. He needs a buddy to show him where to eat, where the classrooms are, where the TV room is. How about it, Ruben? Will you show him around?"

Ruben?

"Andy!" Ruben nearly knocked him over with a savage hug.

"You guys know each other?"

"We were kidnapped together in Los Angeles," Ruben answered matter-of-factly. "He's like my blood brother but without the blood."

The guard, a guy so young he could barely manage a mustache, actually seemed like he might be a decent person, practically the only one Andy had seen the whole time he'd been in custody. "All right then, take your blood brother and get him some breakfast. And stop saying you were kidnapped."

"But we were," Andy said once the guard was gone. "How are you, little buddy?"

"Okay, but I want to go home. I need to know where my Papà is. Gunner said he'd find out but he didn't."

"Gunner, that's the guard that was just here?"

"Yeah, he's okay. Everybody else here sucks, especially Wayne. He's the old guy with glasses. He came in the shower room when I was in there and tried to look at my junk."

"No way! Did you report him?"

"I told Gunner. He said he does it all the time, not to go in there by myself anymore."

Great, so Gunner was a nice guy, but too nice to report a pervert. "That's creepy, Ruben. I'm going to tell my lawyer about him. A guy like that has no business being around kids."

He followed Ruben to the cafeteria where he instantly grasped what made Berks unique—families. A couple of fathers, a few teens, but mostly mothers with babies and small children. Which was probably why they all had separate cells, so the families could sleep together in one room.

"Who do you stay with, Ruben? Do you have a room all by yourself?"

"Yeah, but I hang out sometimes with Cristal. She's nine." He pointed to a girl dressed in pink jeans and a hoodie like Andy's. She was sitting with three other kids and a woman who held a baby on her lap. "That's her. Sometimes I sit at their table."

"This place is way better than where they sent me. I heard them say there were three thousand kids there but they were all teenagers."

"Where was it?"

"Florida. Man, it's hot down there. They had bunkbeds all lined up, hundreds of us in one gigantic room." He decided not to mention the gangs and the stabbing because that stuff was too violent for little kids. That's what his moms would have said. They never let Georgie and Eleanor watch anything like that on TV. "Hey, I might get to go home today. I have another hearing in a couple of hours and this time I've got a lawyer."

"No! You just got here. You can't leave already."

"I'm here by accident, Ruben. They thought I was somebody else but my lawyer has the papers that prove I'm not."

"It's not fair," Ruben whined, his lower lip protruding.

Andy didn't blame him for pouting. He'd be mad too if he was stuck in here while others were getting out. "Did they give you a lawyer?"

"No, just a social worker. She says I have to stay here till Papà goes to his trial. Or till they find my *abuela*."

"Right, I forgot. They took your dad to jail." The government's attorney had said Ruben's father was charged with assaulting an ICE officer, but Andy hadn't seen any scuffles during the raid, just people trying to run away. "What did he do? Hit one of those cops or something?"

"He didn't do nothing. It's bullshit. Cristal's mother says they make shit up so you'll be a criminal. Then they can kick you out."

That sounded exactly like something ICE would do. "They like to lie, that's for sure. Remember when we went to court?

Those guards lied to the judge about calling my ma. And the judge just took their word for it."

"Because they're all son of a bitches."

Andy thought about correcting his grammar, then realized he'd be teaching a seven-year-old kid to swear. "I don't get why they're making you stay here. You said you had an aunt. Can't you go live with her for now?"

He shook his head vehemently. "Cristal's mom says not to tell them about her 'cause ICE will go pick her up too."

"But...you said she was married to an American. That means she has a right to be here. They can't just pick her up for nothing. You should tell your social worker."

"I can't." He covered his face with his hands and grunted. "I only know her first name is Carla. I don't even know what street her house is on."

"Maybe I can get my moms to try to find her. What's her husband's name?"

"You have moms? What about your dad?"

"I'm adopted by two moms. They're married to each other."

Ruben gave him a disapproving look. "That's weird."

"No, it's fun. I have a brother and a sister too. We say it's lucky because our friends only have one mom and we have two." When Ruben said everyone should have a dad, Andy described his grandpa and Hal. "Hal has a huge boat. Sometimes we go out fishing and we sleep on the boat, Jonah and me. He's my cousin."

"I don't got nobody like that, just Papà."

Andy wished he could help Ruben the way he'd tried to help Santos. He didn't know any lawyers in Pennsylvania, but maybe his ma did. For now though, it wasn't fair to promise something like that and get Ruben's hopes up.

A woman's voice over the intercom announced the start of classes in the activities room for all "guests" between the ages of five and seventeen.

"There's a magazine on that table over there," Andy said. "I think I'm going to grab it and head back to my room."

Ruben grasped Andy's sleeve and tugged. "They won't let you. School is mambatory for everybody."

Andy groaned. The only thing *mambatory* was getting out of here.

* * *

Lily swilled her glass of sparkling water and finished it off, sucking an ice cube into her mouth. Her speech garbled, she said, "You probably shouldn't have chartered a private jet, Anna. I'm never going to want to fly commercial again."

Anna had balked at flying from Miami International into Philly and renting a car to drive another hour and a half. Their jet from Homestead Executive Airport to Reading shaved nearly three hours off their trip.

"I said the same thing after my jaunt over to Mesa to meet Shelynn Kelly. God, was that just three days ago?"

"Amazing, isn't it? Think about all we've been through in the last week. And poor Andy. God, I'll be so glad to see that kid."

Arturo had messaged them only minutes ago to confirm that he'd secured Andy's release. They were to check in at the main entrance with their documents and wait for him to be escorted out.

"How do you think he'll be?" Lily hadn't even wanted to broach the subject until they were sure he was getting out. Now that he was, they had to prepare for the worst. "He might need therapy for this."

Anna snorted softly. "Good, we can go together."

"I'm serious, Anna. To this day I get flashbacks from some of the things I went through before I was adopted." Like men with beer breath and dark, confined places. "It's not just the stuff that happened…it's the feelings they dredge up. Remember last month when our power went out at home? I was in the laundry room by myself and it scared me half to death. All I could think of was Karen putting me in that closet and saying she'd whip me if I came out."

"Oh, Lily." Anna stretched across the table that separated them in their luxury seats and grasped her hand. "It breaks my heart to think about the things you went through. I'm so grateful to Eleanor for taking you away from all of that."

"She saved me." It was Lily's automatic reply when she spoke of the woman who'd adopted her and given her such a wonderful life. "But I don't want Andy to have to feel that way about us for the rest of his life. I'd rather he didn't remember that time at all before he came to live with us. And that's what worries me, that this experience will trigger some old feelings of anxiety and loss of control that he's forgotten about."

The copilot, a twenty-something named Dustin, did double duty as their flight attendant. He exited the cockpit to collect their glasses and tell them they'd be landing soon.

"Anna, have you given any more thought to my suggestion of getting away for a few days with the kids?"

"In a tent? Yes, I've thought about it." She visibly shuddered. "But I wouldn't exactly call them pleasant thoughts."

CHAPTER EIGHTEEN

"Yeah, I could totally get used to this," Lily said over her shoulder as they descended the stairs in the bright sunshine.

"I wouldn't if I were you. I'm ready to spend all the proceeds from the sale on lawyers like Arturo who can start putting these families back together." It was the first time in days Anna had thought about her business.

Dustin waited at the bottom to help them off the last step. "We're scheduled to be wheels-up at two forty-five, but don't worry if it takes you longer than that. We've got an hour or two to play with, and we could always lay over and go tomorrow. Either way, we won't leave without you."

Anna had paid extra for two pilots so they could fly home to LAX tonight without worrying about flying time restrictions. "With any luck, we'll be back on board in under an hour. *Three* of us."

"We'll try to be ready."

Her lightweight trench coat, which she hadn't needed even once in Miami, was all but useless against Pennsylvania's cold

March winds. *Under an hour.* She could stand anything for under an hour.

Reading Regional Airport handled general aviation and charter services but no commercial jets that Anna could see. After a short walk across the tarmac, they entered a quiet lobby area where a young man in a too-large brown suit and tie sprang to his feet holding a placard with their name.

"Right on time," Lily said.

"Welcome to Reading. I'm Jack, your driver. I understand you're going to Berks. Would that be the nursing home or the…"

"The ICE detention center," Anna said, almost laughing at his surprise. To be fair, it probably wasn't every day two women cruised in on a private jet to pick up an ICE detainee. "They're expecting us at the main entrance. Do you know where that is?"

"Sure. Are you with the federal government?"

"No, I'm an angry mother who's had it up to here with ICE." Anna made a gesture of slitting her throat.

Once they climbed into the back seat of his black SUV, Lily took mercy on the poor fellow and explained the purpose of their visit, how their son had been picked up by mistake.

Anna added, "So when you drop us off, keep the motor running. We'd like to get back to the airport right away so we can fly home."

"Yes, ma'am," he said with a cursory salute. "People around here, they've got mixed feelings about this place. It's jobs and all for the community, but there's a lot of Hispanics in Reading. Sixty percent."

"I had no idea."

"Yeah, Puerto Ricans and Dominicans mostly. There's tons of protesters out here every weekend, and not just Hispanics. Nobody likes seeing families locked up. They aren't hurting anybody. All they want's a better life for their kids. Who doesn't want that?"

They turned off a quiet rural road into a government complex that included the aforementioned nursing home and a multistory "residential" center. To Anna's surprise, there was no gate or fence surrounding the cluster of buildings, just a large visitor parking lot in front of a building marked Administration.

"Wish us luck," Lily said to Jack. "But watch out. If they don't hand over our son this time, we're going to start a riot."

As they neared the door, Anna took Lily's arm. "Can you tell I'm nervous?"

"About what?"

Anna shrugged. "I don't know…seeing Andy. What if he's mad that it took us so long to get him out?"

"Arturo would have said. By the way, if I faint when he comes out, I want you to throw me over your shoulder and carry me out of here. I don't want to wake up in this place."

An unseen receptionist buzzed them into a lobby and appeared moments later behind a glass enclosure. "May I help you?"

Lily stepped closer to a microphone embedded in the glass. "We're here to pick up our son, Andres Kaklis. Your records might show him under another name, Andres Casillas. I have the necessary paperwork to take custody."

The woman disappeared into another room for what felt like an eternity. Anna's impatience turned to irritation after fifteen minutes. "I swear to God, if she comes back and tells me he's not here—"

A door opened behind them.

"Ma!"

Anna whirled to see Andy fly into Lily's open arms. His hair curled in every direction, as if it hadn't been combed all week. And was it her imagination or had he lost weight? From behind, his jeans looked loose and his gray pullover hoodie swallowed him.

Lily beamed with joy as they rocked from side to side. Without breaking their embrace, she dipped her head to look him in the eye. "I've never been so glad to see someone in my whole life."

"You're not half as glad as I am."

The seconds piled up as Anna waited her turn. Andy hadn't even looked in her direction, stoking her fear that he blamed her for something. Or maybe he'd been seething all this time over her broken promise. For not believing in him and treating him like an irresponsible kid. She was determined to make up for all of it. Andy had gotten through this awful ordeal on his own. No two ways about it, he was far more mature than she'd given him credit for. He absolutely deserved her trust and respect.

When he finally turned to face her, he broke into a broad smile and his eyes welled with tears.

"Hey, pal," she said softly. To her relief, he didn't hesitate at all, leaping from Lily's arms into hers. She pulled him into a hug, cupping his head against her shoulder as they both began to sob. Whether he knew it or not, he was comforting her. "God, I love you so much. Do you hear me? I love you, Andy."

"I love you too, Mom."

There were so many things she needed to tell him but that one mattered most.

She loosened her hold and steered him toward the door. "We've come to take you home, pal. Are you ready?"

He sniffed loudly and nodded. "Yeah, but can we please stop and get a pizza? I'm starving."

* * *

Despite the chilly air, Lily cracked the window in the back seat of the SUV to let some of the garlic smell out. Watching Andy scarf down a large pepperoni pizza by himself might have been funny were it not for the fact that he truly was ravenous. He'd confirmed the worst of the horror stories, of being served frozen and spoiled food, and going to sleep hungry every night.

Anna had cracked the window on the other side. "Sorry about the garlic, Jack. I'll make it up to you."

"Not a problem." He pulled to a stop in front of the airport lobby well ahead of schedule. "I'm glad I got the chance to drive you and hear your story. It does my heart good to see a family reunited."

Dustin met them in the lobby and escorted them to the plane, which was being serviced by a fuel truck. "Come aboard and relax. We'll be ready to roll in a few."

"Wow!" Andy was clearly impressed. "This is majorly dope."

Lily let him choose his seat first, then sat facing him. "That seat folds all the way back into a bed if you get sleepy."

"Are you kidding? I'm staying awake so I can enjoy every minute of this. Our own private jet. I feel like a rock star."

Anna laughed. "You'll definitely have a few stories to tell about what you did over spring break."

"No shit." He immediately slapped a hand over his mouth.

"It's okay, pal." She flashed Lily a conspiratorial look. "I think under the circumstances, that one's pretty mild. You should have heard some of the stuff I said."

"That's right, Andy. And your mom hardly ever swears so you know she meant business."

Lily saw no reason to rush Andy back to school on Monday. After almost a week in custody, it wouldn't hurt to have him checked out by a medical doctor, despite his insistence that he was fine. The crowded, unsanitary conditions of ICE detention centers made for a breeding ground for viruses and bacterial infections.

And then there was the matter of Andy's mental health. It could be several days or even weeks before problems began to manifest. Complicating matters further, the signs could be almost anything—irritability, anxiety, difficulty sleeping or concentrating.

"By the way," Anna said as she reached into her handbag, "Tony recovered your phone and your wallet from the ICE detention center in LA. I already called your grandpa and Serafina while we were waiting for your pizza, but you should give Jo-Jo a call."

"He's not going to believe this." He snapped a selfie before scooting to the back of the plane where he had privacy.

"And make sure he tells Aunt Kim and Uncle Hal," Lily added. She leaned across the aisle and whispered playfully, "Do you want to look over his shoulder and check for swear words or should I?"

"You mean to see if he spells them right?" Anna laughed, but then lowered her voice. "I honestly don't care if he swears, as long as he doesn't do it around the customers."

"What customers? Last I heard you were selling the business."

"Mmm…I might be having second thoughts."

Lily answered haughtily, "I guess that means I have to find someone else who can keep me in this lifestyle to which I've grown accustomed."

"Knock yourself out, woman. But you won't find anyone *anywhere* who'll love you more than I do." Anna punctuated her challenge with an air kiss.

Lily answered in kind but made a mental note to encourage Anna later to think through the Premier Motors situation carefully before making an emotional about-face she might regret. This was no time for snap decisions.

"Sweetheart…that's your phone," Anna said.

Lost in thought, Lily hadn't heard it ring. "It's Arturo."

"Tell him we have the package. I always wanted to say that."

"Hi! Anna says to tell you we have the package. We're getting ready to leave for LA."

"That's great. How's Andy? Did he get that pizza?"

Lily peered around her seat to see Andy smiling as he furiously texted. "He did. He ate the whole thing in one go. Though I think he missed his phone more than his family. We'll all be glad to sleep in our own beds tonight. Arturo, we can't thank you enough for taking on his case. If Anna and I can ever help you in the future, I hope you'll ask."

"Thanks, I might just take you up on that." He definitely sounded like a budding politician. "I wanted to touch base about Andy's friend Santos. It turns out they're pretty keen on cutting him loose."

"I bet. Nobody wants to take responsibility for him, especially if he has enemies inside."

"Exactly. But here's the problem. His uncle's his only relative in the US and he works at a hospital in LA. Ten days on, four off. It'll be eight days before he can get to Miami, and DHS refuses to put Santos on a plane by himself."

During the quiet pause that followed, Lily anticipated the request he seemed hesitant to make. "You're saying someone needs to receive custody because he's a minor."

"Correct. And with you being an officer of the court…"

It was a huge ask, since they were eager to get home and end this fiasco. The pilots were ready, the plane was fueled, the flight plan filed. She hated to say no—they were *so* grateful to Arturo—so she decided to pass the buck and let Anna do it.

"And by the way, I spoke with his probation officer. Santos has definitely stayed clear of his old gang. She thinks he's a good bet."

"Umm…hold on a sec, Arturo. I need to talk this over with Anna." She muted her phone and explained the situation to Anna. "Bottom line is he wants us to turn around and go back to Homestead so we can pick up Santos and take him back to LA. What do we tell him?"

"I think it's Andy's call."

She put it to Andy, who didn't dither at all. "I don't think anybody's ever given Santos a break. Let's go get him."

* * *

"You guys ready for dinner?" Lily asked from her seat at the front of the cabin.

"Yeah," Andy replied, drowned out by Santos's "Yes, ma'am." Andy snickered and called him a suck-up.

Despite his vow never to return to Florida, he was glad his moms had agreed to fly back and pick up Santos. He felt bad that only a few days ago he'd thought Santos deserved to be kicked out of the country just for joining a gang. If he'd grown up where Santos did, he might have joined one too.

Andy had done a lot of thinking about his life during his time in detention. He didn't remember much from before he was adopted but it couldn't have been good. Most of his childhood memories were happy times with his Kaklis family. Being around kids like Santos and Ruben made him realize just how lucky he was.

The charter airline had called in a second crew that was ready and waiting when they arrived back at Homestead. Instead of having to stay the night, they were able to collect Santos and return for an evening flight to LAX, due to land around midnight, which was only nine o'clock Pacific Time. A long day for sure but a day Andy would never forget.

Santos wasn't likely to forget it either. When he'd walked out of Homestead with Ma, Andy had met him with a fat beef burrito that was "cooked all the way through, man." Now the two of them had claimed the back end of the cabin so they could talk out of earshot of his moms and the flight attendant Josie, who was preparing a gourmet dinner.

"What do you call 'em? They both the same," Santos said.

"That one's Mom, the one with the dark hair. Her name's Anna. Don't let her sweet face fool you. She's a badass."

He nodded thoughtfully. "She look like a boss."

"The other one's Lily. I call her Ma. Used to be Mama when I was little. She's kinda low key but I've seen her be a badass too, especially in court."

"Yeah, she basically told me if I fucked up she was sending me back to jail. Like now I gotta go to school or start looking for a job." Still wearing the shorts and T-shirt they'd issued at Homestead, Santos sat wrapped in a blanket against the cabin's cool temperature. "Which one your real mother?"

"Both of them. Neither of them." Andy was used to such questions. He'd learned long ago that some queries, like this one from Santos, were out of genuine curiosity, while others were a pretext for making fun of his parentage. "My natural mother was killed by the police in San Francisco. Accidentally… or so they said. Ma says they were reckless 'cause she wasn't even doing anything."

"That's a lie, man. You shitting me."

"Swear to God. I don't remember anything about her though. I was living in a foster home 'cause she wasn't taking care of me. That one"—he pointed to Lily—"she's my real mother's sister. And they're married, so they both adopted me. I'm legally their son."

"You lucked out, man."

"Tell me about it." As he told about the rest of his family, he couldn't help but notice Santos's somber look. "Do you have any brothers or sisters?"

"Naw, just me." He stared out the window, his silence all-consuming until he finally said, "Don't tell nobody, okay? My ma's not my real ma neither. She my sister…my half-sister. We got the same father. My real ma was murdered in Honduras and that's why he brought me to live with her. I was about four. I used to didn't know. Some days I wish I still didn't." He added a sarcastic laugh. "She only told me 'cause I was being a pain in the butt and she threatened to send me back. Wait till she hears ICE almost did it for her."

Andy's rough start didn't hold a candle to that, but he still felt a strange kinship with Santos that he hadn't shared with anyone. The difference between them was exactly what Santos said—luck. A few years ago his quest to learn more about his personal history had been satisfied when his moms sat down with him to go over his records. The only specifics were that he'd been neglected and possibly abused, and he'd lived in six different foster homes by the time he was four years old. His life changed forever when he moved to LA and became a Kaklis.

"ICE thought I was some guy named Andres Casillas. Whoever that is, he better hope those motherfuckers don't catch him." Andy jumped at the sound of his ma clearing her throat as she swiveled her chair to face Santos. "Oops, sorry."

She ignored him and addressed Santos, "How are you feeling, Santos? Any pain in your belly?"

"It's okay. Sometimes it hurts when I cough."

"I think that's normal. The doctor said you needed to keep the area clean and change the bandage every day. Do you have bandages at home?"

"My uncle say he can get some. He works at a hospital."

"Oh, right. You looking forward to going back to school on Monday?" She let him dangle in awkward silence for several seconds and then laughed. "Why do I get the feeling school isn't your favorite thing?"

"I'm just not very good at it."

Anna turned too so the four of them were facing each other. "Here's a news flash, Santos. Everybody struggles in school sometimes. Even this guy." She pointed to Andy. "The key is finding the thing that really interests you and pouring your whole heart into it. Right, Andy?"

"If you ask me, the key is to get help when you need it. I should have done that with math. Instead I just acted like everything was okay, like I was too cool to need help. Then I got behind and it was hard to catch up again."

"I think it's a little of both," Lily said. "We should set up a meeting with your PO and talk about what's next. One of my colleagues at the courthouse has a program for kids your age so they can get a GED and start a career path. I bet I can pull some strings and get you in it. You interested?"

"Yeah." He corrected himself immediately. "I mean, yes ma'am. I don't want no more trouble. I'm done with that."

"Tell me about this gang stuff at Homestead. Arturo said you got stabbed because of a gang fight."

No way was Andy going to volunteer what Santos had said about needing to take sides. "It was my fault, Ma. I gave him my rugby shirt to wear 'cause he liked it and it was too big for me. I didn't know it was gang colors. If I'd been wearing it, I might have been the one who got stabbed."

Lily shuddered and blew out a breath. "Don't even say that. You'll give me nightmares."

"I'm done with gangs," Santos repeated, pounding the arm of his chair for emphasis. "I promise. I won't go nowhere ICE be picking up kids."

Anna, in her typical badass fashion, said, "I'm done with ICE. If it were up to me, I'd shut down the whole force. Or I'd at least make it illegal to take minors into custody, especially off the street."

That gave Andy an idea. "Hey, you could help Ruben too! Ruben Ibarra. He's at Berks."

Santos made a face. "That little pipsqueak that kept kicking my seat?"

"Cut him some slack. He's only seven. His dad had a green card. Instead of letting him go, they arrested him and said he assaulted an ICE officer. Ruben says they just made that up. It's not fair how they lie."

Lily traded looks with Anna. "Tony told us about that, remember? They charge people with a bogus crime so they can justify deporting them."

"They do. I seen it," Santos said. "Or they lock you up for nothing and hold you so you miss your check-in day. That's it then—you broke the law." He snapped his fingers. "Bam! You deported."

"And the stupid judges always believe whatever they say," Andy grumbled, before it dawned on him his own ma was a judge. "I'm not saying all judges are stupid. That judge in Phoenix though, he believed every lie that came out of that lawyer's mouth." He looked to Santos for backup. "Remember those two a-holes who drove the van? They told the lawyer they checked out my story that my name was *Kaklis*, that my ma was a judge. They said they couldn't verify it. They didn't even try."

"'Course they didn't. Just like they said I was hanging out with F-Thirteen. I know the guys in F-Thirteen—they weren't even there that night. ICE just looked me up and lie. That's how they do all Latinos."

"He's right, Ma. They treat us Latinos like crap. That's why I want to help Ruben and his dad."

"I understand, Andy. But we don't know the facts there."

"Except the facts are whatever ICE says they are. And the judges act like ICE agents are...*impallible*."

"I think you mean infallible," Anna said. "They don't ever make mistakes."

"Yeah, that."

Lily would be the first to admit the judicial system had serious flaws. "Andy, I hear what you're saying—and you're right, it's not always fair—but judges have to work with what they're given. That's how the law works. The real problem is that detainees aren't given attorneys who'll push back. Or the attorneys they have are so overworked they can't mount an effective defense. If you'd had access to appropriate counsel, the judge would have received evidence of who you were and you'd have been released on the spot in Phoenix."

"Then somebody needs to fix it 'cause court ought to be fair...even if you're not a citizen."

"I agree completely," Lily said. "Tell you what...I'll call Tony tomorrow and ask him to look into Ruben's father's case. Ibarra, right? Even if we can't help him beat the assault charge, maybe we can get Ruben released."

"Cool!"

Santos snorted but smiled. "He still a pipsqueak."

* * *

Anna closed the bedroom door and leaned against it. The thrill of having Andy home again—and of watching Georgie, Eleanor and Serafina listen raptly to his story—had kept her going for the last couple of hours, but the crash was imminent. "I don't know how either of us is still standing. Twenty-one hours, three states, three time zones."

"Can you believe it was just this morning we were eating breakfast in the Everglades? Feels like last week."

"And it feels like a month that Andy was gone." She followed Lily into the bathroom where they readied for bed. "I was struck by something he said on the plane. 'Us Latinos.' I know he's been teased about it at school, but it never once occurred to me what that really means. We need to have The Talk with our whole family."

"You mean like the one Black parents have with their kids? How they have to be hyper aware of what they say and do when it comes to the authorities."

"Exactly. And how they need to stay focused on one thing—doing whatever it takes to come home safe." That her children's wellbeing might be at risk from entrenched prejudice ignited a fury stronger than she'd ever known. "We dropped the ball on that, Lily."

"I agree. At least we get another chance. I noticed you were in his bedroom a long time with the door shut. Is that what you were talking about?"

"That...plus he was telling me about one of the guards at Berks, some guy named Wayne. His little friend Ruben said Wayne followed all the little boys into the showers so he could look at them naked. I promised him we'd report it."

"Damn right we will," Lily said. "And we can use that to try to get Ruben released to a caretaker right away while his father awaits his trial. Did you happen to mention the psychologist to Andy?"

"I did…He didn't think he needed one, but I convinced him to humor us. Then we went online and made an appointment at the DMV for him to take his driver's test next Tuesday. He still needs twelve hours behind the wheel, but I promised him we'd knock those out this weekend."

"You're quite the negotiator." Lily stared back from the mirror, her mouth open and toothbrush in hand. "I bet he's over the moon."

"Yeah, I'm proud of the way he handled himself. All this time I thought he wasn't mature enough for the responsibility, but clearly I was wrong. And I told him that."

In return, Andy had promised never to do anything stupid or irresponsible. While she appreciated his commitment, she reminded herself that any sixteen-year-old was sure to have plenty of foolish mistakes ahead, no matter how sincere their promises.

Anna stripped off her shirt and bra and turned away. "Scratch my back, would you?" As Lily complied, she moaned her approval. Sometimes a good back scratching was almost as good as—

"We get to sleep in tomorrow," Lily said. "I heard Serafina promise the boys she'd make them pancakes…though I doubt seriously Andy will be up before noon."

"Tomorrow's Saturday. We've got tennis and STEM camp. And I need to take Andy driving."

Lily finished with a kiss between Anna's shoulder blades. "Nope, all that's canceled. Except some driving. Officially we're still on vacation till Sunday, remember?"

Anna shimmied into a satin nightshirt and finished her ablutions. She found the bedroom dark but for a flameless candle on each nightstand.

Lily lay naked on her side, her hand smoothing the sheet. This was her superpower, the unfailing ability to make Anna forget work stress, family worries, even exhaustion, with just a soft pat on the bed. "Come be with me."

She fell into Lily's arms and slid a knee between her legs, their bodies fitting together as perfectly as the tricolored wedding rings they wore. "I'm always with you, no matter where we are."

EPILOGUE

June 2019

As she set out plates and utensils for dinner, Lily overheard a squabble kicking up in the family room.

"That's my pencil, butthead," Andy said sternly. "Stop taking my stuff."

Georgie replied, "I'm telling Ma you said a bathroom word."

"Good, then you might as well tell her I called you crap face too."

"Ma!"

"Georgie, please come to the kitchen," Lily called. Before he could tattle on Andy, she handed him a box dinner from the drive-thru at KFC. "Take this up to Serafina's apartment. Knock on the door and wait for her to answer. And don't stand around and talk. She has to study for her exam tomorrow, so we need to give her some peace and quiet."

"How come she gets to eat already and we don't?"

"Your mom will be here soon and we'll have dinner together."

Eleanor appeared in the doorway, a longhaired tortie kitten literally on her heels in pursuit of a dangling shoestring. "Silly Hedy. Rafa chases her and she chases me."

Rafa was Georgie's all-black kitten, named for tennis player Rafael Nadal. They were loads of fun but kittens came with only two gears—park and turbo.

"Sweetie, go with Georgie and take Serafina this piece of lemon cake. But first, tie your shoe. And be careful not to let the kitties out."

Anna had texted that she was on her way home, so Lily went ahead and set the food out in the breakfast nook. "Andy, would you come in here please?"

He sauntered in and sank into his usual seat at the table without looking up from his phone. Though he'd been home for half an hour, he still wore his much despised school uniform but with his tie hanging loose and his shirttail out. Lily was surprised he hadn't stripped it off in the car since this was their last day of school.

"That's two bucks for the bad word jar, young man." She unscrewed the top off the plastic jug and set it in front of him.

"Aw, I was hoping you didn't hear that. When Georgie gets back I'm going to kick his *butt*ered biscuit, that little *cra*fty boy."

"Why, you little *smartas*—a whip kid. Just for that, I'm going to *ass*ault you." She bopped his head several times with an empty paper towel roll until he wrested it from her in a fit of laughter.

Since Andy's release from detention three months ago, he'd been noticeably happier and more engaged with the family, his verbal jousts with Georgie notwithstanding. In fact, Anna thought all of them had drawn especially close after saying their sad goodbyes to Martine last month. It was as if her passing, heartbreaking though it was, had released them from the cloud of dread.

Andy drew the covered bucket of chicken closer and inhaled. "Mom better get here soon. I'm not going to last much longer."

Lily tugged it away as she joined him at the table. "There was an article in *The New York Times* today about the detention center at Homestead. They're talking about closing it down. I'll send it to you if you want to read it."

"Heck yeah! Somebody ought to burn it to the ground. What are they going to do with all the kids there?"

"Let's hope the idea is to stop taking them in. They made a mess and now they don't know what to do with it. Mark my words, when it's all said and done they're going to have loads of kids without parents because nobody's kept up with them."

"No sh—no kidding. They didn't even have my name right. And these little kids, some of them don't even know their parents' names or where they're from."

"That's another thing…your friend Ruben and his father. Tony called me today." Tony had taken on Miguel Ibarra's criminal case, which proved thornier than usual. ICE was claiming the assault occurred in the lavatory at the detention center, away from security cameras and other witnesses. "The assault case came down to his father's word against that of two ICE officers. You know how hard it is to prove your innocence when law enforcement testifies against you."

"Because they lie and the judge always believes them. It sucks."

"Yeah, sometimes it really does. Ruben's dad decided not to take his chances in court. He was facing the possibility of eight years in prison for assault, and they were going to hold Ruben at Berks the whole time. Tony got them to offer a deal instead—plead guilty to disorderly conduct instead of assault. Instead of sending him to jail now and deporting both him and Ruben when he got out, they're deporting them now." In fact, Ruben was on his way back to Phoenix today so ICE could dump them at the Mexican border together.

"But that's not fair. He didn't assault anybody. He should have fought it in court."

"Honey, that's a huge roll of the dice when the system's stacked against you. Can you imagine Ruben having to stay at Berks until he's fifteen years old?"

"But it's blackmail."

More like extortion or coercion, she wanted to say. Prosecutors did it all the time to extract guilty pleas, even from people who weren't guilty.

Andy folded his arms on the table and rested his head in the crook of his elbow. "Poor Ruben. He's going to think I let him down."

"I'm sure his dad will tell him you tried to help. You did all you could do. One good thing happened though. Remember that one guard Ruben said was looking at him in the shower? Tony got him transferred out of there. He's at the adult prison now. That was the best he could do without concrete evidence."

"At least it's something."

She rose to stand beside him and hug him to her chest. "I'm really sorry, honey. It was good of you to try to help. In case I haven't told you lately, I'm really proud of the young man you've become. I can't think of a better feeling for a mom than to know her kid's grown up to be a good person."

The tips of his ears burned red as he hugged her waist tightly. Their sweet moment was shattered when the twins burst through the back door and ran to chase the kittens. Behind them the back gate opened to Anna, who sauntered across the patio with her suit jacket slung over her shoulder.

"There's your mom. Go wash your hands so we can eat."

Anna entered the kitchen with the broadest grin Lily had seen in quite some time. Instead of a hug, she lifted Lily off her feet and swung her around.

"Someone's in a good mood. I take it Hal said yes?"

"You should have seen him. I think he's even more excited than we are. But they want to do their Puget Sound trip first."

"I don't blame them. They deserve some time to relax."

"That means we can start work in July. We're going to love this, Lily. All of us."

After weeks of soul searching, Anna had decided to pass on the opportunity with Helios. As stimulating as it would have been to break new ground in automotive technology, she couldn't see herself working for someone else. Instead, they were going to use the proceeds from the sale to launch a new enterprise—the

Kaklis Family Foundation—to help fund some of the causes they cared about. Legal aid for immigrants, Alzheimer's care, STEM for girls. They'd look for opportunities where small grants could make a big difference.

"It'll be a wonderful legacy, Anna. I'm surprised you didn't want to go out to Empyre's to celebrate." Their biggest events were usually marked with a big family dinner at their favorite Greek restaurant.

"I sort of wanted tonight to be just us," Anna said.

Since the ordeal with Andy they'd spent more time with their kids, enjoying games and movies at home, and fun outings like the Santa Monica Pier. Even camping at Malibu Creek with Sandy and Suzanne. The first time Andy went out with his friends, he'd texted all through the evening to set their minds at ease. Even so, Anna had spent the whole time in the alcove in their bedroom watching the driveway for his return.

"Hi, Mom." Andy returned from washing his hands and rose on tiptoes to kiss her cheek.

"Mommm!"

As Anna stooped to hug the twins, Georgie excitedly shared news of his practice with Coach Bobby and Eleanor related the latest antics of Hedy and Rafa. It was a poignant moment for Lily, the realization that these childhood moments would be behind them all too soon as the kids grew too cool to hug their moms and too secretive to talk about their days. They'd be adults in eight short years—no time at all.

"I've got some news," Anna said, rubbing her hands as she took her seat at the table. "You know the Schumacher house? Across the street, two doors down. Aunt Kim and Uncle Hal bought it. They're going to be our neighbors."

"Wow!" Andy said.

Eleanor clapped with glee. "Yay, this means I can see Alice whenever I want."

"And we can play ping-pong," George added.

"That's wonderful news," Lily said. "I bet they're excited about having their own place again. What did George decide about the Big House? It's too much for him by himself."

Anna's feelings about the old mansion were decidedly mixed, she'd told Lily a couple of nights ago. Wonderful memories, and now sad ones too. It had been in her family for over seventy years but was in dire need of major repairs and renovations. "Dad's putting it on the market. Kim's going to help him find a place to rent for a year or so until he figures out where he wants to be. I think it's the right thing to do but it's bittersweet."

"Maybe now your sister will stop trying to steal this house out from under us."

"Let's hope. But wait, there's more," Anna said, doing a cheesy imitation of a late-night TV huckster. "I signed all the papers this afternoon to sell the dealerships to Pinnacle...all twenty-one of them."

Lily winked at her as they watched Andy's face for a reaction. He was too busy fishing through the chicken bucket to find a drumstick.

Only Eleanor caught the slip. "There's supposed to be twenty-two."

"Right, I decided we ought to keep the BMW dealership in Beverly Hills. That was your grandpa's idea. He was worried Andy and I might not know what to do with ourselves if I sold it."

Andy's eyes went wide with delight. With half a biscuit in his mouth, he managed, "Are you theriouth?"

"Yeth, I'm theriouth. What do you think of that?"

He pounded the table with excitement before taking a drink to wash down his food. "I think it's fan—frickin'—tastic!" He whipped out his wallet and tossed a five-dollar bill on the table. "That's in case frickin's a bathroom word. What made you change your mind?"

"It's in my blood, I guess. I figure as long as there's a Kaklis who wants to sell cars, we should keep the doors open."

Lily spoke up, "But if you get to college and decide you want to...oh, I don't know...go to law school? All bets are off."

After his release from detention, he'd talked vaguely about the possibility of becoming an attorney like Arturo. *Not like his ma*, Lily noted. She and Anna had been pleased to hear that he was open to other venues after all, though they doubted anything could tear him away from his love of cars.

Andy was practically bouncing with excitement. "Does this mean I get to run the dealership some day?"

"What about me?" Eleanor asked pointedly.

"You don't know anything about cars," he replied, punctuating his remark with an eye roll.

"I know how to calculate engine displacement. That's how much air gets pushed out when the pistons go down. The higher the engine displacement, the more power a car has."

Andy stared at her, mouth agape, then turned to Anna with a questioning look.

"She's right, pal."

Having secured her automotive engineering bona fides, Eleanor took mercy on her brother. "It's okay, Andy. I want to be a scientist. But you can call me if you ever need any help figuring out stuff like that."

Lily had never seen him quite so flabbergasted, as if downright embarrassed that his ten-year-old sister had schooled him on something he should have known.

"You're sweet to offer, Ellie," Anna said, "but I was kind of hoping Andy would take me up on a job offer now that school's out. That would give him a chance to learn the business from the ground up."

"A job?"

"You know, that thing where you show up for work every day at a certain time and do whatever your supervisor tells you to do till it's time to go home."

He gave Anna a tentative look. "A real job? Like…would I get paid?"

Anna helped herself to a chicken wing and a biscuit. "Of course. You'd be an official tax-paying employee. Fingerprints, credit check, the whole nine yards. What I wanted was for you to work with Javier doing routine service." She addressed the twins. "That's oil and filter changes, tire rotation, fluid top-off."

"A grease monkey," Georgie proclaimed.

"That would be so cool!" Eleanor said, causing Lily to laugh. It was scary how much like Anna she was.

Anna turned to Andy again. "But our insurance won't let you work in the shop till you're eighteen. I gave that job to your friend Santos instead. He turns eighteen next week. I'm pairing *you* with Megan this summer so you can learn how we price trade-ins. Sound like fun?"

"Yeah…yeah, it actually does. How much will I make?"

"Personally, I'd pay you in M&Ms but California insists on twelve bucks an hour as minimum wage. I expect you to work your tail off for that."

Georgie looked up from his plate, which was loaded with mac and cheese. "How come tail isn't a bathroom word but B-U-T-T is?"

Lily chuckled. "Good question, honey. Your mom and I will discuss that later. What time does Andy have to be at work?"

"Megan starts at seven, so…"

Andy wrinkled his nose. "That's pretty early. You don't usually go in till nine. Can't I go then?"

Anna shook her head. "Sorry, pal. It's called paying your dues. But I guess we should talk about getting you a car so I won't have to drop you off at that ungodly hour. You think you're ready for that responsibility?"

His eyes widened with excitement. "Totes!"

Lily laughed at Anna's bewildered look. "That's short for totally."

"Ahh. I didn't realize *totally* was so labor intensive. Anyway pal, getting your own car means following all the traffic rules. Seat belts, speed limits, all that. No showing off, no clowning around, no losing your temper behind the wheel."

"No taking it out of LA without permission," Lily added. "And no letting anyone else drive it—including Jonah."

"*Especially* Jonah," Anna said.

"Cross my heart." He gestured with an X over his chest, then clasped his hands in prayer before finishing with something that looked like Scout's honor.

"Your mom and I talked it over, Andy," Lily said. "To be honest, we didn't see eye to eye on which car to get. See, my first car was an eight-year-old Toyota Tercel. My mom bought it for me when I turned sixteen so I could go to my job after school. It wasn't much to look at but it got me where I needed to go. Whereas your mom…"

"My first was a brand new M3 Cabrio convertible, Diamond Black. Really hot stuff. Your Aunt Kim got one too. You'd have loved hers—Misano Red. Dad wanted us to drive them to school so the other kids would be envious and get their parents to buy them one too. And it worked. We sold a bunch."

Lily sighed and shook her head. "You guys…there's never an off switch when it comes to selling Bimmers. Andy, I told your mom I didn't think a sixteen-year-old has—"

"I'm seventeen in two months."

"I don't think *teenagers* have earned the right to drive fancy new cars unless they've worked for them."

Georgie and Eleanor ate in silence but it was clear they were listening, as if storing the information for the conversations they'd have six or seven years from now when it was their turn to drive. Lily was big on fairness, though Anna had convinced her a car meant far more to Andy than it likely would to Georgie or Eleanor. They had their own passions.

"You know what I said to that, pal? I told her you've been working at the dealership since you were this high." Anna held out a hand. "You wipe down the cars in the showroom without even being asked. You run errands for Uncle Hal and me, you keep the media room clean. All that and you've never gotten paid."

"And sometimes I help wash and dry the cars when people bring them in for service," he volunteered.

"Right, so I thought you deserved a really nice car, but we agreed it should be one you'd already driven."

"The 230i demo?" He clearly was trying to play it cool but couldn't hide his grin. "It's a great car. Mark Whitaker got one for graduation. His is Jet Black. I like the Melbourne Red though. It stands out."

"Yeah, that's what I told your ma. Personally, I've always gone for the darker shades but red suits you. It has a certain cachet." Anna fished a set of keys from her pocket and slid them across the table. "It's in the driveway. You can drive it to work tomorrow."

Lily caught him by the shirttail. "Not so fast, kiddo. I think your first new car calls for family photos."

They waited—not all that patiently—for Georgie to finish eating before walking out the back door together to the side gate. Anna hung back, taking Lily's hand and whispering, "Someone's about to lose his bathroom word."

Andy swung the gate open to find his new car on majestic display. "Oh, my God! Is this for real?" Instead of the 230i, Anna had brought home a Z4 roadster, a slick two-seater convertible in San Francisco Red.

"Anna!" Lily said through gritted teeth as she held her smile in place. "This is not what we agreed to."

Anna was obviously pleased with herself at seeing Andy over the moon. "Shouldn't you be taking pictures?"

Lily hurriedly snapped a few of Andy as he slid behind the wheel, and with Georgie and Eleanor taking turns in the passenger seat. She had to admit she'd never seen Andy so happy and proud. But still… "Seriously, a convertible?"

"I knew you'd say that so I brought you a copy of the Insurance Institute's study. Want to guess what it says?"

"Why do I get the feeling this is a trick question?" Especially considering Anna's satisfied smirk.

"They're actually safer…which makes sense if you think about it. They're heavier than a hard top and low to the road, so they're less likely to roll over. Do you feel more vulnerable in my car with the top down?"

"Yeah, maybe."

"So do I. You probably wouldn't notice but it makes me more careful, more aware of my surroundings. From the way Andy's driven my car, I think it has the same effect on him."

Lily couldn't help being skeptical but she trusted Anna's opinion. "At least talk to him and make sure."

"That's a deal."

"And it has a stick shift!" Andy shouted. Suddenly he jumped out of the car and ran toward them, his arms wide enough to catch them both. "I love you!"

"We love you too, pal," Anna said, her voice matching his joy. After Andy's ordeal, she'd told Lily she hoped never again to let those words go unsaid.

"Can I go show Jonah?"

"Absolutely. And your grandpa too. Tell him I learned from the best."

"Remember the rules," Lily yelled.

As Andy carefully backed out of their driveway, the twins ran back inside yelling about dessert.

"Look at him go," Anna said. "Top down, cooling off his brain."

"Cooling off his brain?" Lily playfully backhanded her belly. "I distinctly remember us agreeing that it would be best to give him one he was used to driving. That was the 230i."

"He's driven this one too. Not as well, though. It's the one he wrecked in the parking lot." She wrapped an arm around Lily's shoulder and delivered a kiss to her temple.

"I should have known you'd give him the car *you* would have wanted."

"Not true. Mine would have been Mediterranean Blue."

"But a Z4? You have to admit that's pretty extravagant."

"I know, but you've seen the parking lot at his school. It's full of luxury SUVs and sporty coupes. But a really hot sports car? If anyone's going to drive that it ought to be the son of somebody who sells BMWs in Beverly Hills. Did you see his face?"

Lily knew she'd already lost this argument, and honestly, she no longer cared. Andy's excitement trumped all of her objections.

"By the way, you were right," Anna said. "As usual."

"Oh, I love conversations that start like that. What was I right about?"

"Brat." Anna hip-checked her as they walked inside. "You were right that I haven't been giving Andy enough credit. I was too hard on him, and yes, it was because he wasn't more like me. Instead of encouraging his strengths, I came pretty close to giving up on him. Sixteen years old and I essentially decided he didn't have a future in the one thing he cared about most. If that doesn't make me a terrible parent, I hate to think what would."

Lily leaned into her shoulder and said, "Trust me, sweetheart. I've seen some truly bad parenting in my day and that wouldn't even register on the scale."

"It registers on *my* scale. I plan on proving to him that I have faith in him to take over the business someday if that's what he wants to do. After all he's been through, it's obvious he can handle it."

"Just like it's obvious you could no more sell that dealership than you could lop off an arm. It's part of you…and part of Andy too."

Anna walked her back through the gate and stopped for a kiss. "I won't deny that, Lily. But the biggest part of me will always be you."

Bella Books, Inc.

Women. Books. Even Better Together.

P.O. Box 10543
Tallahassee, FL 32302

Phone: 800-729-4992
www.bellabooks.com

9 781642 472813